The Good Deed

a novel

Helen Benedict

 Red Hen Press | *Pasadena, CA*

Book design by Mark E. Cull.

Library of Congress Cataloging-in-Publication Data

Names: Benedict, Helen, author.
Title: The good deed: a novel / Helen Benedict.
Description: First edition. | Pasadena, CA: Red Hen Press, 2024.
Identifiers: LCCN 2023047092 | ISBN 9781636281124 (trade paperback) | ISBN
   9781636281131 (ebook)
Subjects: LCGFT: Novels.
Classification: LCC PS3552.E5397 G66 2024 | DDC 813/.54—dc23/eng/20231010
LC record available at https://lccn.loc.gov/2023047092

The National Endowment for the Arts, the Los Angeles County Arts Commission, the Ahmanson Foundation, the Dwight Stuart Youth Fund, the Max Factor Family Foundation, the Pasadena Tournament of Roses Foundation, the Pasadena Arts & Culture Commission and the City of Pasadena Cultural Affairs Division, the City of Los Angeles Department of Cultural Affairs, the Audrey & Sydney Irmas Charitable Foundation, the Meta & George Rosenberg Foundation, the Albert and Elaine Borchard Foundation, the Adams Family Foundation, Amazon Literary Partnership, the Sam Francis Foundation, and the Mara W. Breech Foundation partially support Red Hen Press.

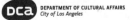

First Edition
Published by Red Hen Press
www.redhen.org

Printed in Canada

For Eyad

لأجل إياد عونان

Glossary

Daesh is the Syrian term for ISIS or ISIL. The word has no literal meaning in Arabic, but because it sounds similar to the words for trample or crush, ISIS supporters object to its use.

The Arabic phrases I have converted phonetically to the Roman alphabet are all common terms of endearment, such as my love, my heart, my eye, my little moon.

Frontex is the coast guard of the European Union.

Oh, black clouds
Passing borders fearlessly
I am neither Odysseus who returns home
Nor Aeneas who makes a homeland in exile.

—Majid Naficy, "Escape to Lesbos," 2015

BOOK ONE

JULY 22, 2018

1

HILMA

The sea around this island is so brazenly blue it puts even the unblemished sky to shame. How mystifying it is that the ancient Greeks had no word for the color. *Wine-dark sea*. Like living in a forest and having no word for tree.

I am without canvases here, my brushes forever abandoned, but were I a painter still, I would be afraid of this blue. Afraid that I could never render it, even in abstract, because the sea here is an ever-spinning whorl of blues—turquoise, aqua, cyan, indigo, cerulean, slate—all overlayed by darts of black and white, amethyst and silver, verdigris, rose, and violet, constantly changing with light and current. To capture this, one would need a moving painting—not video but oil. A flood of multicolored oils streaming over the canvas, lit by an Aegean sun.

I'm watching these blues from the mountain apartment I rented through Airbnb, its stone terrace veined in gold. Every evening, I sit here with a glass of wine, looking over the bay to Vathi, the town on the far side heaped like a jumble of sugar cubes at the bottom of Mount Thios—a town that my host, a gnarly Greek with the voice of a frog, lost no time in telling me holds the most overcrowded refugee camp in Europe.

"These people, they come here from Africa to get rich, and so many are thieves, Miss Khilma!" he insisted, pronouncing the *h* in my name with the same guttural splutter with which my grandmother used to pronounce Hanukkah. In fact, as a quick Google in my phone affirms, by far the majority of the people in the camp are Syrian. "They took the honey from the beehive of a poor little old lady—her very own honey! And two of them, they broke into an empty house to sleep and left their rubbish all over the floor!"

Tut-tut. But then those hives were not mine, and nor was that house. I'm not a Greek islander trying to scrape by on tourists who won't come anymore or on the honey I can barely sell.

When he's not spouting misbegotten opinions, my host, Kosmos Constantinides, seems a kind enough man. Somewhere in his early seventies, more than a decade older than I, he's just past the age of handsome, skin a fine nut color from the sun, hair the silver of an olive leaf, eyes small and murky blue, face square if sagging. On the day I arrived, he was proudly showing me his view when a furious wind sprung up out of nowhere, inciting a nearby pine tree to pelt us with cones and needles—surprisingly painful. Mortified, he rushed me inside his disorderly kitchen, sat me in a wooden chair, and bustled about, his squat, muscular body moving with the confidence of a laborer, preparing me a plate of perfectly cubed honeydew and watermelon while explaining that Samos is prone to these sudden squalls—Poseidon throwing his tantrums. Kosmos's flaw is that he listens to his neighbors too much: a flaw that many of us, of course, share.

But I didn't come here to argue with Airbnb hosts or anyone else. I came to recuperate. Doctor's orders.

Why I chose to do my recuperating on an island with a refugee camp is simple. I didn't know. I don't read about tragic matters anymore. I used to, when I was the person before the person I am now. Not any longer. No, I chose to come here to Samos because I'm interested in the mathematician and philosopher Pythagoras and this was his supposed birthplace. Because I fancied the view of the Turkish mountains poking up behind Vathi. I came because myth has it that Aesop of the fables talked his way out of slavery here, and because this is Greece and therefore timeless. I came for the Aegean blues.

If Theo, my son, had not stopped speaking to me, I would invite him to join me here. As a boy, he had a passion for the sea, the sing and sway of it, the fish little colorful packages put there, he used to think, just for him. He would have loved the beaches with their multicolored pebbles as perfect as eggs, the sea as clear as a mermaid's eyes.

Linnette would have loved it here, too. But Linnette is forbidden.

Theo not only refuses to speak to me, he won't look at me, either. The last time I was in his presence, in a Manhattan courtroom, he turned his head away and stared at the wall.

Theo is a lawyer for Amnesty International, a job that takes him to the most godforsaken corners of the earth to help the most godforsaken people. I used to see the toll it took reflected in his face, back in the days when he let me see his face—the withdrawals, the impatience with trivial conversation, the grim exhaustion. Were he here with me on Samos, he would be over at that camp already, advocating for any and all who asked. I might go there myself. Just to see what I can see. And maybe—if he ever talks to me again—tell him about it.

Part of my recuperation program is not only to avoid arguments, but to swim. Strap on my mask and snorkel, dip myself into the turquoise, glide into the cobalt, churn through the aqua. The marble stones on the seafloor here, pale beige and fuzzed with blond weeds, hide many a treasure. Tiny striped fish wagging their way lazily through the current. Urchins balled as tight as hedgehogs.

In the month I've been here, I've found two beaches within easy reach of my Airbnb, one a short drive away and "official," which means littered with rentable umbrellas, deck chairs, and half-naked Germans sunning themselves like pink whales; the other just below the house and "unofficial," which means untended and isolated. Today I'm in the mood for the latter, a small cove I can only reach by clambering down a stony, ankle-twisting path lined with thornbushes and the promise of snakes, but where at least I can be alone. All the beaches on this side of Samos are shingle, covered not only by those egg-like pebbles but rocks the size of melons, so on with my water shoes and most practical swimsuit and down the rubbly path I go. The only sign of civilization down here is a small white house, which has remained deserted during my entire stay, and the little rowboat I've noticed before anchored near the shore, bobbing in the waves.

The sea is choppy this morning, last night having delivered the most brutal storm I've witnessed yet on Samos, the wind yowling and hammering at my shutters like a banshee, the waves sucking in great breaths and spitting them out again with a crash against the pebbled shore. But the air is already heating back up to its July highs, so in I wade, battling the surf, and after an initial flinch at the cold, head out to deeper waters, where it looks calmer.

How I love the weightlessness of swimming, the exhilaration of cutting unfettered through the waves. Water crystalline and clean, those wagging fish. The sun projecting a light show on the seafloor, a spangling honeycomb of hexagons dancing over the sand; the brown seagrass rippling in the current like a field of wheat in the wind. I lose all sense of time and fly through the water as though it's as yielding as air.

A splash dives into my snorkel tube, so I raise my head to empty the water out and take in where I am. Far—a great deal farther than I thought. The little rowboat has shrunk to the size of a bath toy. I'm not tired, but I am sensible. Time to turn back.

Just as I do, my eye catches a spot of color, an orange object bobbing a short distance away . . . a buoy perhaps, or else a polluting plastic bag I feel obliged to remove. I swim closer.

It is not a buoy. Or a bag. It's a life jacket. With somebody in it. A pitifully small somebody.

A fist closes around me, pulling me to a halt, my breath suddenly short and airless.

Not again. Please.

The little figure is ominously still—no sign of swimming or flailing. No movement at all.

The fist grips tighter.

Not this time, Hilma. You can't.

With an effort, I wrench free of my paralysis and push myself closer. Then again, the fist.

The water, too, is resisting me now, no longer as yielding as air but viscous and stubborn, as though I'm swimming through glue. I look around for a rescue boat. There is no rescue boat, no sign of anything but the endless azure, the ropes of waves and spume of whitecaps. A sea as wide as the earth.

Fighting away the fist, I force myself to keep swimming. I've lost all my weight-lessness now. I'm as heavy as cement.

Be alive. Please.

When I'm close enough to call out, I spit away the snorkel. "Hello?" My words feeble against the great seethe of the sea. "Hello?"

No response.

"*Yassou!*" I try in Greek. "Hello?"

Nothing. I swim closer, able to see the figure's face now, a tiny oval under a long tangle of wet black hair. A girl, a very little girl. Her eyes are closed, lips gray. She hangs suspended in the life jacket like a collapsed marionette.

Then begins a macabre chase like something out of a fever dream because the nearer I draw to her, the more the waves caused by my strokes push her away. Again and again, I reach for her life jacket only to send it spinning beyond my grasp. So I speed up and circle her like a shark, spiraling in closer and closer, the fist still trying to stop me, still trying to drag me away. Again, I make a grab for her. Again, I miss.

I dive underneath her instead.

Her legs dangle as limp as seaweed, swaying in the current. Chubby little girl legs. Pink leggings. Bare feet as pale as the underbelly of a fish.

Oh god, please.

Coming up beneath the life jacket, lungs ragged, I reach out yet again, trembling so violently I can barely control my hand. This time, though, I manage to grasp hold of a strap. Pull her to me.

Please, please be alive.

I touch her arm, my fingers shaking. Her skin is a hard cold, but not, I think, the cold of death. Treading water, my legs throbbing now, I feel for the pulse in her neck.

She *is* alive. But so cold and still . . . how long could she have been here—all night? All the way through that storm? I stroke her baby cheeks, rub her head. Nothing. So I touch her eyelids.

That does it. She jerks back, her eyes flipping open, liquid brown and terrified, and vomits a spurt of seawater. Only then does some color return to her lips.

"You'll be all right, sweetie, I promise, just don't fight me," I babble with no idea of whether she will understand. Lying on my back, I pull her face up onto my chest and wrap my left arm around her. Using my right to stroke, I start the swim back to land, frog kicking to avoid splashing more water into her mouth. *Kick gently but firmly*, I remember from my high school lifesaving class. *Remain calm but steady.*

Calm but steady.

The way is long, the water cold and colder, the wind picking up, and far from fighting me, the child is entirely limp and growing heavier by the minute. Gone is my welcoming Aegean, its soft and cradling hands. It only drags on me now, no longer a friend but an adversary, its steely waves slapping and punching.

If I can't make it to shore, I'll swim to the rowboat.

Kick and pull, kick and pull, heart straining, lungs searing, legs burning, mouth raw with salt. How could I have swum so far out? Whenever I crane my head around to see the rowboat, it looks no nearer than it did before. The harder I pull and kick, the longer I seem to stay in place.

The girl still hasn't made a sound. *Keep breathing, please.*

Kick by kick, stroke by stroke, legs trembling with the strain, I inch closer to the boat, although it seems to take hours. And finally, the breath almost gone from my lungs, I reach it.

My plan is to heave the child aboard, swim to where I can stand and pull the boat in by its rope. But I've lost the strength to lift her and am still out of my depth, so have nothing to use as leverage. I try, over and over I try, only to sink and splash more water into her face. Her eyes are closed again, the gray back in her lips.

The only choice is to keep swimming.

My arms are burning as much as my legs now, as if every muscle is tearing from its bone, and whenever I reach a foot down to feel for the seafloor, I sink and have to flail to the surface again, terrified that I've pulled her down with me. Only after scrabbling and kicking even longer do I feel stones beneath my feet.

This part is harder than the swimming, carrying her out against the powerful suck of the sea. Normally, when the surf is this rough, I crawl out, but that's not possible now. I nearly fall countless times, staggering wildly as I try to stay upright with her in my arms, the waves pummeling and pulling in their effort to knock us over. She has grown even heavier now without the water to hold her up, her life jacket and clothes sodden, her body as inert as a sack of sand. When I manage to stumble out at last, clutching her to me and gasping, the waves still snatching at my ankles, I collapse with her onto the stones.

Quickly, I flip her on her side to let her vomit out more water, and then onto her back, preparing to pump out what remains of the sea in her lungs and give her mouth-to-mouth, not that I really know how. But she is breathing normally, thank god, although every breath comes with a shudder. Her eyes are still closed, lips no longer gray but purple.

She is so young. Four or five at most.

As fast as my frigid hands will allow, I unstrap her life jacket—not a real life jacket but some cheap knockoff that I'm amazed held her up at all—and peel off her clothes: the leggings and, oddly, three dresses. Wrapping her in my towel, mercifully warm from the sun, I hold her close and rub her all over, both of us shivering violently. The towel is losing its warmth already, the wind lashing us as if to punish.

She moans, opens her terrified eyes again and stares at me, although what she sees I can't tell. Struggling to my feet, I carry her up the stony path to the house, a path that had seemed as short as a stumble but now feels as long as a mile. Only later do I wonder where I found the strength.

Rushing into my apartment, I turn on the shower and step under the warm water with her, clutching her to my body, rubbing her gently all over with a washcloth, careful not to let the temperature get too hot or cold. She hangs in my arms like a waterlogged doll, but the purple does gradually recede from her lips, although her skin is still clammy and her eyelids keep drifting closed. I vaguely remember that hypothermia must be handled extremely carefully but can't remember what carefully is, so all I can think to do once I've dried us off is to get into bed with her, swaddle us both in warm covers and pillows, and hold her close with one hand while frantically Googling what to do on my phone with the other.

I learn that I must keep her awake, still and warm; cover her head; elevate her feet. That I should exhale into her mouth so she can inhale my warm breath. That we must stay here for a long while. That as soon as she is fully awake, I should give her something warm to drink, a dribble at a time.

She shivers for many minutes before she flips open her eyes again. Deep brown, huge.

Mama.

I see the word form on her lips, although she makes no sound.

"Little Linnette," I whisper, half unconscious myself, "don't be scared, I have you safe now, sweetie. I have you safe with me."

BOOK TWO

JUNE, ONE MONTH EARLIER

2

AMINA

Down in the town here, old men sit in their cafés smoking cigarettes, playing dominoes, dice or cards, drinking ouzo or metaxa, coffee or sugar-laced tea. Talk and braggadocio, grizzle and gristle, legs spread to display the dangling insistence of testicles. Women swing past, lips glossed, shopping bags heavy, hair dyed a rusty red, their children, sleek and fat, careening by on bicycles, sucking on ice creams. Tourists come and go under sunhats and sunglasses, snapping photos, applying lotions, spending money.

We, on the other hand, stay high up on the hill in a metal box, packed onto rows of bunk beds with thirty-four other people, like rolls of carpet on a merchant's shelf. Leila found us two bunks in a back corner, she and I on the lower levels, her sons Hazem and Majid, boys as small and sharp as thorns, above, our only privacy the gray blankets we hang around our bedframes and the clothes we use to cover our bodies. Inside these we pretend to have a home.

Sometimes we look down at ourselves, shocked at how this place has changed us. Leila, a widow of not even forty, has grown bloated from the foul air and food here, her face as pale as wheat, hair greased for want of water. Our friend Nafisa, who sleeps alone in a tent outside, is not much older, but with her skin ashy and cheeks sunken, could pass for eighty.

As for me, I am only nineteen, yet since I lost Mama and all I know, I feel as old as the moon.

Leila's children, too, have been transformed here: Majid, seven years old and pinched-faced; Hazem, who even at nine has the chary eyes of an adult. Once well-groomed and fed, they now look like the children of the poor, clothes faded, skin wan, bodies scrawny. The heel of Majid's flip-flop has been broken off for weeks, forcing him to hobble.

Leila has a daughter and granddaughter, too: Farah, little but fierce, and her child, Dunia, a girl of five, but they were snatched from us on a Turkish beach. We have not heard from them since.

This morning, in my usual sleeplessness, I watch Leila rise just before dawn and dress in the semidarkness. I know what she's about to do: slip her feet into a pair of the plastic sandals piled by the door, run down the narrow concrete path to the camp police office, cling to the cage that holds the newcomers and search for Farah and Dunia. She does this every time she hears of a new boat arriving, just as she stands for hours by that office every day, using its Wi-Fi to read the Boat Reports and count the drowned.

When she returns a short time later, her back slumped yet again in defeat, we wake the boys and tell them to dress, even though it's not yet light, because our mornings are long and full of waiting. First, for one of the only two working toilets at the far end of the metal box, the children yawning and gripping their crotches. Then, for a shower, clutching our optimistic towels and shampoo, praying to the water not to cut off. And then again along the narrow cement path that circles the restaurant—also a metal box—where we stand for three hours, Hazem and Majid dropping to the ground with groans, young men as ribbed as street dogs pressing in around us, the stenches of hunger and anger enveloping us like a gas. Only after we finally reach the serving window and pick up the miniature juice box and crescent of bread that make our daily breakfast do we haul ourselves up the stony mountainside to join Nafisa.

"So here you are, my sisters." She raises her gaunt face to us. "You took your time this morning."

"I swear the lines grow longer every day," Leila grumbles, bending to kiss her. We drop onto a log under our olive tree, its trunk as twisted as a knot of old rope but its branches generous with shade. Hazem squats beside us, his tangle of dark hair flopping over his brow, knees around his ears like a grasshopper's, drawing letters in the dust with a twig—I've been helping him practice his writing in the absence of a school here. Majid tries to imitate him, squinting in concentration, but his letters come out as nothing but scratches. By their ages, I'd been reading and writing for years. Neither of them mentions the missing: their sister Farah, their niece Dunia, their dead father and uncle. Neither of them says much at all.

For a time we sit in silence, gazing down the mountain at the glistering sea below, its turquoise and silver, the thread where it melts into the horizon. Yawning, I pin up my hair, heavy and hot in this heat. Leila glances around the steep hillside and, seeing no men nearby, pulls off her hijab and ruffles the short brown hair beneath. Without the scarf, she looks ten years younger, even in her faded galabeya, but then she ties it back on with a sigh. Nafisa sits as still as the wood on which she's perched, her spine upright, high-boned face drained, hair cropped and graying. Her long limbs fold inside her tunic and trousers like a bundle of sticks.

We scratch at our skins, stippled with bedbug and mosquito bites. Empty plastic bottles skitter by our feet in the wind. "You look troubled today, little Amina," Nafisa says at last, her voice rasping and worn. "What is it, child, you are thinking of your mama again?"

I nod. The past is an ocean of sorrow for those of us trapped in this camp, yet somehow I need to plunge into it again and again.

Mama and my brother Tahar, I tell her. It is because of him that I am here.

Tahar, skinny as a sapling with frizzy brown hair that stuck out all over his head, was the youngest of my three elder brothers and the only one who was kind to me. Whenever our father was in one of his rages, shouting at Mama or me or at someone on the phone, Tahar would take me aside and wipe away my tears with his thumbs, blinking behind the huge glasses that he thought made him look like a rock star but really made him look like a mouse. "Don't cry, little sis," he liked to say. "You don't want Baba ever to know he can make you cry. Come." And he would put a kite in my hands, one of the airy diamonds he made from tissue paper and ribbons, and lead me out to the dusty road beside our house, where we would run with the string until the kite seemed to scoop all the clouds from the sky.

"I had two brothers myself, you know," Leila tells Nafisa, who is not from Syria like us, but Sudan. She glances at her boys hunched over the parched earth. "I lost them both to the army and the war, Allah bring rest to their souls. I lost my husband and son-in-law, too. Bashar al-Assad took them all, curse his evil head."

Nafisa rests a sympathetic hand on her knee. Leila spits and stands to kick away a wad of used toilet paper. "God, I'm sick of living in this filth." She sits back down with a grunt.

My brothers also were forced to join the army, I say then. First Abdullah, the eldest, and then Zakoor, the middle one, even though they had wives and children to support. And as soon as Tahar turned eighteen, Bashar took him as well, leaving me the only child in our home.

Once all my brothers were gone, dread moved into our house in their stead. As terrifying as it was to lie in bed listening for the scream of a missile or whistle of a bomb that would send us scrambling to the basement, that was nothing compared to the fear we felt waiting for the knock on the door or ring of a phone that might bring bad news. My father suffered terribly, never mind that he had supported Bashar and hustled my brothers into the army with pride. Baba had always stood tall and confident before, big-bellied and old though he was—much older than Mama—but the more brutal the war grew, the more his fears for my brothers bent his back and shriveled his flesh. His only comfort was to gather the family in front of the television, if the electricity was working, and listen to the government's reassuring lies. Mama's thin face as gray as her hair in the television's light. Baba fingering his counting beads and mumbling prayers. The pock-skinned girls Abdullah and Zakoor had married huddled under their galabeyas, eyeing him warily and hushing their children. How I wished we could all shake free of that room, the war and the lies, run out into a sunshine free of bombs, and breathe.

We lived with that dread for four years, each new phase of war bringing us new secrets to keep and new dangers to dodge. When the rebel Free Army pushed Bashar's forces out of our city of Manbij, Mama and I privately celebrated—"Better to live as a free dog than a caged lion, no?" she whispered. But Baba was even more distraught because now he could no longer boast about his sons in the army but had to hide their affiliations instead. And when, two years after that, the rebels were in turn defeated by Daesh, and Baba had to grow out his beard, bow and scrape, while we women were forced to bury ourselves under burqas, he couldn't even mention my brothers without putting all our lives at risk.

Fate is so perverse. Why is this, Aunties? I know religious scholars have their theories: God testing us or punishing us for our sins. But to me God is nothing but caprice, manipulating our fates to bless or torture us for no reason at all. Look at how he treats us in this camp. Thousands of us squeezed together like crated chickens, forced to shuffle through filth and rats just to find food or fresh air. What have we done to earn such treatment? Is it a crime to try to stay alive?

"Ours is not to question Allah's wisdom," Leila answers, massaging her legs. She slides her eyes again to her boys, who are still poking in the dirt a few meters away. "He has his reasons for everything."

"Nonsense." Nafisa pulls up a tuft of yellow grass with her long fingers and braids three of its blades into a string. "Of course we must question. Why else would Allah give us brains?"

Baba was the one who brought Tahar back to us, with the help of two of Tahar's fellow fighters disguised in civilian clothes. A bullet to his boy's throat, another to his left eye, more where we couldn't see. "We were fighting in Idlib," they had told Baba over the phone. "Please, *Abu* Abdullah, come." That was how we discovered that Tahar had defected from Bashar's forces to join the rebels and fight for our liberty instead, which meant that my tender Tahar, still only twenty-one, had been killed by the comrades of our own brothers, while those brothers, who licked the anuses of the powerful and enforced the murderous policies of our president, had come home unscathed. What reason, Auntie Leila, would Allah give for that?

Leila looks at the ground.

Mama said not a word when Baba and Tahar's friends carried my poor brother into the house. She didn't even cry. She only stood silent and upright in her black abaya, as though she had turned into a rod of iron. But I saw the light die out in her eyes. Even the light that looked at me.

Tahar's comrades, boys no older than nineteen, laid his body on our back room table, while Baba stood beside them, wringing his meaty hands, the folds of his face collapsing. "Tahar was a good man and a loyal fighter, may Allah bring his soul to rest in peace," the boys murmured—boys who should have been playing football, studying and laughing and looking for girls to kiss. Then they handed me Tahar's mouse glasses and hurried back to war, leaving Baba, my brothers, and me as still as Mama.

That is when she broke. With a shriek like a tree tearing from its roots, she flung herself on Tahar and clasped his body to hers, kissing his ruined eye and pressing her lips to what remained of his throat. "Talk to me!" she cried. "Come back, my beautiful boy!"

Her grief for the moment froze mine. The more desperately she wailed, the less I could make a sound or move or even think. I gripped his glasses and stared.

My father and brothers wanted to bury him right then, with no washing or shrouding. "Tahar died a martyr and so is already purified," Baba insisted, barely able to speak through his tears. "Move away, Hana, and let us give him a soldier's burial. We need to hurry before Daesh finds us."

But Mama refused to move or even let them come near to Tahar. "He's my son! Leave him with me or my curse will doom you all to die in shame! My Tahar had a heart as white as a child's, and not one of you men is worth a single hair on his head."

My brothers and Baba stared at her for a long moment, unsure of what to do. I stared too. I had never seen her this defiant. Mama, orphaned at thirteen, whose uncle had sold her to Baba, already old and fat, when her breasts were still tiny cakes on her chest and her hips as narrow as a goat's. Who, until then, had always been so submissive.

Finally, the fear of God—or maybe her curse—won the day. Baba and my brothers turned and left the room.

"Men all over the world are afraid of a mother's curse," Nafisa says, leaning forward to brush a line of ants off her sandaled feet.

Leila scratches a swollen ankle. "It's their own weakness men fear, nothing more."

Either way, Aunties, Mama only truly began her mourning once they were gone. How gently she caressed Tahar, rebuttoning his blood-soaked shirt, smoothing down his sleeves, straightening his trousers, all the while talking to him as though he were a little boy. "Here, *habibi*, let me clean your face." Pulling off her hijab, she used it to dab his gouged eye as carefully as if he might wince and turn away. "There, my beloved, isn't that better? Does it hurt? Please tell me it doesn't hurt." Yet when I reached out to caress him myself, she stopped me. "You're too young to touch a body, *benti*. Step back."

"But I need to touch him! I love him more than anybody!"

She looked at me a long moment, the tears on her cheeks threaded with his blood, her blouse and even her mouth stained with it, too. "All right, but only from the knees down, you understand?" I hugged and kissed his legs, the only part of him that had not been torn by bullets, while she lifted his lifeless body to her own with a strength I'd never before seen in her, as if he were, indeed, a small boy again, and held him to her, rocking him and crying out her *dua* for the dead.

Ya Allah! Write my beloved's name in the Book of Good Deeds, for he has done such good in the world.

Only then did she give Baba and my brothers permission to return. They looked shocked at the sight of her smeared in so much blood, and tried to avoid meeting her eyes as they laid Tahar out on a plank. Together, we recited Mama's favorite *sura*, and once our prayer was replaced by silence, they lifted Tahar to their shoulders and carried him away to a grave, as only men are allowed to do, tears no different from mine running into their beards and prayers no different from hers tumbling from their lips.

After they left, Mama pushed me aside and stumbled to her bed, where she lay moaning and wailing, the empty house echoing with her heartbreak. I rushed from room to room to escape the sound, but her wails followed me to every corner, clinging to me like a beggar child. Finally, I abandoned her and ran upstairs to my bedroom, where I plugged my ears with cotton and did what I'd long since taken to doing when in need of comfort: I wrote a poem.

For one, two, three entire days I wrote, until I'd carved all my grief and outrage into an elegy for Tahar. Every minute I could steal from sleep and the hours I had to help Mama cook for the relatives and neighbors who streamed through our house to pay their respects, I wrote. Bitter and furious, my poem railed against the waste of Tahar's precious life, the readiness of old men to destroy families by sending their brothers and sons to slaughter, the senselessness of war.

"Mama," I said when I was finished, bringing my poem to her in the kitchen, "what do you think?"

She put down her cooking spoon and read it, her knotted hands trembling with sorrow. "I agree with every word, little moon," she said, wrapping me in her arms, her scents of cinnamon and cooking oil curling around me like a shawl. "But if the wrong people see this, you could be accused of criticizing Bashar. I know it's hard, *habibti*, but make your words a cake of honey in which you have buried blades."

Angry but knowing she was right, I returned to my room to rewrite yet again.

The next version still spoke of youth squandered and families erased, of a brother lost and a future cancelled, but gone were my references to the madness of war and power-hungry old men. My poem was naïve and clumsy, I know that now, but it was sincere. "Yes, this is better," Mama said. "You have indeed buried your blades in honey. Your father and brothers will be impressed."

Oh, the lethal vanity of a mother's heart.

"A mother's pride isn't always lethal," Leila objects, raising her eyebrows at me.

"It can save lives," agrees Nafisa, stretching her long legs out from under her skirt.

Aunties, it did not save me.

Two weeks later, when our official mourning period was over and our guests had at last stopped sneaking through the bullets to visit, Mama suggested that I recite my poem to the family after we had finished our evening meal. My elder brothers, who were on bereavement leave from the army, and their wives and children were all there, including my niece and best friend, Fatima, Abdullah's firstborn, only two years younger than I am.

Once we had cleared away the last of the dishes and served the tea and everyone had resettled themselves on the cushions around Mama's flowered *sofra*, my brothers and father smoothing down their beards and rolling cigarettes, I was allowed to begin. I stood in my favorite dark red skirt and blouse, feeling strong and fierce, the way Tahar had most loved me, certain that I would not only impress everyone with the poem, but move them with the honor I had paid my brother.

After I finished, a hush fell over the room. I looked from face to face—Baba's sagging and purple under the eyes, Abdullah's flushed above his bush of a black beard, Zakoor's sharp-nosed and gingery, their wives' wan and pimpled, Mama's drained, Fatima's smooth and pink—faces belonging to people I'd known all my life. Every one of them had tears on their cheeks. Every one of them but Mama avoided my gaze.

Baba finally wiped his eyes. "Daughter," he said in his smoke-roughened voice, "for all our sakes, burn that poem and never speak of it again."

Two days later, Zakoor suggested that he take me and Abdullah's children, Fatima and her little brothers, to visit our uncle in Aleppo. "Are you mad?" Mama said. "It's much too dangerous with those Daesh fanatics everywhere."

"Oh, be quiet, woman," he replied, his orange beard waggling. "The kids need cheering. Abdullah and I both think so."

Zakoor had learned early from Abdullah never to show Mama much respect, just as he imitated him in every other matter, too: joining Baba's business trading in furniture fabrics, marrying when Abdullah married, taking on his pro-Bashar politics—even enlisting in the same branch of the army. Ever since Zakoor had been a boy, he had lurked in Abdullah's shadow, his skin pasty where Abdullah's was ruddy, body puny where Abdullah's was robust, hair red where Abdullah's was black, a boy destined to fawn over the powerful and take out his humiliations on his village girl of a wife. "Poor Zakoor, his spine is made of butter," Mama had whispered to me more than once.

So off to Aleppo we went.

As Zakoor drove, I gazed out of the back window, trying both to see and not see the destruction around us. A city that's been bombed is like a body that has been crushed, isn't this so, Aunties? Ruptured skin, cracked ribs, splintered spine, scattered organs. Wires dangling like exposed nerves, walls gaping like wounds. Windowless houses like faces with their eyes gouged out. I thought of the day a bomb had fallen on our neighbors' house, killing my friend Rania and her entire family, the remains of their lives scattered for anyone to see: a doll, a chair, a slipper, a toothbrush. A spoon. I closed my eyes, longing for the Manbij of my childhood, the city of roses and rivers where I had run with Tahar—longing for Tahar himself.

"Manbij, city of gold and light," Leila murmurs.

"No offense, sister," Nafisa says, "but nostalgia can gild even a pile of shit." She shifts her long body emphatically on her log.

Zakoor had not been driving long before we were stopped at a Daesh checkpoint—nothing more than a pile of sandbags blocking the road and three sullen *mujahideen* in mud-spattered fatigues chewing on *miswaaks* and fiddling with their beards. When the regime had controlled Manbij, it had always been easy for us to pass through checkpoints, thanks to my brothers' positions in the army, not to mention the wads of liras and packs of cigarettes they would slip to the guards. But now, under Daesh, we knew such tricks would be fatal, cigarettes and bribes being forbidden. I sat beside my cousins in the back of the car, shaking under my burqa, which for once felt like a shield rather than a cage, while I watched the *mujahideen* picking their teeth with those little sticks as though they had all the time in the world.

We had to pass through three such checkpoints that day—three long waits drenched in terror while the cars in front of us edged forward as slowly as caterpillars, until we reached a final barricade in Aleppo itself, this one controlled by the regime army. The wait here was no less terrifying than the others because, just as Daesh liked to drag whoever they wanted off to be tortured or killed for no reason at all, so did our president.

"Don't worry," Zakoor whispered as we crept closer to the guards, "I've got my military ID here." He pulled it from his groin. "And I also have . . ." He held out a hand until Fatima, who was only fourteen, produced the two packs of cigarettes he had forced her to hide under her burqa. He flashed a grin, as if he hadn't just risked his own niece's life.

When, at last, it was our turn to be inspected, Zakoor pulled the car up to the officer in charge with an obsequious smile. I was expecting the man to give us a nod, slip the bribe up his sleeve, and wave us on. But no. "Pull your car over and get out," he ordered in the menacing bark common to all bullies in uniform.

I glanced at Fatima as we climbed out. She looked as frightened and bewildered as I was. Zakoor seemed strangely calm, however, stroking his long beard as though it were a cat. I suddenly wondered why he had brought Abdullah's children and me but not his own. "What's going on, *saydi*?" he asked the officer politely, holding out his ID papers with a stack of liras and the cigarettes tucked underneath. "May I help you with something?"

"That one," is all the officer replied, pocketing the bribe and pointing at me. And before I could grasp what was happening, two soldiers seized my arms, tied my wrists behind my back, gagged my screams silent, and threw me roughly into the wooden hut behind them.

And so, at sixteen years old, I was accused by *al mukhabarat,* Bashar's intelligence agency, of collaborating with terrorists—that is, with Tahar's fellow revolutionaries—and carted away to prison for three years. My crime? The poem.

3

HILMA

"Kosmos," I say to my host on my second morning here as he drives me to Vathi so I can buy toothpaste and sunscreen, "I can't stop thinking about the refugee camp."

He looks at me, the lines around his little eyes wrinkling in concern. "Miss Khilma, you must not worry your mind with such thoughts. I should not have told you, my guest, about this sad thing. You are in the land of the gods, of dark wine seas and Pythagoras, who you said yourself is your hero."

I did say that, true. Pythagoras of the hypotenuse squared, father of numbers, lover of wisdom, influencer of Plato. Pythagoras believed that odd numbers are masculine and even numbers feminine, which makes sense to me, odds being clearly spiky and phallic, evens round and soft. He also believed, as far as history can sort out, in moderation. All over Samos, shops sell a goblet they call the Pythagorean cup, which he supposedly invented and which uses the principal of hydrostatic pressure to spill wine all over you if you're greedy enough to fill the cup to the brim, hence demonstrating the wisdom of eschewing greed in all forms, whether for wine, food, money, fame, or love. A lesson I certainly can't claim to have learned.

"This evening, when you return to my house, come up to my terrace," Kosmos is saying. "Have some of our local wine and watch the sea until she turns this same color of Homer. You need to relax, *Kyria* Khilma, and stop all this plaguing of your mind."

I'm coming to quite like Kosmos, despite his objectionable opinions.

"But I want to see the camp," I tell him then in the car. "Where is it, exactly?"

"It is up, up above the town. You can walk to find it. But it is run by the government, Miss Khilma, so the guards they won't let you in."

"Why not? What are they trying to hide?"

"I think it is for the health." He casts me another worried frown. "Miss Khilma, do your host a favor. Do not go there. It is not safe. Those refugees they bring AIDS and who knows what diseases."

"Kosmos, I can't get AIDS from walking around in the air."

"*Dax.* But that disease, the one they call TB, this you can. So, if you must be stubborn like a donkey, at least please wear a—what you call it, the white bandages those Chinese they put on their faces?"

"A surgical mask?"

"Yes. This I have one of. I can lend her to you. All my friends here who work in the camp, they wear the mask."

"Kosmos, do you ever read the news or check your facts on the computer?"

"I do not like the computer. You want me to lend to you this mask?"

"Thank you. But I'll be fine."

Once he drops me off, I head straight up to the camp, whatever Kosmos says, resolved to keep my unspoken promise to Theo. The distance isn't far but the climb is arduous under the burn of the noonday sun, most of the streets lacking shade, although they are resplendent with perfume and color: jasmine bushes the size of cars, red hibiscus like giant bouquets, technicolor spills of purple and fuchsia bougainvillea. I pull on my practical if unflattering beige sun hat and push on, passing modern shopfronts nestled beside ancient stone houses, an imposing Orthodox church as white as a creampuff, bland cement office blocks. The town rises so steeply up the mountain that some of its narrower streets are nothing but long flights of steps, as precipitous as ladders, which leave me panting. From Kosmos's terrace, Vathi might look like a pile of sugar cubes, but up close it's more like a box of peppermints, its pastel yellows, mint greens, and baby blues topped by undulant terracotta roofs. And, like almost everywhere in Greece, it has its share of skeletal, half-built houses, the concrete ruins of new homes nobody could afford to finish.

A stray tabby dashes across my path, thin as a fishbone, patchy and one-eared. It slinks under a parked car and crouches there, peering out at me with panicked green eyes.

Up I climb, my skin griming with sweat-stuck dust and evaporating sunscreen. On the way I pass three women walking downhill together with two under-nourished boys, all of whom eye me with open curiosity. Most tourists don't venture into this part of town, and I, in my inelegant khaki capris, baggy pink T-shirt and unfortunate hat, am clearly a tourist. I am curious about these women, too, and wish I could think of a way to open a conversation with them, find out who they are and how they live—for Theo's sake, if not my own.

One of the women, an African, whose hair is closely shorn and speckled with gray, is draped in loose black trousers and a slim tunic of forest green. She is strikingly tall and long-limbed, her posture erect, but too emaciated to be healthy. Yet I can tell she was beautiful once, her small face graced with high cheekbones and large eyes, her head delicate atop a long and slender neck.

In contrast, her friend, whom I guess is an Arab, is short and plump, and moves as though she's weighed down by her black robe, her equally black headscarf pinching her round face, so pallid it's almost doughy—how she bears all those clothes in this heat is beyond me. She's holding both boys by the hand, each of whom has a dangle of brown hair over his brow and a face as narrow as a ferret's, the smaller boy limping because the back of his flip-flop has snapped off. Both are dressed in a pair of worn gray sweatpants and a faded T-shirt printed with English words I wonder if they understand. One says, *I ♥ GREECE*. The other: *ON THE ROAD AGAIN*.

The third woman intrigues me the most, maybe because she's really only a girl, perhaps the plump woman's daughter. Like her, she's small, no taller than my own five foot three, but her head is uncovered, her auburn hair pulled back but curling down to her waist, and she's in western clothes: a white T-shirt and stretchy blue jeans, her figure so slight she barely fills them out. She looks tired, stains circling her wide eyes, yet her face is pretty, a little heart-shaped face that starts up an ache in me.

I nod at the women and smile. The young one smiles back, a quick, shy smile, but the older women ignore me and soon pass, the moment over. I wonder which wars they fled, whom they have lost, what they have suffered.

At the top of the town, I finally reach a treeless highway, beyond which an incline of sandy earth, straw-colored grass, and olive trees stretches up the mountain. I wander back and forth, the sun reflecting up from the sticky asphalt as if to roast me from both sides at once, the occasional car zipping by in a gust of hot wind, but for the life of me, I can't find the camp. I do come across a narrow concrete pathway flanked by hurricane fences, however, down which people are pouring—teenaged boys, shrouded women laden with bags or babies, old men bent and shuffling. Yet as soon as I approach, a mustachioed cop jumps out of a booth and stops me, just as Kosmos predicted.

"*Apagorévetai I eísodos!*" he shouts. "*Pigaínete étsi!*" He points to his left and waves his arms in passionate circles, his mustache jumping excitedly. "Go there!" he tries in English, and waves his arms in circles again.

Is this a camp or a prison? I ask myself, aware that this is not an original question. The guard may be incomprehensible, but a sign on the hurricane fence beside him is clear enough: a picture of a camera with a red line struck through it. Again, I wonder what his government is hiding.

Defeated, I plod back down the hot hill, strangely disappointed, given that I don't really want to go into that ghastly camp at all. I just resent being thwarted.

At the seafront, I head to the main square, gratifyingly named Pythagoras, a wide plaza paved in black marble and circled by sprawling outdoor cafés, all overlooked by an imposing marble lion who strongly resembles a kitten with a perm. In Arabic, the word for lion is Assad, the adopted name of the man responsible for at least two thirds of the refugees right here on this island, three of whom happen to be sitting at the same café I've chosen. Young and lanky— mere boys, really, their chins free of beard—one is rolling a cigarette as thin as a toothpick, another is squinting into his phone, the third petting a scrofulous kitten whining at his feet. But when the waitress, a motherly type whose hair is dyed the same maroon I see on many local women here, brings my coffee and the men politely ask for one each, too—in Greek, no less—she retreats into her doorway. "You no stay here!" she shouts at them in English, pointing at the sea, her arm flab wobbling. "Go!"

The men look bewildered.

"Go or I call police!" she shouts again, shooing them away exactly as she might the flea-bitten cat I saw earlier. "*Μαλάκα!*"

They leave, holding their heads high but saying not a word.

"Why did you do that?" I ask her after they've gone.

"My clientele, they do not want those people here."

"I'm your clientele and I don't mind."

She eyes me with frank disbelief. "No. You tourists, you see these people enough in your towns at home. You no want see them here."

"That's ridiculous! Why did you have to be so rude to them?"

Mom, Theo would say, *don't fight with the natives. Listen and learn instead.*

I don't think I'm very good at listening and learning. Anyway, Theo, you would have fought.

I look up *μαλάκα—malaka* in our alphabet—on my phone. It means one who masturbates so much his brain has turned soft.

After leaving Vathi, I take a long swim at an official beach named Limonakia, self-disgust dragging at my ankles like a tangle of seaweed. Not only did I break doctor's orders by arguing with that waitress, I accomplished nothing today beyond behaving like a voyeur.

Limonakia is a few kilometers from Kosmos's house, a small and sheltered bay flanked by cliffs that reminds me of the beach in France where I taught Linnette what to do with waves. If a big one threatens to break over you, I told her, dive through it, don't try to ride it. That way you won't be tumbled about like underpants in a dryer. She giggled at that, squirming in delight. Like all small children, she loved any mention of underpants and all other matters related to bottoms. My little tadpole.

I'm not supposed to think about Linnette. Another of my doctor's orders. *Do not*, commands the psychologist, *think of a white bear.*

How Linnette did love the sea. I first started bringing her to it when she was only a year old, leaving Theo and Megan behind to work and take time alone together. I found a fishing village for us in Provence, cream and peach, the only sounds the cackle of gulls and groan of foghorns, the lick of waves. There, I rented a cottage the size of a fishing boat, so tiny and low-beamed I had to duck into the kitchen, climb a red ladder to the bedrooms. Linnette and I went back every summer.

I taught her to swim there before she was even three. Her baby legs frogging, her tadpole wriggle. She liked best to swim underwater, wagging like an Aegean fish. The summer she was four, she took to roaming the beach collecting shells and sea glass, her little body bent intently over the sand. Sturdy legs, round tummy, ropes of coppery curls falling down her back, her bucket so heavy she could barely haul it up to the house. She spent hours arranging her treasures, measuring the effect with calculating eyes. Soon she had them lining our windowsills and skirting boards, filling the gaps between our books. Scallops and periwinkles, conches with mouths the pink of gums. Cowries, coquinas, and angel wings. The sea glass she put in jam jars, crystals of indigo and ruby, topaz and amber, spinning rainbows all over the house. "Don't move them, Granny," she would tell me. "They're just where I want."

My husband, Nick, came to join us on the weekends he could get off work—he edits a business magazine that has always eaten him alive—while I swam with her and painted, borrowing colors from the pinks of her shells and the blues of the sea. I wasn't afraid of blue those days, but then it wasn't the Aegean. Most of all, I painted her. Fiery curls, fern-green eyes, plump little limbs. I mounted her image on every wall in the cottage.

All those paintings are gone now. Hidden. Destroyed. Erased.

We may hope for forgiveness, I read somewhere, but only a fool expects it.

A fisherman befriended us during our last summer there while Nick was away. Jacques. He would come to sell us his catch, stay for a lingering glass or three of absinthe and tell us the village gossip. He was scandalously beautiful, and were I not faithfully married and nearly twice his age, I would have been tempted, even though his mind was no livelier than the fish he grilled for us each night. Skin tanned to the color of toffee, arms as hard as wood, hair black as a seal's, eyes the aquamarine of a wave.

Jacques was kind to Linnette. Did the things fatherly men do—the things Theo did when he was with her. Lifted her to his shoulders, threw her in the air, romped with her in the grass. I played those games with her, too, but it seemed my lifts were not so thrilling, my throws not so high, my romps not so raucous. She and Jacques would run over the lawn kicking a beach ball, rolling down a hill, she clutching her little belly in laughter, staggering to her feet with her hair full of daises and grass. I grew jealous.

Jaques was a broody sort, though. Not even thirty, yet already in love with the loneliness of oceans. Even while he was drinking and laughing with us, I could see in his maritime eyes the longing for horizons, for the sun crimsoning the waves, the leap of dolphins and kiss of breakers against his prow.

He liked to take us out on his boat and did so often, I trying to smile while my gills grew green. Linnette, though, was a duck to his water. Walking the deck at five years old with perfect balance. Holding a gasping fish as it flapped in her hands, bashing in its head with aplomb. I looked at her in surprise at that, having thought her gentle. But she had not a squeamish thread to her, nor a sentimental one, either. She was fond enough of her pets at home: her bunny, her puppy, her short-lived hamster, balding and crippled by the age of two. But if they died or a butcher hung up a skinned rabbit in front of her in the market, she didn't flinch. "Don't be silly, Granny, it's just nature," she'd say, her little voice as phlegmatic as a farmwife's. "Everything has to die."

On the hot days, she would jump off the side of the boat, my fearless tadpole, her tender limbs disappearing beneath the surface while my heart leapt under my tongue and lay there, quivering. "Come back!" I would call. "Come back!"

The day Jaques stopped visiting, not long after Linnette turned six, she blamed me. "You should have been nicer to him, Granny." She pursed her little mouth in condemnation.

"I was nice to him."

"No, you weren't. You always looked bored when he talked. That's why he liked me better than you."

He did, it was true. And yes, I was bored.

We got over it, Linnette and I, although it was harder for her. She moped. She snapped. She climbed the red ladder to her room and stayed there for hours, reading book after book in her precocious way, playing her electronic games, or scribbling misspelled, furious secrets in her little diary, which of course I snooped through while she was playing outside. "Granny made Jak go way. I luv Granny, but sumtimes she's a grump. I luv Mommy and Daddy to. I mis them."

Her nest of a room. The stuffed animals arranged according to color, a chrono-gram of black to yellow marching along the shelf. Her books of fairytales and intrepid adventuresses. Her jars of sea glass and shells. Her sleek little bathing suits, baskets of hair bands, resolute refusal to own a doll or wear a dress—she hated anything with a frill. Her fierce little diary.

I open my eyes, lost over where I am. Floating on my back in the sea, thinking the thoughts that are forbidden.

4

LEILA

Hellenic Boat Report
June 22, at 6:23 AM

Three boats arrived on Samos this morning,
carrying 166 people: 18 women, 12 children,
136 men.

So far today, 8 boats have been stopped by the
Turkish Coast Guard; 405 people have been arrested.

❧

Dropping my cell phone into the worn pocket of my galabeya, I gaze down at my luckless sons standing beside me. What childhoods I might have given you, my loves, had you not come into the world when you did. Hazem, you could be playing your beloved football in parks and streets, rather than having to make do with kicking pebbles against a fence. Majid, born with the voice of a songbird, you could be taking singing lessons with your friends instead of rubbing your ears and straining to hear. You would both have a father and uncles instead of a family of widows. You would both be in school, learning history and mathematics, penmanship and geography—learning to think.

Such ordinary things for a mother to give her children. Such ordinary things now out of my reach.

Yalla, I say to them quietly, let's go look for your sister and Dunia. And grasping their hands, small and fragile as sparrows, I pull them the few meters over to the cage by the camp police station to search for those eighteen women and twelve children who arrived today amongst the hundred and thirty-six men.

Many other camp dwellers are here to look for their lost ones, too, jostling one another as they push forward to the cage, each murmuring names, not daring to shout for fear of the police: "Maria, Ahmed, Miriam." The names tangle like the words of dreamers. "Hakim, Rifan, Hossein, Liliane, Azita."

Farah, Dunia, I chant with them, as if reciting a prayer. *Farah, Dunia.*

"Farah, Dunia," my boys echo, their voices tiny.

But nobody amongst those eighteen rescued women is Farah. And not one of those twelve children is Dunia. There are only hundreds of frightened, bewildered strangers locked inside the cage and a group of angry police officers outside, shouting at us to go away.

The disappointment drops through me like a stone.

"Why aren't they ever here, Mama?" Hazem asks, Majid watching us with a knot of incomprehension on his brow. "Aren't they ever going to come?"

I crouch down and gather my boys close, these boys who have lost too much already.

Don't worry, my loves, I tell them, your sister and Dunia will come, *insh'Allah*.

And only when I say this do I believe it to be true. They will come.

5

NAFISA

For thirteen months now I have lived in this coffin of a tent, squeezed between one shipping container and the next like a beetle between bricks. The keepers of this place put me here, I assume, because they see me as old and without power. But I am not old, only withered before my time. And I am not without power. I am hiding.

I am able to escape, though, at least when the moon is no more than a curl in the sky and I can wrap the dark about me like a cloak. Rising quietly so as not to disturb my neighbors, I weave up the hill, past the other tents and shipping containers, the towering lights that stare down at us like great angry eyes, and slip through a hole in the fence at the top. There, I climb high above the camp, far out of reach of the town and the keepers, and further than I ever go with Amina and Leila, until I find a quiet spot and a soft patch of pine needles and herbs on which to make my bed.

All night I lie swaddled in the perfumes of resin and sage, searching for you, Amal, in the sky. I trace the invisible lines from star to star until I find you etched throughout the heavens. And there, with you dancing above me, I am content.

You were never a child I was supposed to love as I do, little heart, and I knew what it was to love a child because I gave birth to four before you. Osman, the father you never had, welcomed each of your brothers and sisters into the world with song and celebration, as he would have welcomed you. Osman, a boy to my girl when we married, childhood heartsweets, whose faith in me was as stead-fast as the earth beneath our feet. I search for him in the night sky, too, but can never find him.

When two people have loved each other ever since they were children, as he and I did, it is hard to point to the moment when we slipped from innocence to passion. I only know that I had always counted the minutes until I would catch sight of him walking by, or hear his voice calling me from outside, when my heart would pick up, jump and cartwheel until my cheeks burned and my chest cramped. What a smile he had, so kind it hugged the world. What eyes, shining with a pleasure that could warm a room. What arms, able to hold the whole of me, and I am not small. What a voice, deep and soft like the wind in the night. We could not keep from loving each other until our parents said, enough, marry and marry now. We were fifteen.

I tell you this under the stars, Amal, or I tell it to Amina and Leila under our olive tree. I do not always remember which.

We owned a little farm in the southeastern state of Blue Nile, Osman and I, be-queathed to us on our marriage by my grandfather, the village chief. There, we raised a small herd of cows for milk and breeding, and cultivated vegetables and groundnuts, sunflowers and sesame to sell in the market, our children helping us however they could. Faisal, your eldest brother and our firstborn, tended the vegetable garden. I can see his serious little body now, crouched intently over the small patch of okra we had taught him how to grow, his head bowed, his small hands busy at the weeds, the knobs of his knees scuffed but sturdy. Faisal was my helpmeet, my twenty-sixth rib, the little man-boy by my side.

Your sisters, Yusra and Aisha, had the job of guarding the cows, crying if we had to sell one, refusing to speak to us when one of them died. Yusra was a born commander, with a fierce motherly instinct and a tendency to order her siblings around, even her big brother. By the time she was six, I could already imagine her taking over the family, running the village, keeping everyone in line.

Aisha did everything Yusra did, a cuddly butterball of a child who cried and loved easily and deeply, and who, had God graced her with a long life, would have been adored by her family, her village and her own children, as she would have adored them.

And then the littlest one, Amir, who suckled eagerly at my breast from the instant of his birth, grew fat and round, and smiled earlier than any of his siblings.

And you, Amal, with your spark and determination, your loud laugh, athletic limbs, grace, and kindness. Had you been born among us, you, too, would have been loved by us all.

Osman and I spent our days on our little farm digging wells, mending walls, ploughing and planting. Irrigating when our river swelled, conserving when it shrank. Faisal went to the village school once he was old enough, while we put the younger ones in care of my mother until her death, and then in the care of Samiya, my dearest friend. In short, we lived as our neighbors lived, laughing, crying, working, quarreling, watching our children grow, and trying to pretend that we were not afraid.

Our fears were rooted in the hidden wealth of our nation, and this I want you to understand. For beneath the hardscrabble surface of Sudan, the earth is rich with gold, oil, chromium, and graphite, and so has been plagued by plunderers for decades, the forces of greed and imperialism rending brother from brother until he kills, son from mother until he rapes, while opportunists seize and cling to power as long as they can. It is not always a blessing to live atop riches.

And so it was that only eleven months after Amir was born, the second civil war of my lifetime erupted and our murderous dictator of a president, Omar al-Basheer, sent his forces to our village to slaughter anyone he saw as a threat.

The first set of soldiers stormed in without warning, eyes filmed over like those of the dead, bodies in ill-fitting camouflage, faces wrapped in khaki hoods, as if already shrouded for the grave. Samiya flew up the road to us screaming, "They're killing all the boys! Run!"

Osman seized ten-year-old Faisal by the hand, plucked up little Amir, his stomach as round as a coconut, my milk still wet upon his lips, and run they did. "*Umi!*" I heard Faisal cry as they disappeared into our sunflower field. "Why?"

The second set of soldiers, five of them, same uniforms, same hoods, arrived at my house a few minutes later. Guns to my daughters' heads, orders to me. "Strip or we shoot."

They made your sisters watch. Four-year-old Aisha sucking her blanket, Yusra clutching her hand like the little mother she was. The soldiers held them by the ears and hit their heads with the butts of their rifles if they closed their eyes for even a second or voiced so much as a whimper. Those two warm little heads.

Then, through the terror and pain and stink, I heard it. Three bursts of gunfire from out in the fields.

One.

Two.

Three.

The soldiers laughed and bared their teeth. "That's what you get for resisting us," they jeered, yanking up their trousers as they left. Who had resisted and how, they never explained.

"They never do," Amina mutters, or I think she does.

"They never have to," Leila adds. "Oh, my dear sister."

As soon as I could move, I struggled up, bloodied and filthy and dazed with shock, and pulled on my clothes. "Come," I just managed to say to your sisters, the two of them standing as still as sticks, eyes pinned wide. "Let's find your father and brothers."

Find them we did, lying in our sunflower field; Osman had not managed to run far. He, Amir and Faisal heaped on top of one another like sacks of refuse, the wheeling shadows of vultures crisscrossing their bodies, flies drinking from their lips. Osman's arms were flung out as though trying to snatch our children from death. Faisal's mouth hung open, his last question forever unanswered.

Amir's baby feet, so round and soft, lay still as they had never before, even in my womb.

"*Umi*, why doesn't Baba talk?" Aisha whispered. Yusra hid her head in my skirt.

Six of my surviving neighbors helped me lift the heavy body of Osman and the too-light one of Faisal onto boards and carry them to the graveyard, while I stumbled after them with tiny Amir shrouded and stiffening in my arms. There, we joined the other new widows of the village burying their own husbands and sons, brothers and fathers, after which we held one another and screamed.

"Were no men or boys left at all, not even the newborns?" Amina asks. She squints at me against the sun and draws her legs to her chest; a little egg of a teenager with the face of a prisoner.

No. Not one.

A third group of soldiers came next, the *murahaleen*, another militia working for Basheer, only even more ruthless. Seven men this time, or rather boys, the eldest not even fully grown. The same eyes of death beneath their masks. Same brutal instructions to me. I fell unconscious.

When I awoke some time later, ripped open and ragged, the *murahaleen* were gone. But my daughters lay splayed beside me. Each shot through the temple.

I stared at their little bodies flung across the ground, their eyes open but blind, and could neither scream nor weep. My tears had dried to gravel, my voice to a stone, my prayers to dust. I could only gather my babies into my lap. Cradle Yusra's torn, tender head. Count Aisha's baby fingers. Brush the soil from their round, scuffed knees. And with my voiceless voice, I cursed every soldier on earth, every man who has hurt a woman or a child, every boy who has killed or raped, and swore to wreak my revenge.

"Revenge, like water washing out a wound," Amina spits when I say this, her eyes burning. How her spirit reminds me of yours, Amal, so fierce and determined.

Leila shakes her head, adjusting her soft body on her log. "Vengeance only triggers more vengeance. When will it be enough?"

Vengeance or justice, I reply, what's the difference?

A day later, or perhaps two, Samiya and four other women came to fetch me, each of whom had been treated as I was. They found me sitting on the floor of my house, my dead daughters still in my lap, my thighs still stained with gore, our bodies crawling with flies. The women gently pried Yusra and Aisha from me, lifted them into their arms and coaxed me upright, leading me again to the burial grounds, which had now grown larger than our village. There, we laid our murdered daughters beside their brothers and fathers, uncles and grandfathers; washed and stopped up our torn vaginas with rags; gathered what belongings we could balance on our heads in baskets and bundles; and joined the thousands of others fleeing Sudan for Ethiopia.

We walked all and every day on that journey, Amal, thirty, forty kilometers at a time. Blistered feet, swollen ankles, knees crying at every step, backs throbbing, necks aching. We washed in rivers and slept in the bush, rotated as lookouts for animals and men, and took what food we could find—sometimes as gifts from villagers, sometimes by scavenging from fields and trees. Samiya remained my companion throughout, a woman with the same strength that had graced little Yusra. And on the days I felt so crushed by grief that I wanted only to lie down and die, Samiya was always the one to stop me. "If you leave this earth, Nafisa," she would say, "your memories will leave with you and Osman and your children will be wiped from the world forever." So on I would stumble, trudging the dusty roads of history, as so many women have before me, faces drawn, feet cracked, bodies reduced to sinew and bone, eyes emptied of hope. Rivers of women running.

We ran for three weeks, my companions and I, many of us lost to murder, abductions or exhaustion on the way, until we finally reached the Ethiopian border. There, we threw ourselves on the mercy of the police, who packed us into huge, rattling buses and drove us south for hours, until we reached a place unlike any I had ever seen. It was called Fugnido and housed thirty thousand refugees, white tents and rickety shacks stretching over the barren land all the way to the horizon, the air dense with the same stench of sewage, loss, and sorrow that I and my sisters breathe here on Samos.

If only these memories would slip away from me as the sea below the camp here slips from the shore. If only it were so easy.

It was at Fugnido that I discovered I was carrying you. "Abort," the other women hissed, "or smother it at birth." And often they did just that with their own children of rape, creeping into the night with a bundle, returning with none. But I knew that you were not to blame, just as I knew that your face would never remind me of your father because I did not know which of my attackers your father was. I also knew that those very murderers who had tried to take everything from me had left me this greatest gift instead: you. And so when you were born, I named you Amal: one who gives hope.

After your birth, those same people in the camp who had advised me to abort ostracized us—me for keeping you and you for your anonymous fathers. But I was impervious because the spirits of my murdered children had already told me that they loved you, their littlest sister, and that I was to do you no harm. Osman, too, came to me in a dream and gave us his blessing. "I will look over her," he promised. "I will love her as my own."

This is how I know that you will always have an invisible chorus of the dead looking over you, Amal, gracing you with all the life of which they were robbed. Faisal gave you his loving heart, Yusra her protectiveness, Aisha her bubbling laugh, and little Amir his future.

Yet now, as I sit up here on the mountainside listening to Amina with her bitter history and longing for her mother; to Leila with her missing daughter and granddaughter and counts of the drowned, I wonder if I have burdened you with more than you can bear. The weight of war and death is heavy enough on our adult heads. Why, I ask myself now, did I ever expect one as little and fragile as you to carry for me all my memories, all my ghosts?

6

HILMA

The man who runs my favorite stationery store in Vathi is a chatty little fellow with a point of brown beard who reminds me of an elf. I drive there this morning in my rented Fiat, green as a pea and not much bigger, both to enjoy his company and to buy a hiking map and a second batch of ballpoint pens. Mine keep running out of ink, perhaps because of all the writing I'm doing here, this obsessive recording of my days, whether to offer a confession or a plea for forgiveness after all, I'm not sure.

A confession. Let's call it that.

The elf is complaining about the dwindling number of tourists in Samos when the shop door pings and in walk the same three women I noticed before: the tall but sickly African, the long-haired teenager, and the head-scarfed woman with her two skinny boys, the smaller one still limping in his broken flip-flop. They are dressed much as when I last saw them, except for the African, who's wearing fitted black slacks and an immaculate red button-down shirt that looks freshly ironed. I wonder how she keeps so pristine in a camp.

"May I help you?" the elf says to them in English, that being the lingua franca here, the bridge between Greek and all the other languages swirling about this island. Even the sun-scorched Teutons have to use English much of the time.

"Yes, please. You have cover for this?" the teenager replies, also in English, her accent heavy but her voice soft and clear. Flicking her curtain of hair over her shoulder, she holds out a thrice-folded white card, worn and tattered. "I need, what it is called, the coat you put on it?"

"Lamination?" I interject. Everyone turns and looks at me blankly. "You know, where you seal it in plastic?"

"Ah, no, I have something better." The elf disappears down a trapdoor in the back, and while he's gone, I take the opportunity to chase after Theo's coattails again. "Hello," I say to the girl, adding the only phrase I know in Arabic: "*Salaam aleichum.*" I flush, sure I've said it wrong. Or maybe I shouldn't have said it at all.

The girl, who is carefully smoothing out her card as if her life depends on it—and perhaps it does—looks over at me quickly. "Found it!" The elf pops up again, holding the sort of foldable plastic pocket in which we all used to keep wallet photographs back before we lost our photos to cell phones. "Now you can take the ID out when you need."

The girl thanks him. "The cost, please?" She pulls a handful of coins from her jeans pocket and carefully picks out the two euros with slender fingers. "Goodbye, madam," she says to me in English. She and the older woman beside her, who hasn't spoken a word, each takes the hand of one of the boys and leads him out of the shop, their willowy friend following.

"Why aren't those boys in school?" I ask the elf once they're gone.

He drops the girl's money into his cash register and shuts it with a ringing clank. "There is no school for them. Well, *ochi*, there is one, but it takes only few children, so everyone waits on long list. Most never get in."

"Can't they go to the local schools?"

He shrugs. "The parents here, the Greek ones, they do not want. They say the children bring disease. The government, it fights them. Outcome not decided."

I happen to know from Theo that it's written into international law that every refugee child has the right to go to school. But then most of everything that happens to refugees flouts their rights, including trapping them on this island. As Theo would say, human rights are an ideal, not a reality.

After leaving the shop, I head to a nearby supermarket to buy an easy dinner and a half bottle of wine. On the road, I pass an elderly man and a youth I take to be his son searching bins of garbage by a church, both with the broad Mongolian faces I've sometimes seen in photographs of Afghans. The men are neatly dressed but painfully lean in that way that comes with hunger—Kosmos did say that the camp sometimes runs out of food. The older man is carrying a bulging plastic sack of empty water bottles, the younger a rusted birdcage. Perhaps they'll take the cage up to their tent, trap a crow and fatten it up for dinner. Theo's told me of worse.

In the supermarket, I'm trying to decide what to buy for my own dinner when the same African woman I just saw turns into my aisle. She obviously recognizes me because she says in accented but perfectly clear English, her voice low, "Good day again, madam. Do you know if this is good? I cannot read the ingredients list." She holds out a granola bar, its packaging covered in indecipherable Greek.

I squint at it and look up at her—she's a good seven inches taller than I am. "I can't read it either. Try this." I hand her a brand I at least recognize, and maybe because of my earlier curiosity about her, or maybe because of Theo, something makes me invite her for coffee.

She steps back, her eyes taking me in with suspicion. But then, to my surprise, she accepts. So, after she pays for her bar and I forgo my own shopping, we walk in silence to Pythagoras Square and its goofy lion. This time I avoid the shouting waitress and instead choose a café where I've seen refugees served without being shooed away. Indeed, two are at a table in front, sipping tiny cups of Greek coffee, thick and black as sludge, and staring at their cell phones—their only portals, I presume, to whatever remains of home and family. Each is wearing the style I see on almost all the young men here: hair shaved at the sides but long on top, skinny jeans fashionably sliced at the knee, immaculate T-shirts over their slender, boyish chests.

Theo, too, was built like that before he reached his thirties, when he suddenly broadened and sprouted like an old tree. He also has my olive skin and tight curls, along with Nick's doleful brown eyes and endless legs, all of which give him more than a passing resemblance to the young men at this café. I've been shaken several times in town thinking I see him when it's only a refugee. Only.

I used to paint Theo all the time, hoping to capture the exact mood of those eyes, the elusive tint of that skin, the intent expression he always wore when concentrating. He liked to paint me, too, even when he was small, making my arms stick out like twigs, my eyes as big as plates. All the way through his childhood and teens, he would come with me to my Brooklyn studio, where we would work together in quiet companionship, his curly head and narrow back bent over the table, I standing at my easel, while the radio played Brahms or Miles, Mozart or Joni Mitchell—or, his preferences, Outkast or Nirvana. How I relished his childhood paintings, so much freer than mine with their haphazard colors and wild lines—I pinned them up all over my studio walls for inspiration. I relished his guileless criticism, too. "Mom, you put a face right there and you don't even know it," he once told me about one of my abstracts. And later, when he was a tall and rangy seventeen, "Mom, that painting is so depressing it'll make people want to jump off a bridge. At least give it a splash of red. And that line there on the left? It needs to be bolder."

Ah, Theo, what a serious person you've become, so determined to fix the world. You were the saving of me and your dad, you know, our love for you rescuing us from our respective self-absorptions. I scrambling up the ladder of the art world, courting galleries, enduring openings, hustling Instagram; your dad dodging teapot office politics and trying to write. How diminished we would have been without you. How diminished I am.

At the café, I notice my companion eyeing the youths nearby uneasily, so choose a table as far away from them as possible and ask her what she would like to drink. "I will take coffee, black. Thank you." She sits opposite me while I order, her back upright and her high-cheeked face a mask of wariness atop her long neck, which makes me wonder again why she came. Smoothing down her tidy red shirt, she waits for me to speak. So I introduce myself and open with what I hope is a safe question.

"I'm from the United States—New York. May I ask where you come from?"

"Sudan, madam."

Sudan! Darfur, decades of civil war and slaughter. Darfur made Theo despair more than any other mission I've seen him work. Is that what she fled? But I'm afraid to ask.

"Please," I say, "call me Hilma. Do you mind telling me how long you've been here?" I take a sip of coffee.

"Thirteen months. I am awaiting my interview for asylum. But it is not to come for another year."

I look up from my cup. "That long? Is that normal?"

"For many it is longer." She gazes directly into my eyes. "I came here because four of my children, they were killed, as was my husband. I came because death would have caught me if I had not. But in this place I am treated like a criminal."

Her voice is as expressionless as if we are still discussing granola bars, but I am shocked into silence. Four children killed? How can she even breathe?

"The animals on this island, they are treated better than us," she continues. "I wish you to tell the people of America this. Tell them that we are not criminals, we are not terrorists, we are human beings who only want to live as human beings should live."

She falls silent after that. Her gaze is still on my face but her eyes, large and round but bloodshot, have turned disconcertingly unfocused, as if she no longer sees me at all. And suddenly, I am blurting out my own story, a story I have never told anyone before.

When I stop speaking, she regards me without reaction. "What is your name again, madam?"

"Hilma Allen."

"I am sorry if you told me before. I have no memory left."

"And yours?"

"Nafisa Abbas." She stands. "Thank you for the coffee. I leave now. Goodbye."

"Wait, please." I jump up and ask for directions to the camp.

She looks at me with no interest. "The police, they will not allow you in." But she tells me how to get there and with that walks away, leaving her coffee untouched.

I gaze after her a long while, too shaken to know why I said what I said, or who took from whom. Almost every person in that camp must have a story as tragic as hers. What was I thinking, burdening her with mine?

As I toil again up the hill toward the refugee camp, I realize that I am once more out in the hottest time of the day. The shops are shuttered, the cats asleep along walls and in doorways, and the streets empty of people, the town being sunk into its long siesta. Two mangy tortoiseshell kittens wake for a moment to snarl at each other but otherwise all is quiet.

Up and up. Turn right. Tromp along that same hot highway I reached before. Turn left and left again—now I know why I couldn't find the camp before and why that cop was waving his arms in frenetic circles. But at last I reach a crumbling dirt road carved into the side of the mountain, where some dozen uniformed soldiers and cops are leaning against a row of parked cars, talking and smoking. Above them, on the mountainside, a scattering of families sit under olive trees, listless and silent. Women in headscarves and long skirts. Children lying inert in their laps. Men gazing into space. Teenagers with faces as blank as slammed doors. As I walk by, their eyes turn to me and watch.

Below the road, a crowd of tents spills down the hill sloping toward town. Some are not even tents but merely tarpaulins or blankets held together by pins and battened down with rocks. The stink of sewage wafts through the air.

At the end of the road, I finally reach the camp itself, squeezed onto a narrow strip of land seared into the side of the mountain. At first, all I can make out are concrete walls and chain-link fences topped by coils of razor wire, their blades flashing in the sun. But as I near the entrance, nothing but an open gate, I glimpse dozens of white shipping containers shoved end-to-end and stacked in rows up the hill like dominoes. And crammed into every inch of space between are thousands of tents in all shapes, sizes and colors, draped in laundry and swimming in garbage and mud.

This is no camp. This is a slum.

A cop is glaring at me from inside a booth by the entrance; it seems I've come too close. I smile at him like the American I am, turn and retreat. The watching eyes of the families on the mountainside follow my every step.

I came here for Theo but I don't have his courage. He would talk his way past the police and into this shameful place, somehow. He would do something.

☙

Back at Kosmos's house, I find him sweeping my terrace clean of pine needles and dust, as he does twice a day, although given how windy this island is, I don't know why he bothers. He looks exactly as I've always imagined Odysseus's sailors to have looked: blocky and bowlegged, arms thick, hands hairy, skin as sun-beaten as an old hide—a master at the pitch and dip of a ship but no doubt easy prey to the songs of sirens.

"*Kyria* Khilma," he says when he sees me, looking unusually stern. He straightens up, holding his broom in both hands like a musket. "I must ask of you again a question. Please do not leave your waste at my door. You must take him to bins. As I told you."

I'm not keen on being scolded like a schoolgirl but I blush anyway. The waste he's talking about, to my chagrin, is the used toilet paper one is forced to collect in a plastic bag here instead of flushing it down the toilet. "I tried," I reply defensively, "but as far as I can see, you don't have any bins."

"She is down the road—up." Kosmos waves his arms in vague circles, much like the police officer at the camp.

"You mean I'm supposed to carry it out into the village?"

"Yes, *Kyria*. All Greeks, we do this. Or you can drive."

The idea that I should not only hoard my excreta like some sort of Howard Hughes but walk up the road with it for all to see, or, even worse, pack it into my nicely perfumed little Fiat and go searching for a dumpster is not something I'm prepared to entertain. "Why is your country so absurd about plumbing, anyway?" I grumble.

Kosmos frowns, a tuft of his silver hair waving wildly in the wind. "'Absurd'? What is this word?"

"It means ridiculous. I'm asking why your toilets are so bad."

"Oh, that." He shrugs. "It is all the fault of Englishmen. In the 1930s they come, they find our bars open all day and our wines cheap. They drink, they lie on beach, they fry their brains like eggs in a pan, and they put in pipes only four centimeters in diameter. Only the shit of a mouse could pass through such a hole, if you excuse my language."

"But why hasn't this ever been fixed in eighty years?"

"Why you think, Miss Khilma? No money. You must understand that Greece she is poor because we had to start twice over from nothing. And because the *poutsa* Germany he buggers us. So bad toilets, no jobs. No job for me, no job for my friends, and no jobs for your refugees."

I'm about to say something about government profligacy, reckless investments, rampant tax evasion and over-borrowing, not to mention the four-hour siesta and early retirement—but again, I'm not here to argue. "You haven't got a job?" I say instead.

"*Ochi*. Why you think I air-bee-and-bee my own home? But now, enough about jobs and the shit, it is time to watch the sea turn to wine. Come." And putting his hand firmly on my waist, he pushes me up the stone steps that lead from my lower terrace to his upper one, sits me in a deck chair facing the view, pours me a tumbler of the local red, thick as blood, and returns to his sweeping, the whisk and scratch of his broom blending pleasantly with the buzz of cicadas in the pine trees around us.

Stretching out my bare legs in the last of the day's sun, I raise my glass to the view. The valley of olive trees, their leaves flashing from silver to pale green in the breeze; the bay; the creams of Vathi beyond. A small church is perched on the side of the hill across from me, its walls as white as salt, its dome a rich ochre and its shutters the exact blue of the sea—the very blue I'm afraid to paint.

I wish Nick were here with me so this could be romantic rather than medicinal. I wish he could see these impossible blues, the houses like knucklebones scattered up the hills, the lavender shadow of the Anatolian mountains beyond. I wish he could hold my hand, sip his own wine, kiss and, yes, forgive me.

Nick is an unusually kind man, if prone to melancholy. We met in Paris nearly forty years ago as art students, not in a museum or classroom but because I sprained my ankle dancing down the Sacré Cœur steps in my Indian bangles, long skirt and sandals, fancying myself graceful and free. Tumble, twist, and plop, I landed in a gasping heap of elbows and pain. Seeing me fall, he approached, auburn hair dangling into matching eyes, the flash of sun on his knight's armor blinding. "Are you all right?" he said in a Tennessee drawl that promised long nights of sex in every position. "Don't try to stand till you're ready."

An alarm bell was pulsating in my head by then, and the pain was shrinking the pavement into a vanishing black dot.

"You've gone pale. Here." He handed me his water bottle and I drank, feeling a pleasant sensation on the back of my neck: his fingers, massaging. "Put your head between your knees. And don't worry."

I awoke naked on his bed. No, that wasn't until later, until after he'd roused me from my faint, carried me to a taxi and offered to take me to his studio apartment, mine being on the opposite side of Paris. I must have agreed because next I knew, I was lying on his couch while he wrapped my ankle in ice packs and lifted my foot to a pillow, my skirt riding up my thigh, revealing a hint of underwear as flimsy as floss. He undulated about the spartan room, the drawl of his body, lank of his voice. "Wine or wine?" he offered me, as if it were a night of candles and violins and not a summery morning with the sun pinging off the powdery zinc rooftops outside. "You need to numb the pain."

We drank until the throb in my ankle became a forgettable ache, and I was sweeping desirous eyes over him, allowing my skirt to ride ever higher. His buttocks like two cantaloupes cozied together, the tightness of his jeans hugging low-slung hips and a promising tubular bulge.

Two glasses, three, we finished the bottle; he opened another—no Pythagorean moderation for us. We talked the talk of foreplay: a *soupçon* of philosophy and history, a sprinkling of confession, while his fingers slowly unbuttoned my shirt, caressed my nipples. The taste of rose and vinegar on his tongue, the tangy lime of his skin, his hand discovering the ready wetness of me, his low grunt of pleased surprise.

Three days in his bed, my ankle still propped on the pillow, legs spread. His body replete with willing and urgent sperm, I, the happy receptacle, *L'Origine du monde*.

Enter, Theo.

Nick worked tirelessly at getting me to marry him once I had returned to New York and told him I was pregnant. Sent me pleading messages on the backs of wittily chosen postcards. Giacommetti's emaciated war figures—*I am starving for your love!* Picasso's looming cubist women—*You overwhelm my thoughts.* Hopper's lonely bedrooms—*My heart without you.*

I resisted. Not for me that retro nonsense about wedlock, lock in wed, and all its tea-cozy respectability. The art world had shown me enough of men's vanity, of that towering "I" casting its shade across my canvas, to borrow from Virginia Woolf. I was afraid that Nick would try to make our child a reflection of himself, as I feared he would me. Little mirrors dancing at his feet, sending up rays of praises. *Oh, the darlingness of you!* Anyway, I hardly knew the fellow, so quickly had he impregnated me.

Yet, when my belly rounded, my breasts turned to watermelons and my nose thickened to a sponge and his devotion remained steadfast anyway, I realized I had him wrong. So lock in wed we did. And not a moment's regret, either.

Thirty-nine years we had together. Our little apartment on Riverside Drive, two poky bedrooms but a glimpse of the Hudson. My studio in Bushwick, my eventual gallery in Chelsea. Our travels, our dinner parties, our Sundays at art museums, our visits to his eviscerating parents in Nashville, our family cuddles on the marital bed, licking one another's wounds. Our Theo. Our Linnette.

Thirty-nine years.

Shivering, I stand and pull on a jacket, the incorrigible Samian wind having picked up again and with it a chill. Already the olive trees in the valley below are waving their branches in a frenzy while pine cones skid past my feet as if bowled by an invisible hand. Hardly the weather for living in one of those tents I saw today, let alone a jury-rigged shelter held down by nothing but stones.

I move to the edge of the terrace to watch the storm mount. On placid nights, I usually see minute dots of light bobbing in the distance, little fishing dinghies with no more than a pair of oars, a lamp, and an outboard motor to bring a man home. But the only dinghy visible now is anchored a few yards out from the unofficial beach below, a little wooden rowboat bucking so violently in the surf it looks about to flip over and smash.

How terrifying to be a fisherman in a squall like this; even more so a refugee on an inflatable launch. No rudder, no frame, just a flimsy slab of rubber at the mercy of every wave and current, so overloaded with people it lies only an inch away from sinking.

Shuddering, I turn and go inside.

7

LEILA

Hellenic Boat Report
June 25 at 5:45 AM

A wooden boat, believed to have carried as many as 160 people, mostly Syrians, sank between Turkey and Cyprus at 05.00 today.

Reported rescued: 103.

Bodies picked up from the sea: 19.

Still missing: 38.

ॐ

"*Teta*, see if you know this one: 'My finger is yellow. Bite me. Yikes, my shirt comes off!' What am I?"

"I don't know, *hayati*, what are you?"

"A banana! Isn't that a good riddle?" Little one in my arms, smelling of rose soap and her mother. I can still smell those scents even as my arms close around nothing.

I take my boys down to a small playground on the seafront this morning in the hope of finding them exercise and distraction. The children playing here are all refugees like us, the locals preferring their own company, and all are shouting and screaming as children do. Their mothers and grandmothers sit on nearby benches talking to one another, looking at their cell phones or staring into the space that holds their memories.

Go on, I tell my sons, don't be afraid. Play.

But they hang back, hiding behind my legs. "Mama," Hazem says after watching for a time, "the children here are too noisy." Instead, he and Majid want to wander by the edge of the sea to search for treasures: dropped coins, lost toys, silver buttons, gold beads—who knows what they think they will find.

So wander we do, walking the wide pavement that separates the bay from the road, seeking the shade of the few palm trees planted along the way. The sun glances off the white concrete and glassy water, dazzling my eyes until they ache. The waves knock against the wall of rocks piled along the shore, releasing wafts of salt and decay. Sweat runs out from under my hijab, stinging my cheeks.

Hazem meanders ahead half-heartedly kicking a pebble, his shoulders two little knobs under his faded red T-shirt, his loose gray sweatpants sliding down the narrow spout of his hips. Majid, once plump, now stringy, and still so small he only reaches his brother's chest, hobbles to catch up in his broken sandal, stopping every now and then to stoop over something on the ground. My sons have turned into old men.

Once we reach the jetty, a curved pier of stone off which the locals like to fish and dive, we see a gray shape lying near the end of it, heaped like a giant jellyfish on the ground. "A whale!" Majid exclaims, my fanciful boy, and he and his brother run toward it in rare excitement, I following.

It is not a whale, of course, but the remains of a rubber dinghy, half deflated and patched with fraying squares of black tape. We stand beside it, gazing at the contents of its collapsed insides. A yellow sweater, twisted and sodden. A bottle of sun lotion floating in a puddle. A black garbage bag that must have served as somebody's suitcase. A purple sock. A child's life jacket.

Hazem and Majid back away from the boat as if it might reach out to snatch them. It is exactly the same kind of boat on which we crossed the sea. The boat that took us away from Farah and Dunia.

I take my sons' hands and squeeze them, lifting my head to look out at the bay beyond. The water is such a penetrating blue here, the blue of promises and forever. But it stinks of putrefying fish and rotting seaweed. It stinks of the grave.

8

AMINA

Last night, a hundred or so of my fellow camp dwellers were ordered with no warning to gather their belongings, board a ferry at sunrise, and leave this island forever. I was not lucky enough to be among them, but I'm determined to see them go. I like to watch the ritual of farewells, the sorrow so naked, the heartfelt hugs and passionate promises, never having had the chance to say such a goodbye myself. Not to Tahar. Not to Fatima or my family. Not to Mama. Not even to my prison mates.

At the port, the sea beyond gleaming like the back of a fish under the feebly rising sun, I join the crowd of people weeping and waving. We all dream of breaking free of Samos like this, of moving onto the mainland, and after that, to Germany or Switzerland, Belgium or the Netherlands. Yet as much as we envy those who are leaving, how bitter it is to watch our friends pack up their meager possessions and sail off to the horizon, most likely never to be seen again.

Most of the people around me are young men who arrived on Samos alone, either orphaned, sent ahead by their families, or desperate to escape execution, imprisonment, or conscription into one murderous army or another. They walk in town together all the time, these motherless boys, clinging to one another like brothers. To outsiders they might look like boys anywhere, laughing, teasing, strutting in their grins and loudness, biceps and tightly trimmed hair. But they are not like boys anywhere. That skinny one there was kept prisoner by Daesh for two years and starved to the point of death many times over, until he escaped. This stocky one here was flayed by a Taliban whip in a public square, his back stripped raw. That little one there was arrested by Assad and tortured within an inch of his life. That shy one over there from Ghouta left his house for bread and returned to a pit of smoke and stones, the bodies of his baby sisters flung into the road like mutilated toys.

The boys laugh, drape their arms around one another, keep an eye out for police and girls. But I know.

One young man I do not recognize, however. He towers over his friends like one of the palm trees along the seafront, his jaw long, cheeks bony, nose a great arc over a beard like a cloud of wool—he would look fierce but for the kindness in his eyes. This tree of a boy hugs his departing friends long and hard. I think I'd like these boys if I weren't afraid to speak to them. I so miss companions of my own age. But just as they have their friendships, I have my reputation. And my memories.

After the ferry churns away across the water, leaving all of us on the dock feeling bereft, I am just turning to go when the tall-as-a-tree boy takes a step toward me, smiling from inside his beard, as if to offer the very friendship I so crave. For a moment I almost respond. But then my skin shrinks and my body flinches. I turn and hurry away up the hill to meet Nafisa, angry at myself and yet afraid.

I find her sitting against the trunk of our olive tree, eating an orange. She's wearing a blue tunic over one of Leila's long black skirts—we borrow one another's clothes all the time—and looks more rested than usual, eyes clearer, face less drained. I know she carries a deadly disease, although she won't say what it is, because at times I see it sapping her energy, while at other times it recedes. Today must be one of her strong days. Still, she needs good medical care and fresh food. A clean place to sleep. A home.

"*Marhaba*, little sister, what time is it?" she says as I hand her a bottle of water.

Nearly eight. There was another evacuation this morning. I went down to the port just now to watch.

"Amina, you should not walk about by yourself like that. You know it's not wise."

I don't care. My father and brothers aren't here to stop me anymore, are they? And nor is war or Mama. Anyway, Auntie, what could happen to me here that would be any worse than what happened to me in prison?

She shakes her head but says nothing.

When do you think it'll be our turn to leave on a boat like that? I ask her then.

"How would I know? We might as well be packets of socks the way they ship us about without telling us anything." She takes a swallow of water and offers me a segment of orange. "Don't stand there, Amina, sit. You look tired. Could you not sleep again?"

I almost never sleep, you know that, Auntie.

I sit, my legs clammy in the still-damp jeans I washed last night. Popping the orange in my mouth, I fasten my hair into a knot on top of my head as relief from the already gathering heat, and tell Nafisa that I am confused by the nature of memory. Mama's growing so misty, I say. I can only see her face as a blur of wrinkles and scars—I can't find her eyes or her smile anymore. But in my dreams, I see her clearly. Do you understand this, Auntie? Because I don't.

"Memory never follows time or reason, it does what it wants with us." She finishes her orange and tucks the skin into her shirt pocket—she'll make a perfume of it later.

But why are my dreams about Mama so full of love while my thoughts about her are filled with anger?

"Because you haven't forgiven her, little one. But you must. She's your mother. And didn't the Prophet Muhammad, peace be upon him, say that heaven lies beneath a mother's feet?"

An ache tugs at my chest.

But Auntie, Mama left me. The only reason I resisted death in prison was for her sake. Other women were killing themselves or being killed all around me.

Yet when I came home and said, "Look, Mama, I'm alive, I'm alive for you," she deserted me only a few days later. How could she have done that?

Nafisa shifts against the tree and brushes off the ants and dust that have collected on Leila's skirt. "She must have had her reasons. Mothers usually do."

Even a reason to abandon me?

Nafisa bows her head at this. But offers no reply.

Seeing that I've caused her pain, I change the subject.

Auntie, do you remember that old woman tourist we saw the other day? The one who nodded at us?

"The one with the ugly hat? Yes, she took me for coffee."

She did? Why, what did she want?

Nafisa shrugs. "I neither know nor care. But what about her?"

I only wonder what it would be like to change places with her; for her to be me and me her.

"You wouldn't want to be that woman." Nafisa sucks her teeth. "Anyway, we're born to the fate Allah gives us, Amina. There's no use pretending otherwise. Look." She pulls a crumpled envelope from the pocket of Leila's skirt and passes me the single photograph inside, creased and faded. "This is the only picture I have of my family. It's me and my little Faisal in his last year of life, Allah protect him."

A tall and youthful woman gazes out at me, dressed in a sky-blue wrap, the folds of its soft cloth wafting gracefully down her body, a matching scarf loosely draped over her head. She's smiling, her skin aglow, her arm around a gawky boy of about ten, his head leaning against her hip, his own face serious and sweet.

"My husband took that photograph. He's the one who made me smile so foolishly."

You don't look foolish, Auntie, you look beautiful. Did you always dress like that?

"We did. In the brightest colors we could. That's how we celebrated the glories of Allah." She puts the picture back in her pocket. "All that's lost now, as you know. This is what I mean about fate." She glances at me out of the sides of her eyes. "Now, tell me what happened to you down at the port today? Your face is full of secrets."

I must be blushing because she laughs and says, "Is it a boy?"

I'm not interested in boys.

She raises her eyebrows at this and I wonder if she thinks I mean that I'm interested in girls. But all she says is, "Amina, you can't live all your life sealed away. Nor can you let those prison guards steal your chance at love. Don't ever let them win like that."

I scowl and scratch the bedbug bites on my hands and wrists. I don't believe in love, I mutter.

She looks at me tenderly. "Then tell me instead what happened to you after you came home from prison. I still haven't heard that part of the story."

Do I have to?

"Of course you don't. But I think it might do you good, little one."

I look down, torn between the pain of telling and the pain of silence. But my need for a listening ear, especially Nafisa's ear, pulls the words from me.

I was only released last January, I begin. Five months ago.

"That recently?" She gazes at me a long while, then pulls her back up straight. "Why did they let you go, do you know?"

No. They never told us anything except that our families were dead even when they weren't. All the guards did was drag me out at dawn, throw me into a van blindfolded, drive a short distance, and throw me back out.

For a long time after they left, I was too dazed by my sudden freedom even to move. The streets around me spun and blurred, the sky was so vast it seemed about to swallow me whole, and my vision had become too weak from my three years in a dark cell to make out the shapes around me. I had to sit down right there on the side of the road and wait for my eyes to clear before I could know what to do next.

Only once they had did I recognize that I was on the outskirts of my own Manbij. The war had horribly deformed that part of the city, burning its golden stones black and pulverizing many of its buildings. Still, these were the same streets in which I'd flown my kite with Tahar, with the same rivers running through them that dried in the summer and flowed in the winter, so I understood where I had to go. Just as I understood that all these years when I had thought myself impossibly far from home, I had been locked up only a few kilometers away.

Wrapping my tattered prison abaya tightly around myself against the winter wind and eyes of men, I darted from shadow to shadow, desperate to reach Mama, yet with no idea of what I would find. In all the years I'd been gone, she had never been allowed to know where I was, let alone visit or write to me, so my greatest fear wasn't the snipers or shells or even the hate-filled eyes of fighters, but that she and my home might no longer exist.

When I reached our street, it looked as though a giant had rampaged through it, carrying away windows and doors, leaving holes that gaped like tongueless mouths. Many of the buildings I remembered were now no more than hollow shells pocked with bullets, while others had either been pummeled into craters or shorn in half, exposing carpets dangling off the edges of vanished floors, curtains hanging over nothing, wardrobe doors flapping open like broken jaws. Cars lay tossed into courtyards, burnt black and twisted, and the street was so empty of life it seemed to lack even air. I ran through this wreckage as wild with fear as if I were running through my own nightmares. And then, at last, there was my house, half-demolished and almost unrecognizable, rubble piled all the way to its front door.

For a long moment I froze, too afraid to approach. But finally, I forced myself to clamber over the mess and knock, my hand trembling, my heart rising in hope. Who would answer? A stranger? A soldier? My mother or a ghost?

I heard a movement inside. The spyhole lifted. A long, terrible pause. Bolts slid and groaned. Locks clanked and clicked. The door creaked open a crack. And there Mama was, peering cautiously out. She stared at me, and I at her, both of us suspended in time, joy and uncertainty chasing each other all over her dear face. Then time broke, she let out a cry and pulled me in, locking the door behind us and flinging her arms around me, holding and rocking me with all the tenderness I had so longed for in prison.

Nafisa emits a small noise.

Auntie, are you all right? Shall I stop?

"No, no." She lowers her head. "Go on. I want to hear."

You sure?

She insists, so I do.

Over the next two days, Mama held and fed me, bathed my wounds and cried over my body, which bore the marks of all the guards had done to me—and everyone knew what was done to women in Bashar's prisons. "At least they didn't shave off your hair," she murmured one night, washing and combing it gently. I didn't tell her that was only because the guards liked to use it as a rope.

Nafisa lays her hand over mine.

Yet even as I basked in her care, Auntie, I couldn't shed a single tear. "Why don't you cry, *habibti*?" Mama kept asking. "If you hold all this pain in, it'll eat you alive. You need to let go and cry!" But my tears had long since drained away. They have never come back since.

Baba, too, wept with relief when I came home, for he did love me in his distant way. He even hugged me to his breast, withered now and frail. He was not a bad man, Auntie, only a man who lacked the courage to be better. But my brothers were a different matter.

I had been home for only three days when they started in on me. The two of them appeared at my bedroom door, Abdullah as big and fat as Baba used to be; Zakoor hovering as usual behind him, petting his gingery beard. Why they weren't on duty with the army these seven years into the war instead of lurking about at home nobody explained, but I assumed it had to do with their usual bribes and connections.

"Mother, now that Amina has come home, you must take her to see a doctor," Abdullah insisted. "Her virginity must be proven and our honor upheld. She's brought enough shame on our family as it is."

I glared at him and Zakoor until their eyes darted away, and that is the moment I knew what I had suspected all along. My brothers were not the types to care about my virginity, let alone what it said about their honor—they were too modern for that. No, they were afraid that my return would once again mark them as targets, the way Tahar's defection to the rebel army had. Back then, I surmised, they had protected themselves by offering me to *al mukhabarat* in their stead. Now they wanted me gone again, this time for good.

"You mean your brothers were the ones who betrayed you over that poem?" Nafisa asks in outrage.

I do.

"Scorpions! Didn't they know that he who plants evil will only harvest it himself?"

If they did, they didn't care. But that wasn't even the worst of it, Auntie, because instead of resisting Abdullah's demand or going to Baba for support, as

I expected, Mama only agreed. "The clinic is closed today," she told them, "but we'll take your sister to the doctor first thing tomorrow, as long, *insh'Allah*, as the streets are safe." And when I cried out in protest, she put her hand over my mouth. "Shush, *benti*. You know this must be done."

Abdullah nodded but he looked suspicious. "All right. We'll come get you in the morning and go with you. Just in case." And with a last warning glare, he left, Zakoor trotting after him like the lapdog he was.

"Mama, how could you?" I whispered once they were gone. "They'll kill me!"

"Pack your most essential belongings and one change of clothes," is all she replied. "Dress warmly, stay silent, and wait." Mama was more cunning than I knew, more cunning than I ever would have suspected.

"What sort of cunning?" Nafisa looks at me sideways, her sunken eyes sly, as if she already knows.

The cunning of the powerless, Auntie. The woman with the medicine, the man with the magic. The judge who can be bribed, the doctor seduced. The husband who can be bamboozled, the policeman cajoled. The friend who can lie. The master who can be tricked. The treasures that can be stolen. The networks that run underground like veins.

That afternoon, Mama put her cunning to work. She fed my father a heavy lunchtime soup laced with a crumbled sleeping pill so that his usual nap would last all afternoon, and while he slept, she rifled through the house taking anything he wouldn't miss for days: his old watch, several discarded silver rings, the antique copper coffee pitchers he liked to display on the bathroom shelves, the cash he kept for bribes in a drawer of his desk he thought secret but was no secret to her—even her golden bangles, the only wealth she had of her own. Her thievery done, she slipped out and returned an hour later empty-handed but with, I was soon to discover, money sewn into the hem of her galabeya.

She sat on my bed and took my hands in hers. "It's time to go," she whispered.

"Go where?"

"Shh, just hurry." I refused to look at her or speak, I felt so betrayed. But within the cup of her hands, my own were shaking.

Telling me to hide my bag beneath my abaya and wrap myself against the February cold, Mama peered down the afternoon street to make sure it was clear of fighters and up at the sky to make sure it was clear of death. Then we slipped outside, keeping to back alleys and away from squares, which always seemed to be controlled by snipers, no matter which army was in power.

"Mama, this isn't the way to the doctor," I said as we hurried through deserted and crumbling alleyways. "Where are you taking me?"

"To a woman I know."

"What woman? Is she a different doctor? Are you going to bribe her to say I'm a virgin?"

"Shush. The walls have a thousand ears." Mama took my hand, exploring it with her fingers, as if she were trying to memorize every crease in my palm, the shape of every nail and knuckle. Still angry, I pulled it away.

When we reached a part of the city I had never seen before, she led me through a keyhole arch and down a narrow peach-colored alley, flanked by workshops displaying piles of giant copper pots and basins outside their doors. The war seemed to have hardly touched this place. Men were fearlessly squatting in the street, beating the copper softly into shape with padded hammers. Bare-kneed boys rubbed the copper into a dazzling orange gleam, filling the air with the tangy odor of metal and polish instead of the usual stench of scorched plastic and putrefaction. Underfed children no older than Majid darted around our feet like lizards, selling bits of metal and canisters of cheap petrol. "Mama, where are we?"

"You'll understand soon enough. Hurry." We walked on for some time until she stopped at a wrought-iron gate in a wall of chipped white plaster. There, she pushed me inside.

I thought we had entered a ruin. The courtyard was cracked and clotted with weeds, while the house in the back, painted a faded rose, was missing half its roof, a sheet of corrugated tin draped over it like a lopsided hat. Looking around quickly, Mama hurried up to the thick wooden front door and knocked. I stood beside her, shooting questions at her from my eyes.

After a pause, a sturdy little woman answered, dressed in an embroidered galabeya the color of violets and a matching hijab, her face wide and pink. Beckoning us in with a kind smile, she bolted the door behind us and threw her arms around Mama. That woman was Leila.

"Leila?" Nafisa repeats in surprise. "You didn't know her before?"

No. Mama had kept her a secret. I had no idea who she was.

"Wait here," Mama told me, and pulling Leila through the door to somewhere I couldn't hear them, she left me staring at the tiled floor of the hallway, my stomach sick with confusion and dread.

Soon they came back in, holding hands like little girls. Mama was smiling, although her smile looked sad. "Good news, *habibti*. Leila's agreed to help us. You're to travel with her, *insh'Allah*."

"Travel?"

"Yes, my love. Leila's bought passage across the border to Turkey for herself and her children, after which they're going to try to reach Europe. She's agreed in her kindness to take you with them."

"But . . . but you're coming too, aren't you, Mama?"

She slipped her eyes away from me. "I can't, my love. Not yet."

"Not yet?" I looked at her in a panic. "In that case, I won't go. I'll just hide here till my brothers forget me."

Mama's eyes filled but she shook her head. "No, my heart, they'll hunt you down if you stay."

"Then come with me! It'll be too dangerous for you at home if I disappear."

"I'll join you later, *habibti*, don't worry. I just can't now. I'm sorry."

"But what will you tell Abdullah and Zakoor?"

Ignoring me, Mama bent and tore open the hem of her galabeya, extracting, to my astonishment, a thick wad of liras, which she handed to Leila, saying, "I hope this will pay my daughter's way, but it's not enough to repay you for your kindness. May the blessings of Allah be upon you." She gave me an envelope containing my birth certificate and high school identification card. And with that, she left.

"Wait!" I cried. "Mama, where are you going?" But she was gone.

I turned to Leila. "I don't understand!"

"You will soon enough." She reached over to pat my hand, her own broad and strong. "Be patient, Amina. We must put aside the past now, even the past of three minutes ago, and concentrate on the present. We leave at dawn."

"Dawn? But when will Mama join us?"

"You'll see. Come now, say hello to my children."

That is when I first met not only Hazem and Majid, but Farah and Dunia, too. Farah is even smaller than Leila and round-cheeked like her, only darker complexioned, with an upright spine and a womanly figure. She is also very pious—I think you would like her, Auntie. And her little Dunia is such a funny child, so full of spark and mischief. She took one look at me and said, "Can I tell you a riddle, Auntie? I like riddles."

Distressed as I was, I picked her up, a sweet little bundle of freshness and warmth, her dark eyes quick, hair long and black. "I would love to hear a riddle," I told her. She smelled new and sugary, of everything the prison was not.

"'A house with no door. Inside we are four.' What am I?"

"I've no idea. You tell me."

"A walnuṭ! Do you know any riddles, Auntie?"

"Not right now, but if I think of one, I'll tell you."

"Dunia, stop bothering our guest," Farah said with a smile.

"No, no, she's like honey on my heart," I said, giving Dunia another hug before putting her down. "But how did you meet Mama?" I asked Leila then. "Was it at the market?"

"That is where I first met her, yes. But we became friends in our sewing circle."

"Sewing circle?"

"Yes. Farah is an accomplished tailor—she gives lessons in our house. And if a woman needs to escape her home, we help with this, too."

This only further bewildered me. "But when is Mama meeting us? Tomorrow?"

Leila would give me no more answers. She only said that she'd collected enough money to pay the many bribes and fees necessary to buy us passage to Turkey and then to Greece. I wondered how much of that money was Mama's. I still have no idea if Mama paid Leila extra to bring me here or if Leila was acting out of charity, because as pressed up against one another as we are in this camp, we each have our secrets, too.

"So we do." Nafisa wraps her thin arms around her stomach as if to hold the two halves of herself together. "But paid or not, Leila must love your mother dearly to have brought you all this way."

But Auntie, I never asked to come.

Later that night, after I had peppered Leila with many more questions she refused to answer, she had us sit around the bedsheet Farah had made into a *sofra* to eat an astounding gift of a meal, given the scarcity of food in Manbij at the time: rice mixed with almonds; her own *baharat* of cardamom, cinnamon, allspice, pepper, and cumin; weeds she'd collected herself for a salad; radish soaked to scarlet in beetroot juice; and dried apricots collected from the fruit trees spared by bombs. Yet, as welcome as the meal was, it lay inside me like a slab of iron. In prison our daily ration had been a spoonful of rice swimming in rancid oil and the occasional potato tunneled by worms, so my stomach had lost the ability to accept anything as rich and varied as this.

In preparation for our journey, Leila sent us all to bed early. I wrapped myself in a quilt on the cold family room floor, bare of furniture and even a carpet, and fell asleep to a writhing in my stomach and the sound of Farah rolling out her kilim to pray.

Long before light the next morning, Leila roused us all, gave Farah and me each a purse of liras to hide with our identification papers in our bras in case we were robbed, and told us all to put on as many layers of clothes as we could. "Look at me, three dresses!" Dunia crowed, the poor child having no idea of what was happening. I had only the one extra shirt and skirt Mama had made me pack, so I pulled those on under the black abaya in which I had arrived. Farah piled on four outfits, Leila fastened several skirts under her galabeya, and the boys bundled up like Bedouins. Finally, she handed us all knapsacks of food and water to wear on our backs. We looked like a collection of tortoises—particularly Dunia, whose pink backpack was almost as big as she was.

Yet still Leila would answer no questions. She only said, "Now, children, all of you—you too, Dunia, *hayati*—not a word. We leave the house in silence and we travel in silence. This is very serious. I want each one of you to promise not to talk unless I say you can."

"I promise, *Teta*," Dunia said gravely. The boys nodded solemnly, too. Farah muttered a plea to Allah to protect us all.

As soon as dawn began to silver the sky, and while the war was still sleeping, we crept out of the house and across the same weed-tufted courtyard that Mama and I had walked the day before, the only sounds our footsteps and the distant yelps of dogs. I still had no idea who Leila was, or what had happened to her and Farah's husbands, but I did see little Dunia's face closing like a flower in fear.

We eased through the courtyard gate, wincing as it creaked, and into the alleyway. I was still hoping to see Mama turn a corner to join us but the street remained deserted, except for the dark shape of a cat huddled in a doorway. The twilight cast such an eerie glow over the walls on either side of us that they looked more like cardboard than stone and mortar, as though it would take only one push to topple them over.

A long, tense wait ensued, all of us pressing our backs against a wall in an effort to make ourselves invisible, barely daring to breathe. But at last we heard the rattle of an engine, and a battered brown van lurched around the corner and pulled up in front of us. Farah and I drew our hijabs across our faces.

The driver, his own face muffled under a red and white keffiyeh, jumped out and opened the back doors. But just as Leila began to lift Hazem inside, he stopped her. "This one I didn't expect." He looked at me. "You told me you had only one grown daughter, not two."

Leila reached into her bodice and pulled out the thickest roll of liras I had ever seen, even thicker than Mama's. That, I thought, was why Leila's house was so empty. She must have sold all her furniture and gathered her life savings, too, to pay for this journey. Peeling off a handful of bills, she told the smuggler, "I'll pay the rest when you take us across the border, but we need to hide this girl. Here is extra if you can do it. Can you?"

The man looked at me again, or rather he looked at my breasts, and grunted assent. His van was carrying a heap of burlap sacks full of coffee beans but he explained that under the sacks it had a false bottom, beneath which I could hide. We agreed, so he helped me in, although not without sliding his hand under my skirt to probe my buttocks. I dared not slap him away, even though his touch provoked the retching horror I had felt so often in prison. I'm sure he would not have done such a thing if Mama had been there. He didn't touch Farah.

The only way I could fit into that hiding place, which was permeated with such an overpowering smell of coffee that I've never been able to drink it since, was to lie in fetal position, my neck bent at an excruciating angle, the coffee sacks and Leila's family sitting on top of me as if holding down the lid of a coffin. Panic flared inside me every time I thought of my brothers discovering me gone, of what they might do to Mama if Baba failed to protect her or turned out to agree with what they had done, of what might happen to me if I were caught, while every jolt of the van as it bumped over potholes or swerved to avoid landmines and checkpoints sent a burst of terror through my veins.

Before long, all this conspired with the lurching van, lack of air, clashing odors of coffee and diesel, and the previous night's meal to turn my weak stomach against me. I swallowed and clenched, swallowed and clenched, but in the end could control it no longer. Groping frantically in the dark for a container, I found what felt like a man's jacket. Holding the pocket over my mouth, I expelled all that was in me, folded the jacket and tucked it away. "I'm sorry, I'm so sorry," I whispered, wondering if Leila and her children could hear me or smell the reek filling the tiny space.

The van blessedly stopped soon after, and once I had endured an excruciating wait, the door to my coffin lifted, letting in a wave of bitter wind that I gulped like a hooked fish. I crept stiffly out, legs quivering. The driver reached for me as if to help, only this time squeezing my left breast. I handed him his jacket and smiled.

Nafisa chuckles and stands to stretch. "May all such men find vomit in their pockets." She sits back down and rearranges her skirt. "Go on."

We had arrived at the border of Turkey by then, but any relief we might have felt was thwarted by the sight of a looming gray wall blocking our way, too high to scale and too long to walk around. Yet our driver seemed unconcerned. "You have thirty minutes before the border patrol returns," he whispered and ushered us in silence along the wall until we reached a tunnel that someone had dug underneath. There, he lay on his belly, indicating that we should follow, and wriggled through, tugging us out on the other side like a bird pulling worms from the earth.

"Freedom!" Leila gasped, brushing the soil from her skirt, but still we faced a muddy ditch, a barbed-wire fence, a road patrolled by armed guards, and beyond, a wide expanse of vineyards stretching to a distant olive grove. My heart cramped. How could we, with our bags, our heavy clothes and the children—or Mama, when she came—possibly cross over so much open land without getting shot? But the driver only pushed us forward, making us duck, scramble, and run as fast as we could, Farah carrying Dunia, Leila and I dragging the boys by their hands, while the paid-off guards in the distance supposedly looked the other way. I ran, pulling Hazem behind me, as I had never run before, my throat ragged with the effort, my heart galloping in terror, my every muscle knotted in expectation of the burn and pierce of a bullet. I ran and ran until I had gained the shelter of the olive grove, where I collapsed with the others on the ground, breathless and muddy but blessedly alive.

As soon as we stood up again and brushed ourselves off, the driver took the rest of his money from Leila and handed us to a second smuggler, a small and wiry Turk. This one pushed us into his car without a word and drove away from the border and all its dangers to deliver us to a bus in the town of Gazientep. "We're out of the war now, do you realize this, my darlings?" Leila told us as we settled into the bus, tucking her diminishing wad of liras back under her now filthy galabeya. "We have escaped!"

"Is this where Mama's meeting us?" I asked her.

"Shh."

The bus took fourteen hours to cross from the north of Turkey to the southern coast and Izmir, the town that would feed us to a beach and a boat, but on the way, we were at least given food, rest stops, and warmth, all of which Hazem, Majid, and Dunia welcomed with giddy relief. When they were not pressing their stubby noses to the window or sucking on juice boxes or bread, they were curled like hamsters in their mothers' laps, asleep. The sight of their little faces so at peace, so oblivious, sent through me such longing for my childhood days with Mama and Tahar that I had to turn away.

In Izmir, Leila handed over yet more money to yet a third smuggler—they work in chains like this—who took us by taxi to a hotel, where he left us to wait. "Wait for what?" I asked Leila. "For Mama?"

"No, child. Wait for the man to find us a safe boat to take us to Greece. We're almost in Europe! Have faith!"

I looked around the dank and windowless hotel room we were to share with three other families and four single men. Bedsheets streaked with brown stains. Cockroaches crawling brazenly over the walls. A stink of feces and fear. "Can we trust these smugglers?" I asked.

Farah looked at me out of the corner of her eyes. "Of course not. That's what Mother means by faith. All we can do is pray."

Nafisa sucks her teeth and nods slowly. "Leila's daughter spoke the truth there," she says.

That's not what I was thinking, Auntie. I was thinking what flimsy devices faith and prayer are on which to hang a life. As flimsy as the rubber raft that brought us here.

We lived in that verminous hotel for two weeks, waiting for space to open on a boat, an ordeal that Leila and Farah and even the children endured with much more patience than I did. "Yes, this is horrible," Farah acknowledged, "but there are no bombs or snipers here, so how can we complain?" Twice we were called to a boat, each time having to spend hours crouched in the woods by the beach waiting for nightfall and trying to keep the children quiet, as hungry and frightened as they were, only for Leila to take one look at how overloaded the boat was and how worn its rubber, and refuse to let us aboard. "Are you trying to drown us?" she said in outrage to the smuggler. "Do you take us for fools?"

Finally, at the end of those two weeks, he told us that he'd found a solid boat leaving from Kuşadasi beach for no more than fifteen passengers. "I come with a van at midnight," he said in Turkish-inflected Arabic. "Be ready."

The van turned out to be windowless and already stuffed with people but he crammed us in anyway, our faces pressed up against the backs and bellies of strangers, our throats struggling for air, our stomachs heaving from the stink of one another's hunger-breath and anxiety. I had heard enough stories of people suffocating to death in vans like this not to fear the same fate for us. I clutched Leila's arm, Hazem's head in my stomach, Dunia whimpering into Farah's shoulder, Majid clinging to his mother, and mumbled prayers to the god I no longer trusted to keep us alive.

The smuggler took off at such a speed he made the van rock wildly from side to side, throwing us against its walls and one another. He drove for at least two hours, the air growing increasingly stinky and stifling. When he finally stopped, we all moaned with relief and pressed forward, desperate to be let out. But then he made us wait inside for yet another hour, still so tightly packed that three people fainted, including a pregnant woman. At last, the back doors slid open and we burst out, retching and gasping.

Darkness had already closed in by then, it still being the short days of February, the moon a mere wisp in a sky clotted with clouds, and because it was too dangerous to light up a torch or a telephone, we could see little beyond the sand and stones beneath our feet. A rough-looking man appeared out of the night, almost invisible in black clothes, and hustled us into a cove crowded with people. I could just make out the shape of a gray, inflatable dinghy on the water about seven meters long; too small for even the fifteen passengers we'd been promised, let alone the dozens waiting on the shore. I glanced at Leila, my skin tightening.

Shadowy figures moved about distributing orange life jackets to those who paid. Leila managed to buy one for each of the children but the jackets ran out before she, Farah or I could buy our own. None of us knew how to swim.

"Look how fat I am, Mama!" Dunia said with a giggle as Farah buckled the jacket around her chest.

The man in black walked over to us while we were strapping the boys into their own jackets. "No bring so many people 'less you pay," he said to Leila in pidgin Arabic. I couldn't see him well but I could see that he was large and muscular. Dunia edged closer to Farah and gripped her leg.

Leila straightened up, her hand on Majid's shoulder. "But I already did pay. And this is not the boat I was promised."

The man only replied, "Pay more or one stay here." A finger of steel ran down my spine. Was this the moment Leila would abandon me? I was, after all, not her child. And where was Mama?

Leila pleaded as best she could, but this only enraged the man further, so she finally handed over the money. By now, I was sure, her wad of liras must have dwindled to almost nothing.

Tucking the cash away, the smuggler stepped aside to let us pass, but just as we did, he lunged forward, snatched up Dunia and turned to run.

Farah screamed and threw herself at him, catching him by the arm. "Give her back, son of a pig! Give my child back!" she yelled. Leila and I tackled him as well, all three of us screaming while Dunia shrieked and struggled in his grip.

Kicking us away, the man clamped his hand over Dunia's mouth. "Shut up! You want bring police?"

"Let her go!" we screamed again, still wrestling him; only this time we screamed in a whisper.

"If I do, mother and child stay. Boat full."

By now the other passengers had noticed the commotion and were gathering around us, also pleading with the smuggler to let Dunia go. But then two new men approached brandishing pistols. "Be quiet or police come!" they hissed, and seizing Leila and me by our arms, they dragged us away, each of us clutching the hand of one of the boys, who stumbled beside us, sobbing in fright. We tried to turn and see what was happening, but the smugglers only thrust their guns into our backs, forcing us and the other passengers into the frigid water and up to the boat, where they heaved us in like netted fish. "Farah!" Leila cried, scrambling to the side as the smugglers shoved the boat away from the shore. "Farah!"

"Allah have mercy!" the passengers wailed. "For pity's sake, turn back and let them come!"

The smuggler piloting the boat only barked at us again, waving a gun, and although his Turkish was incomprehensible, his message was clear enough. We could do nothing but look on in helpless silence while the figures of Farah and Dunia and the others who had been left behind stretched out their arms to us, weeping and calling. As the boat motored away, we watched them grow smaller and smaller on the shore until all we could see was the orange dot of Dunia's life jacket. And then even that was gone.

"So that's how Leila lost them, Allah help her," Nafisa murmurs.

It is, Auntie. But, you know, she never cried. Once Farah and Dunia were out of sight, she simply cleared us a spot on the floor amongst the seventy or so people crammed into the boat with us, and made us sit, wet and cold as it was. "Mama, are those men going to hurt Dunia?" Hazem asked, his eyes big and frightened, his hair dripping.

"Mama, will you be angry if I peed myself?" Majid whispered between his chattering teeth.

"What's going to happen to them?" was my question.

Leila said nothing for a long time, she only stared out at the black water surrounding us. But at last, she gathered the boys under her arms, pulled our sodden bags closer and spoke, her voice thick with sorrow. "We must put our trust in Allah, children. Now, no more talking."

The boat churned on, the passengers still calling to Allah, although quietly now, when a small speedboat appeared out of the night and pulled up to our side. We thought it was the police and a new terror seized us. But then our smuggler let go of the outboard motor, jumped into the boat, and sped away.

A fresh shout of horror arose from us. None of us had the skill to steer; none of us had even been in a boat before, most having lived our lives in cities or on farms. How were we to prevent ourselves from being washed helplessly out to sea and drowned? But after the first panic passed, the men forced a teenager of seventeen, timid and alone, to take hold of the outboard motor handle. He was called Ali from Aleppo, a woman beside me told us, and Daesh had beheaded his entire family before his eyes. "Steer west," one of the men ordered him, consulting the compass on his phone. "If you refuse, we'll throw you overboard." So steer Ali did. Why the other men would not help him I only came to understand later.

I looked at the passengers crushed up against me, wondering if they felt as near to death as I did: a grandmother in a black embroidered *zabon* so heavy it would drag anyone to the bottom of the sea. Three stick-limbed children, wet and shivering. The pregnant woman who had fainted in the van as pale as frost, her young husband trying to shelter her from the cold. A crowd of boys my own age, jaws clenched, eyes narrowed. We might have each held a history and a hope, a name and a family, but here we were nothing but prayers in the wind.

We sailed through the dark for some six hours, the rubber boat swinging and heaving with each slap of a wave, the sea writhing around us like a herd of monstrous snakes. At first I couldn't understand why the journey was taking so long, Kuşadasi beach being less than an hour away from the shores of Greece. But then I realized that the winter wind was driving us in haphazard directions, just as it was battering our bodies, and that neither Ali nor anyone else would be able to steer our rubber balloon of a boat against such force.

Human beings can learn to endure almost anything if we have to, isn't that so, Auntie? In prison I had learned to endure the loss of any sense of the sexual act as tender or loving, which I knew from poetry but had never experienced. I had even learned to endure much of the pain inflicted on me. But one thing I could never bear was the theft of my will, of my sovereignty over my mind, my control over my body. That is the thing above all else that tempted me to take my life.

On the boat, the division between what we could and could not endure was much the same. We could bear up under the cold and wet, the stink of vomit and diarrhea, the nausea and even the stinging salt and thirst that made our tongues swell and our throats as abrasive as sand, although the thirst was the cruelest. We could also withstand being pressed so tightly together that we could hardly move—the old woman in the *zabon* had been leaning against my leg for so many hours it had turned numb. But our inability to control whether we would be tipped out of the boat at any moment or captured by those who would drag us back to prison or death—that was a torment that gripped us in its teeth like a wolf and would not let go.

Yet even in the face of this, there were heroes among us. Women who sang soothing songs to their babies and so to anyone close by. Men who organized us so that we could not hoard water but had to share it. A young woman who entertained the children with stories. Peacemakers who prevented fights between the men, many of whom were crazed by anger and the horrors of war. An old woman who sent up constant prayers to Allah to protect us all. Leila, who shared our dates and biscuits with the other passengers and monitored our spirits despite the loss of her own—as she does to this day.

I was no hero, though. I'd forgotten how to tell stories. I could no longer sing or pray, and I had no food to share. The most I could do was cradle one child or another, yearn for Mama, and sway in my own urine and fear.

Only when the night began to pale and the sea to lighten from black to dark gray did we draw within our first sight of land. It was nothing but a craggy gray rock bristling with black trees but it was enough to make my fellow travelers break into shouts of relief and joy and cry out their thanks to Allah. Even Hazem and Majid joined in the excitement.

Leila and I, however, remained silent. She knew how very far from Farah and Dunia we had come by then, just as I finally understood that Mama would never join me and had never intended to—that I had lost her not only for the moment but forever.

Nafisa leans forward under our olive tree and, without a word, folds me into her arms.

9

HILMA

"*Kyria* Khilma?" Kosmos peers down at me from his upper terrace, his sly expression and white eyebrows giving him the look of a rascally satyr. "What is it you do to my tree?"

I whack the pine once more with his broom. "Making the cicadas shut the fuck up." The cicadas here are much louder than they are at home, deafening and relentless, and they occupy every tree from sunup to sundown, rasping away like a million tiny saws. I haven't minded until now, under the enchantment of the Samos summer, but this evening their racket is suddenly as maddening as a chorus of car alarms. So I've been slamming the tree for some time now; the same tree, it so happens, that attacked me with pine cones the night I arrived.

Kosmos breaks into unnecessarily prolonged laughter. "Crazy *Amerikanikh*," he says, wiping his eyes, "you cannot battle the cicadas of Greece. They were here long before you and they will be here long after you are gone. Come drink my ouzo with me. Your nerve she needs soothing."

Indeed she does. Last night I was visited by the same dream that's been plaguing me for two years now, each time leaving me shaky and raw. So I mount the stairs, settle into one of his cushioned deck chairs, and look out at the sunset as it turns the Turkish mountains purple and Vathi the pink of a blush.

Kosmos sits beside me, fills two stubby glasses with ouzo and dashes water into it, transforming it from clear to cloudy white. He lifts his glass and we clink.

"Never take a drink without first toasting the health of a friend or very bad things they will happen to you," he says solemnly.

Bit late for that, Kosmos.

In the dream I'm always walking the streets of our French village, the beach of our sea, searching for Linnette. All is leached of color. The water lies murky and still, the sand as gray as asphalt, the pastels of the fishing cottages washed out to mud. The glass in her jars have lost their color, too, the shells their shapes. Her diary lies discarded and dusty, and each time I open it, the pages drain to blanks. My paintings taunt me, the portraits turn their backs. Something tumbles out of my chest, a slimy, gray thing scurrying up to my face.

"Go on, drink." Kosmos sits back with his legs splayed. He's dressed in a pressed blue linen shirt and spotless cream trousers. Kosmos, I'm discovering, is something of a dandy.

I gaze into my glass, wondering at the wisdom of drinking this ouzo stuff, which smells exactly like pastis, a drink I've always abhorred. I try a swallow. It nearly knocks me out of my chair. "Whoa."

"Have more until your urge to battle cicadas it is quenched." Kosmos smiles a smile that takes me by surprise, Greek men being more prone to scowl—a smile, I might add, that looks suspiciously flirtatious. I blush even pinker than the town. Nobody has smiled at me like that for years.

"Miss Khilma," he says after we have each taken a second sip, "you eat only with yourself again tonight?"

"I'm eating alone because I like it," I reply snippily. "But you're here alone too, right?"

He half shrugs and looks out to sea. "Yes, my wife she died last year. Eleni. She was only fifty-four."

"Oh. I didn't mean . . . I'm so sorry." I blush again.

"Why? The fault it is not yours." He turns his milky eyes back to me.

"No, that's not what I meant . . . Um, do you have children?"

He looks surprised at the question. "I do, yes. A boy and a girl. My daughter Sophia, she lives in Australia. I never see her. My son Yiannis, he is in Athens."

"It must be tough to have your daughter so far away."

"Is not my choice. And you, Miss Khilma? You have children?"

I pause. "A son." I can say no more on that.

Kosmos is back to smiling now, his leathery face aglow. "Crazy *Amerikanikh*," he says yet again, which is beginning to irritate me, "you go with me to a movie?"

"Movie?" Isn't there a rule somewhere forbidding Airbnb hosts from dating their customers? "No, thank you. I'm much too tired."

He dismisses this with a wave. "I will show you how we in our villages entertain ourselves. The village it is in the mountains, the cinema in a garden. We leave at half past twenty, we go, we sit, we eat, we drink, we watch."

"We drive?"

"I, Kosmos, will drive. You, Miss Khilma, will relax."

And so, telling myself I need the distraction, I ouzo-wobble down to my apartment, pull on a green sundress and, still feeling somewhat disoriented by this abrupt change of plans, off to the movies I go.

On the way in Kosmos's black Peugeot, which is somewhat battered but considerably bigger and sturdier than my green pea, he wastes no time, unfortunately, in starting up again about refugees. "Three years ago, *Kyria* Khilma, they are landing everywhere. Big heaps of life jackets you will see on our beaches, like orange hills."

"Yes, I've seen pictures. Terrible."

He ignores this. "The families, little children, walking for many kilometers along the roads, you see them also. But you cannot stop to help even if you want because the police they catch you and lock you in the police station all night."

"Why?" I don't believe a word of this.

"Because the Turkeys they have *malakas* all over this island who make the money from the refugees. What is the word . . . exploit? You understand?" Kosmos heaves a dramatic sigh. "The Turkeys and the Greeks we have always been enemies. You know this, Miss Khilma?"

"Yes, Kosmos, I know."

"Do you know also that Samos was once the most rich island in all of Aegean? But then, in fifteenth century, Turkey pirates come many, many times to rape and pillage and murder. In end, Samos stays empty for one hundred years."

"Yes, the period of desertification."

Kosmos glances at me. "Ah, you read our history. I am pleased. There are good Turkeys and bad Turkeys, of course, but the smugglers, this is why the police they will arrest you if you help a refugee."

I agree about good and bad Turkeys but all this still sounds far-fetched to me. So, to test him, I tell him about Nafisa.

Kosmos looks grim. "I hope this African you meet she is not come from Nigeria. The Nigerians they are thieves. I have been to Africa many times and they make the connections with the gypsies here on this island to steal, you understand. A ring of thieves I think you call it? Or gang? I see it in Athens also."

I guffaw so obviously that I have to turn it into a cough. I wish I hadn't come now. "It's lovely tonight," I say to change the subject, gazing out of the window to watch the last of the twilight wash the sky in gold and silver. We're corkscrewing higher up Mount Thios by the minute, its night aromas wafting headily through the car: sunbaked resin and sage, mint and oregano, thyme and jasmine; the quiet interrupted only by the distant thunk of goat bells and the purr of Kosmos's engine. I inhale and close my eyes.

When we park and clamber out, Kosmos accidentally sets off his car alarm, drops his keys, and spends several minutes searching for them in the dark while the car screeches beside us, wrecking the peace I was just enjoying, not to mention that of the village. Turns out a car alarm is worse than the cicadas after all. People stare. I study my feet. But finally, all is calm.

"Come, *Amerikanikh*," he says, unperturbed, while I wonder about all those ouzos, of which he had several while I sipped my single potent dose. He leads me across the road. "This theater it is run by father and son," he tells me. "The son he is what we call *lougra*—I think your more polite word is gay?" He whispers this last remark, casting me a conspiratorial glance, which I try to ignore, wishing again that Kosmos would keep his bigotry to himself.

The movie theater is indeed in a garden. Rows of chairs cushioned with green pillows, little tables, waist-high flowerpots fragrant with basil, rosemary, and thyme. Rosebushes and palm trees form a wall around us, the stars the ceiling. Despite my irritation I'm charmed. *It's just like* The Secret Garden, *Granny, isn't it?*

"In the US we have outdoor movie theaters too," I tell Kosmos. "But there, we sit in cars. This is much nicer."

He looks smug.

The movie is an American comedy of IQ-lowering idiocy but I do enjoy the sight of bats flying across Jane Fonda's lips, the Greek subtitles and the delayed laughs after Diane Keaton makes a particularly vapid remark. At one point though, the film suddenly flickers and turns off.

"Oh dear, it's broken," I say without regret, picking up my backpack.

"No broken, intermission!" Kosmos beams at me. He's on his second beer. Perhaps I should have taken the pea after all.

The putatively gay son appears before us then, plump, baby-faced and smiling, and presents us each with a plate heaped with what look like deep-fried baseballs drenched in honey. *"Kalispera,"* he greets us, and then in English, "My mother made these. They are called *loukoumades*. Eat!" He gives us each six of these enormous things. The first lands in my stomach like a bowling ball. I push the others over to Kosmos, who makes short work of them.

The movie whirs and starts up once again, having skipped several scenes, although nobody seems to notice, dialing down my IQ even further. Yet all this only occupies half of my thoughts. Like a sleeping duck, I seem to be able to bifurcate my brain, the bright half taking in the movie and this lovely garden, Kosmos's clownish hospitality, and the honey of the *loukoumades*; the dark half shouting of Linnette, the dream, of Nick's devastation and of Theo and Megan, their marriage stunned first into prostration, then into catatonia by me.

10

NAFISA

WE ARE NOT NUMBERS, WE ARE HUMANS

My newest brethren here on this island, a whole crowd of whom recently arrived from the Democratic Republic of the Congo, held their first protest yesterday. A novice's hope of being heard.

WE ARE NOT ANIMALS TO SLEEP IN THE BUSH

They scrawled these slogans in French and English on scraps of cardboard or pieces of wood and paraded them around the streets all morning, chanting and singing, holding up their signs for all to see.

WE ONLY ASK FOR OUR RIGHTS

The police wasted no time in showing up, too, of course, closing in around the protesters, wielding enormous shields, their eyes hidden behind the black screens of visors.

JE NE SUIS PAS UN MOUTON. I am not a sheep.

That sign was held by a child.

The problem these newcomers have, I tell Amina and Leila under our tree this morning, is memory. If all they knew was war, it might not be such an affront to live on top of a puddle or inside a cage. But naturally they had lives before, as did we, lives in cities or villages, with families or friends, work or careers; lives of warm beds and laughter in the next room. So they remember and they rage. The past is such a prison, my sisters. Look at the three of us sitting here between piles of shit, scratching our bedbug bites as dogs scratch their fleas, filling our empty days by telling one another our memories. To what end? To disinter the dead? Revive the pain? Plea for pity?

"No, Auntie!" Amina pulls off one of her white sneakers and bangs it upside-down on the ground to empty out some gravel. She slips it back on. "We tell them to remind ourselves of who we are. To take back the history that war has snatched from us."

"Exactly," agrees Leila, looking over at her sons. "Where would our children be without our memories holding their histories?"

So you say, sisters, but after Osman and my babies were killed, what use had I for memories?

"But don't you recall what your friend Samiya said?" Amina counters. "That only by remembering your husband and children could you keep them in the world?"

I look at her with tenderness. Eyes too big for her face, body so brittle under her white summer shirt and narrow jeans. Little one, I say, do you spend your days trying to remember or forget what happened to you in prison?

She is quiet for a moment, scratching at her thumb. "I try to forget most of it, yes," she concedes. "But I also try to remember the women in my cell who were kind to me, who gave me the strength to stay alive for Mama. Can't you remember your children and husband as they were in life, Auntie, rather than in death?"

I shuffle my feet in the dust. How worn and bony they look in their plastic sandals, how knotted and calloused. I have put them through much, these feet.

At times I can, yes, little one, I tell her at last. But when I arrived at Fugnido, that camp in Ethiopia, this was not so. All around me were children whose bellies had swollen with malnutrition while their limbs had dwindled to twigs, mothers blinded by cataracts before they were even old, sanitation not fit for a goat, and rations so meager I knew I would starve. So I understood that if I wanted to save my Amal from joining her sisters and brothers, I had to push aside any memories that would distract me with either grief or joy and root my mind solely on ensuring her survival.

All and every day in that place, I stood in queues with her infant body strapped to my chest, bartering for the food and clothes, blankets and soap she needed; my already abused feet rotting with damp or cracking with heat, depending on the season. I planted a vegetable patch to provide us with better nutrition than we ever got from charitable handouts. Kept her apart from those who were sick. Made sure she drank only bottled water to avoid the dysentery that was draining the life from babies by the hundreds. Built her a cradle out of scrap wood to keep her safe from snakes and insects. Raised our roof with wooden poles to make room to stand—not like the nylon coffin I occupy here. And when a truck arrived to dump discarded packing crates, I fought the crowd for two and made them into a chest of drawers and a table. Outside, our tent may have looked as ramshackle as all the others, but inside it was a home.

I was only able to accomplish all this because of the money I made from men. I apologize for mentioning this, sisters, but, you see, I no longer cared what I did with my body, the soldiers and grief having stolen that from me.

"Ours is not to judge," Leila replies, retying the knot on her hijab. "Only Allah decides who will be entered into the Good Book."

Amina, on the other hand, is shocked, although she tries not to show it—Amina who believes me wise when all I am is tired.

When those men came to call, I continue, I left Amal with my trusted Samiya, blindfolding my daughter with her own innocence. And if at times my body revolted, and when I later fell sick from those men, I admonished it. *Who are you, Body, to complain? You serve my will and my will is to protect my daughter's life. Do as I bid.*

"Mama, too, blindfolded me with innocence," Amina remarks with lemon in her voice. "I would have known not to write that poem otherwise."

Your mother only wanted to give you what mothers must give.

"And what was that, Auntie? Her own foolish delusions?"

Ah, little Amina. For all she has endured, she has no idea of what it is to be a mother.

As Amal grew, graduating from my breast to a bottle, all fours to two feet, I taught her letters and numbers, told her the ancient stories of my village, and formed a small nursery school in the shade of a banyan tree for her and the children of the other pariah women like me. And somehow, as a butterfly rises in the wind, Amal thrived in spite of the squalor and dangers around us—after all, she had never known anything else. At the age of one, she would spend hours arranging pieces of wood into patterns and structures. At two, she became fascinated by numbers, counting up to a hundred over and over all the day long. By three, she could help me tend my small plot of land and raise the chickens I had bought. Wide-eyed and serious, she had become the kind of child people loved to pet. I truly believe she had my dead children's spirits deep within her because, together with them, she soared.

And if at night I was sometimes sleepless with fever, my skin ashing and scoring with lesions, I hid this from her as best I could. And if I awoke screaming with nightmares, I stuffed a blanket in my mouth. And if I ached for the embracing warmth of Osman, our babies, and my village, I hid that, too, binding it under my ribs until it suffocated into silence.

But even as Amal was thriving, life in Fugnido was not. Almost every week, we were met by a new crisis: an epidemic, a drought, a rape, a murder, a battle. In our fourth year, a fight broke out between the Anou refugees in our camp and the Nuer and Dinka in the surrounding communities. Nearly two hundred people died in that fight, my sisters, and hundreds more were left without shelter, while most of our aid workers picked up and fled.

After that, rumors quickly spread that the Ethiopian government might close down the camp altogether and move us elsewhere, which aroused the interest of Western journalists. Sure enough, soon they were buzzing around us like frenzied wasps, bristling with questions and cameras. "We hear many of you women have been the victims of war rape," some of them shouted. "Anyone willing to talk?"

"How the world does love a tragic tale," Leila observes, clamping her thin lips into a bitter line, "as long as it belongs to somebody else."

Amina laughs. I look at her. I almost never hear her laugh.

Most of the women in the camp turned in shame from the sting of that question but I saw in it an opportunity. So I dressed in my best toab—not the sky-blue one in the photograph I showed you, Amina, but a bright yellow one printed with sunflowers—left Amal in Samiya's care, and approached a tall and portly woman who had the look of my own people. "Do you speak Arabic?" I asked her.

"A little," she replied in a French accent. Hefting a big bag of cameras further up her shoulder, she offered me an encouraging smile.

"I will tell you my story, and you can put it on your television and give it to the world."

The woman's eyes grew bright. "Thank you so much, this is very brave of you."

I held up a hand. "But first, I have one condition. In exchange, you must help me take my daughter away from this camp before it kills her."

The reporter gathered her face into a sour plum. "I'm sorry, but I'm not allowed to promise anything like that."

I regarded her steadily. Tall and well-groomed, skin glossy where mine flaked, eyes clear where mine chafed, clothes new where mine were faded. "My daughter has twelve fathers," I said.

She looked at me with new interest. "I'll see what I can do."

My friends in the camp were disgusted. "You are humiliating us," they spat, "have you no shame?" But who else was going to tell our stories, the stories of women refugees? The veiled figures forbidden to appear on camera or speak to strangers. Those deemed too ignorant to know what they are saying or who were never taught the language or confidence to say anything at all. The ones who, like so many women in this camp here, hide all day in their containers or tents, afraid to talk to anyone or even to take a walk. Turn on the radio or television and we hear plenty of stories about men: men in refugee camps, men who have survived the boats battered by lethal seas, men who have hauled their dead babies from the surf. But where are the voices of the mothers and aunts of those babies, the daughters, sisters, and wives of those men?

"You see!" Amina is triumphant. "Our stories do rescue history."

Be that as it may, little one, it is why I decided to tell mine. I told it again and again, in much the same way as I am telling it to you. And soon, with the help of that French reporter, my face became the face of women in war, not only of my own country but all over the world. The face of captured women, pillaged villages, and genocide. The face of the raped.

As for those who reviled me, I cared nothing about what they said because this face of mine, blown large by cameras, plastered on billboards and television screens, was awakening the guilt of the rich, bringing in donations and invitations to speak, visas and offers of help. I opined, I posed, I was interviewed and advertised—after all, I was used to selling myself. In this way, I rescued my little hibiscus and she never even knew how.

The winter Amal turned four, she and I were taken from the camp at long last, put onto an airplane with no more explanation than if we were our own luggage, and flown to the city of Sofia in Bulgaria, a country I had never heard of, old and quiet, gray and brown, its people sullen, its food as heavy as lead, its weather as dank as a dripping blanket—a country my sponsors must have chosen because it was the poorest and cheapest in Europe. There, we were granted asylum and settled into a building with other rejects and refugees, our home like a chicken battery in one of the vast, raw concrete Soviet towers that poke up from all over the city like pins.

But a towering chicken battery was better than a tent, and solid walls, however dank, were better than plastic sheeting. Furthermore, we had running water, hot and cold; heat in the winter, at least sometimes; windows to open in summer; a flushing toilet down the hall; and two entire rooms to ourselves. Best of all, my sponsors had found me work in a small coat factory in the neighborhood of Luilin, where I sewed buttons and seams all day on a production line while Amal went to a free nursery school nearby, alleviating me of the need to submit to men for money.

And if I coughed and grew weak, and if the fevers came and went, my Fugnido disease rising to attack again, I hid this from Amal as I always had, swallowed the pills I collected from the doctor and said nothing. And if I yearned for the sun of Sudan, for our fields and river and my Osman and children, I swallowed that, too.

Amal had never seen such luxuries as we had in our chicken battery and she was dazzled. It was all I could do to stop her turning the water tap on and off for hours or hanging precariously from our twenty-first floor window to watch the tops of people's heads passing below, as tiny as grapes. "I'm high up as a bird, *Umi*!" she would exclaim, reaching for the swifts wheeling and squealing by our window. I gripped the back of her shirt in alarm, longing for the earth beneath my feet, not twenty floors of echoing concrete, as unsettled as I had felt in the airplane with nothing underneath us but sky.

For many years, we lived in Sofia without strife—at least no more than that of enduring poverty, street crime, and the native suspicion of foreigners, Muslims, and anyone else who was not white or Christian. Our way to survive was to try to blend in as best we could, learning Bulgarian and English, exchanging our bright toabs for dull western trousers and shirts, keeping our religion private, even visiting the Orthodox churches when necessary—although, of course, blending in when one is the brown of the earth and everyone else is as bleached as death was never easy. But we tried, ignoring the stares and the shunning, and even the occasional spit, knowing that we, with our charitable sponsors and all they had brought us, might never find such good fortune again.

By the time Amal was fourteen, her determination had grown as steady as her gaze, and her legs were so long I joked she must be the child of a giraffe—a joke

I stole from Osman, who used to tease me with it as he caressed my own lengthy limbs. "I'm going to be an engineer when I grow up," Amal told me more than once. "I'm going to design bridges to cross the rivers and seas of the world so that people like us can go wherever we want. And some of my bridges, *Umi*, will be made of cut steel that sparkles. Thousands of sparkles, so people will think they're walking over a bridge of stars."

I see those bridges here, sisters, on those nights I climb the mountain. I see them arcing all over the sky.

"Did you ever tell her all you've told us?" Amina asks. "Did you tell her who her fathers were?"

Little sister, would you? No, I told her that her father was not a giraffe but Osman, for had he not claimed her in my dreams?

"So, you lied to her, just like Mama lied to me."

I did. But this is what mothers do, little one. We lie to our children to protect them.

Amina fixes me with wide, angry eyes. "Is that really true, Auntie? Or did you only lie to protect yourself?"

11

LEILA

I am looking for my mother.
I am looking for my sister.
I am looking for my son.
I am looking for my family.

On certain walls around the camp, the Red Cross has pasted a series of small posters, each printed with rows of faces the size of postage stamps. Under each face is one of these pleas. My face is there too:

I am looking for my daughter and granddaughter.

This poster campaign is called Trace the Face. These are the kinds of paper wishes that we are offered in lieu of action.

Were I to describe Farah for such a poster, I would say that she is barely taller than Hazem but as fearless as a lioness. She was fearless when war came to our city, crushing everything she had ever known. Fearless when her father, my beloved Mansour, was killed. Fearless when her husband, Hassan, was killed too, leaving her widowed and pregnant at twenty. And fearless when she gave birth to Dunia six months later in the midst of war.

As for Dunia, I would say that her hair is as black as a river, her face the shape of an olive, and the backs of her knees as tender as blossoms. Every time I see a leaf dancing in the wind here, I think of her.

"*Teta*, what are noses made of?"

"*Teta*, will Mama die one day?"

"*Teta*, are our bones made of wood like trees?"

More than four months have passed since I lost them on that beach, and still not a word.

Nafisa, you tell us stories of your murdered family and your beloved Amal; Amina, you of your brother's death, your imprisonment, and your yearning for your mother. I am sorry for you both, as I am for everyone here, but my heart remains strangely numb, heavy as marble in my chest.

Every refugee's story opens in horror, passes through betrayal, and ends in a question. But, ultimately, the only story that truly occupies us is our own.

12

HILMA

And now have I put in here, as thou seest, with ship and crew, while sailing over the wine-dark sea to men of strange speech . . .

Men of strange speech are certainly a dime a dozen in Samos, but Homer's wine-dark sea remains elusive. There is a moment just before dusk when the sun paints a layer of deep rose over the purpling water, creating a color not unlike that of the local Muscat rosé, but "rosé-dark sea" doesn't quite cut it. I've heard many a crackpot theory about why Homer came up with that phrase, from the sea actually being deep red in his day to him being blind. But maybe this sunset rosé is all he meant.

The man of strange speech in this house is out this morning, much to my relief, his car gone from the driveway, along with his increasing insistence on making conversation. Ever since our excursion to the movies, he seems to have intensi-fied his flirting, although I'm too culturally out of place to be sure. Worse, in his gush of attention, not to mention plying me with more Samian wine, he managed to extract the fact that I used to be a painter; a piece of information I deeply regret having let slip. It amazes me that I am still susceptible to sexy smiles, flirtation, and booze. Does one never grow up?

"Why you not paint here?" he said once he had hooked this confession from me. "Greece she is paradise for artists!"

"That's exactly the problem, it's all a big cliché." I didn't tell him that the painter in me fled long ago, in company with the rest of my former self.

He looked at me in honest puzzlement. "Then if you refuse to paint, Miss Khilma, you must draw. Draw something for me, your host. Draw a boat, a bird, the view." He winked. "Draw a *tzitzíki*."

"What's that?"

"Greek for cicada, Miss Khilma."

I can't, I won't.

I received an email this morning from Nick, the first in ten months. *"I wanted to tell you this before you hear it from my lawyer. I'm filing for divorce."*

I also received one from Theo. The first in two years.

"I thought you should know. Megan is pregnant. We'll send pictures when the baby is born, but we ask you not to visit."

"*Yassou*, Khilma!" Kosmos is back, peering down at me from his upper terrace, his face more satyric than ever in this early morning light. "Today I take you to a magic place where you paint again. The muse there she lies in every tree. You will be, how you say—inspired. Even crazy American ladies will not be able to resist. And the walk it is easy. No mountains."

"Kosmos, the other day I hiked way up Mount Kerkis to Pythagoras's cave and back. I don't need 'easy.'"

He squints at me in amusement, running his eyes over me in a way I'm not sure I like. "*Ne*," he says, which I have to remind myself means yes. "The cave she is fake, *Kyria* Khilma. For tourists. But you are strong in brain and body, this I can see. You are made like a little wire of muscle. It is my own knees for which I have worry."

"Then maybe you shouldn't go." I know this is rude but I really do prefer to hike alone. And I'm annoyed about the cave. It took me hours to get up there.

"I go for you. And for the muse." He gives me that smile of his again and I am disarmed.

As soon as we've both finished breakfast, we leave my green pea and those emails behind and once more slide into his Peugeot. No ouzo this time, thank god, but before long I'm clutching the sides of my seat as he careens around corners and along the edges of cliffs, steering with one finger while leaning over to twiddle the radio dial with the other to find me Greek music.

"It's all right," I say in a strangled voice. "I don't need music."

"Khilma, every human being she needs music."

We zoom on. He roars past a huge truck, its wheels an inch from my ear.

"Where are we going?" I just manage to ask, my voice a wobbly squeak.

"We are going west, little *Amerikanikh*, to the quiet side of the island. To see a waterfall there, to climb a ladder, and to find the muse."

"Ladder?"

"You will see. And I, Kosmos, have brought with me a surprise for you."

I don't want any more surprises.

We plunge on, passing a huge tractor around a blind corner at top speed while a motorcyclist hurtles straight at us. I let out a shriek.

Kosmos swerves out of the way just in time and looks at me sternly. "Do not scream. You will make for me to have accident."

After about forty-five minutes of this, we arrive and park, blocking the narrow road like everyone else. I climb shakily out. He looks me over. "You have on bathing suit?"

"I do." He nods approvingly. I'm also in shorts, a T-shirt, and the water shoes he told me to bring. But whether Kosmos is wearing a bathing suit himself I can't tell because his stocky torso is loosely clad in a dashing turquoise shirt, the sleeves rolled to the elbows, and his legs in floppy linen trousers. Only his feet, which at least are not cloven but do strongly resemble hobbit paws, are bare in their leather sandals.

"Good," he says. "Now for surprise." And out of the trunk he pulls a sketchbook and a box. "In here, brushes, charcoal, paint, everything. You need only for the muse she to kiss you. We go to the *Panaghia tou Patamiou* now. It is eleventh century chapel. There we pray her to come."

I want to tell him I can't paint anymore. That I don't pray in chapels, however ancient, and that I don't believe in muses or god or pagan-Christian mash-ups, either. That I'm going to be a banned grandmother and a divorced wife. But all I say is, *"Efarasto*, Kosmos."

He beams. "Ah, you learn Greek! Beautifulest language in the world. Now, I carry the paints, you walk, I give them to you when the muse she kisses." And chuckling to himself, he slings the strap of the paint box over his shoulder and leads me down a path into the woods.

"Theo, that is wonderful news. I am so grateful you told me. You don't have to an-swer, but I'd love to know when the baby's due," I wrote back.

"Nick, I am sad but not surprised. Thank you for warning me. I'll do everything I can to cooperate." I wrote that, too.

We reach the chapel in no time, so small it could barely house a cow. I've come across many of these miniscule churches here, perched atop cliffs and mountains, their walls the white of whipped cream, their floors mosaicked with pebbles the shape and size of sugar almonds, their interiors hung with tiny icons. The chapels are always immaculate, cared for, I suspect, by one old lady or another who toils uphill every day to sweep and scrub, hoping perhaps to earn her own form of forgiveness.

This particular chapel is half in ruins, its walls crumbling, its roof resting on four Corinthian pillars, no doubt plundered from some ancient temple; Greeks are cavalier about ruins. The door is ajar, inviting us inside, where we find an altar the size of a music stand and a battered pewter chandelier dangling crookedly from what is left of the ceiling. A miniature painting of Jesus hangs on the wall, his face pink-cheeked and chubby under a lopsided golden crown—more Greek baby than Jewish martyr.

Kosmos has fallen silent for a change, so I glance over at him. He's gazing up at the ruined ceiling, his lips moving. I keep quiet in case he's praying.

"Khilma," he whispers. "We must light a candle to call for your muse."

This is going too far, I'm about to tell him, when Theo's words murmur in my ear again. *Listen and learn.* I force a nod.

Kosmos picks up a candle from a stack in the corner, slips a coin into a box and lights the wick. I stand back, embarrassed, while he crosses himself and fits the candle into a holder under a glass-framed icon of Mary, which he kisses, planting his lips most unhygienically on top of the prints of the thousands of lips that preceded his. The icon is festooned with dozens of silvery tin votives, each in the image of a prayer: staring eyes, swaddled babies, married couples, shriveled legs. *Please don't let me go blind. Please save my baby from cancer. Please, Mother Mary, cure my crippled daughter. Please don't let my husband leave me.*

I can't help but imagine how dense the walls would be with votives if the refugees on this island were to hang them. Thousands of little tin stamps, each bearing a tragic plea. A house. A mother. A boat. A town. A child. A country.

"Khilma, you are looking in that blackish way again," Kosmos scolds me, his resonant voice bouncing off the walls. "Come. It is time to enter the land of muses and fairies."

I follow him, wondering why I allow this man to boss me so.

Outside the chapel, a slight little woman with a cap of silver curls is sitting on a low stone wall, making jewelry. Her wares are displayed beside her: beaded bracelets, necklaces, and earrings, along with beach stones painted with bucolic scenes and peace signs. It all looks very leftover hippy to me, just as I was in the days I first knew Nick.

Kosmos stops to talk to her while I browse her wares, but after a quick look at me, she switches to strikingly good English. She used to be a teacher of Greek literature, she tells us, but lost her job when the economic crisis closed her school. Now she spends her days working on the jewelry, while her husband, an engineer who has also lost his job, paints the stones.

"This story it is mine also," Kosmos says to me. "I was a history teacher in a village near Platanos until the government she took the job from me six years ago. The crisis it closed thousands of rural schools like this lady's and mine, Miss Khilma. First no heat, then no books, then no salary, then no school."

I look at him in surprise. I'd thought him a laborer, or maybe a sailor, but now all his lecturing falls into place. A history teacher. Of course. *Listen and learn.*

"Yes," the woman says, waving her jewelry pliers for emphasis, "this is how it was for me."

Kosmos grins. "Khilma, this is a nice lady. I buy you something from her."

"No, you don't. I'll buy something myself."

"You are stubborn like a she-goat. In Greece we give. It is our nature. Ancient tradition. You no say no. Never."

The jewelry seller smiles at this, her pretty face lighting up under her curly fringe of silver. "Your friend, he is right," she says to me. "I will tell you a story about us Greeks. If a German or an Englishman finds he has only five euros left in his pocket, he stays at home and worries about how he will survive. But if a Greek finds he has only five euros, he buys a tomato and some cheese, invites guests over, and they eat for three hours."

Shamed into choosing something, I pick a little bracelet of tiny white cowries alternating with periwinkle blue beads. "I love this color," I tell her while Kosmos pays her six euros.

She nods. "We love it also in Greece. Our word for it is *lulaki*." She fastens it to my wrist.

"Come, Khilma," Kosmos says after I thank her. "We walk." The woman raises her eyebrows and sneaks me a conspiratorial look. She must think we're a couple, but a new one, the man testing his powers. This is the last outing I take with Kosmos.

I must admit, however, that the trail does live up to his promise, leading us through an emerald gorge carpeted in feathery ferns and bifurcated by a silver stream dotted with tiny wooden bridges. A row of ancient plane trees leans over us, each twisted into such a human form it's as if we're surrounded by dancing dryads. Sunbeams puddle our path with gold. Butterflies float about in lazy clouds. I am indeed in fairyland.

Kosmos walks ahead of me, the way men tend to do, his stocky frame bounding over the bridges and his hobbit feet hopping from stone to stone—nothing wrong with his knees, as far as I can see. He stops so suddenly I almost bump into him. "Now." He turns and fixes me with a commanding frown. "Sit. Draw."

He points to a round boulder by the stream.

I sigh, unamused. But sit I do. He unhooks the paint box from his shoulder and hands it to me, then stands back, crosses his hairy arms over his turquoise shirt, and stares at me.

"What?"

"Draw. I wait here."

"Kosmos, nobody can work like that. You have to leave me alone." He looks crestfallen, his grizzled eyebrows knitting together. "Leave me with the muse," I add slyly.

"*Dax*. But first, crazy *Amerikanikh*, tell me what you will draw."

I can't, I want to say. Every pencil line, every brushstroke, every gesture belongs to Linnette. "I don't know," I say instead, my voice weak. "And please stop calling me that."

"I tell you then." He looks around. "There." He points to a dragonfly. Iridescent green one second, Aegean blue the next, it's perched on a pale rock, its gossamer wings and shimmering body momentarily still.

The artist in me balks. I'm not an illustrator. Nor a doodler of cute animals. I don't do Hallmark.

"This insect I love," says Kosmos. "In Greek it is called *liveloula*." He pronounces it with the lilt of Italian. The name of this island, too, is pronounced the way an Italian would, singing the *a* in the middle: Saaamos. "What you call *liveloula* in English?"

I tell him.

"Perfect! Your English it is ugly language. Those flat sounds up in nose. So blunt. Almost ugly as German. But Dragon Fly. This it is not bad."

How gracious of you, I say in my head. Out loud: "*Liveloula* is even prettier."

"Of course it is. I go now. Leave you with the muse, may she kiss you full on mouth." And off he bounds, his bare feet padding away.

Nobody kisses me, but I pick out a soft pencil from the box, and my hand does its work. A few strokes and there it is, the *liveloula* hovering on its rock just before it flies away. To please Kosmos, I shade it in with the blue and green pastels I find in the box. It looks like something I would have drawn in grade school but I'll give it to him anyway, to shut him up if nothing else.

It didn't hurt quite as much as I thought. Perhaps this is the answer. Not to paint as I used to paint, with intent or intuition, vision or inspiration, but just to render mindlessly whatever object that happens to sit in front of me, heart blank.

Dear Theo, will you at least tell me the name you choose for the baby?

Dear Nick, will you ever let me see you again?

Those emails I only write in my head.

Kosmos returns and pops up behind me to look over my shoulder. "Ah," he says and no more. I have clearly failed to either appease or impress him. "Now, Khilma, we walk in water."

I've no idea what he means until we reach a place where the stream widens into a pool and then disappears between two cliff-like rocks. Kosmos strips off his shirt and trousers, to my consternation, revealing a muscular if saggy torso, legs as hairy as a faun's, and alarmingly skimpy Speedos in neon green. He tells me to remove my clothes, too, and hang them in a tree.

"Why? The water's not even up to my shins."

"Khilma, just do it."

At first, we are merely wading, which makes me more suspicious than ever about his insistence on all this striptease, but once we squeeze through the narrow gap between the rocks, the water abruptly deepens until I'm up to my waist.

"Snake," he says calmly, pointing to a black wiggle by my ribs. I emit my second shriek of the day and leap into his arms. Chuckling in ill-disguised triumph, he puts me gently back down. "No dangerous. Come."

We wade on, the water creeping to my chest, and at last I see where we're headed: a natural pool cupped by rocks and fed by a cascade invisible from any other route. We stand in silence, watching the water weave into glittering ribbons as it tumbles into the pool, surrounding us in silver swirls.

Kosmos turns to me. "You like?"

"*Ne.* I like very much. It's beautiful. But I'm cold."

"*Dax*. Now, ladder, lunch, ouzo, sunset."

"No ouzo, Kosmos. It's eleven in the morning. And I can't stay out all day till sunset."

He shrugs. "You will miss the ball of fire into sea. More bad for you. But ouzo we must. Lunch, too. Relax and forget our troubles. *Dax*?"

I hesitate, thinking of the snake. "*Dax*. Can we get out of the water now?"

So we half swim, half wade back to our clothes, and do indeed mount a ladder, or what is really a long flight of vertical steps roughly hewn out of cedar. The ascent is steep and vertiginous but worth it because perched at the top of the cliff like a giant treehouse is a terraced taverna presided over by a tiny old man who so resembles a leprechaun he fits the place exactly.

I've realized by now that Kosmos is the muse, of course. Or hopes to be. But although I've no intention of letting him kiss me anywhere, let alone full on the mouth, I do let him buy me the lunch, the relaxation, a moment's forgetfulness, and, yes, even the ouzo.

13

AMINA

Every day that passes here, Leila seems more hollowed out than the day before, as though her need to find Farah and Dunia is consuming her alive. She hardly ever washes her clothes or those of the boys anymore, or even plays with them, let alone takes her turn at cleaning our metal box, as we and our neighbors have agreed to do. She leaves all that to me. All she does, when we are not waiting in one line or another, is stand by the camp police station for ever-longer hours, scanning her telephone. Another boat capsized, another child dead.

"Two children drown every day trying to cross the sea from war to freedom, do you know that, Amina?" she told me this morning.

I try to help by taking the boys out from under her feet for a few hours each day. We might go to the camp office to rifle through the donated clothes, looking for T-shirts they like or sandals to replace Majid's broken flip-flop, and we did finally find a pair after a long shortage of shoes. Or I might usher them down to swim at the little beach past the port or take them for a walk through the town, although this only seems to make them sad. "Why can't I have a bicycle?" Hazem asked me the other day after a blubbery Greek boy sailed by on his.

Yesterday, while we were in town, we had an encounter I did not expect. The boys were pressing their noses to a window of unaffordable toys, Hazem fixated on a soccer ball, Majid on a set of Lego, saying, "Why can some children have those things and we can't, Auntie? Why do we have to be different?" when a voice spoke behind us.

"You're only different, little man, because you're the best."

I turned around to see who had spoken, and there was that same tall-as-a-tree boy I'd met at the port, the one who had smiled at me so kindly. He took a step toward us. "*Salaam*, again," he said with another of those smiles. "Who are these fine fellows, your brothers?"

Once more I hesitated, my hand on Majid's shoulder, half wanting to stay, half to flee. "No," I stammered. "They are the sons of a friend. Say hello, children."

Majid didn't hear me, his eyes still on the toys, but Hazem obeyed. "You are so high up, Uncle," he said solemnly. "Does it make your legs hurt to be so high?"

The tree-boy laughed and ruffled Hazem's hair. "Sometimes, little fellow, yes. What's your auntie's name, will you tell me? I think she's too shy to tell me herself."

But Hazem was not going to fall for that. "What's *your* name, Uncle?" he said instead.

"Ah, that's a fair question. I'm known as Sadek of the Song. And I think your auntie here is very nice and pretty."

That was too much for me. I took the boys by their hands and fled.

If Mama were here, she would tell me what to do about this Sadek, whether to trust him or turn him away. I love Leila and Nafisa both, but in moments like this it is her I want and no one else. If only I could find out where she is or if she's alive. I've used Leila's cell phone at least a dozen times to call her, praying that I'm not putting her at risk, but each time a voice only tells me that our number no longer exists.

Perhaps they are all dead now, my family, murdered by bullets or bombs. Or perhaps Mama has been imprisoned in one of Bashar's torture chambers, as I was. Yet even as these thoughts cramp my chest and tear open my sleep with nightmares, they bring me no tears. I still have not been able to weep since the prison.

I wonder if Sadek of the Song has also lost his family. Whether he, too, has forgotten how to cry.

Many of us in this place used up our tears before we got here. Now our ways are hard and merciless. Get up before anyone else to be first in the food line. Elbow aside any elderly woman, child, or grandfather who stands in your way. Refuse to let the tent dwellers nearby use the toilet in your metal box unless they pay. Sell a scrap of land beside your tent to a newcomer, even though it's not yours to sell. Try to sell a bed in your box as well, even though that isn't yours, either. Barter without yielding. And never reveal weakness to anybody, lest they take advantage, snatch your children and money, and leave you with nothing—a lesson Leila and I learned only too well on that Turkish beach.

To this day, I don't know where we landed after that terrible journey, only that it was a small, dry island that was not Samos. But once our boat had crunched up onto the stones and we'd hauled ourselves out and collapsed onto the shore like so many flapping fish, I do know that I succumbed to terror. I had no idea what was to happen to us, whether we were to be welcomed or rejected, cared for or sent back to our deaths.

A group of well-fed people in luminous orange vests appeared out of the darkness then, offering water and wrapping the children and babies in silver blankets like falafels in foil. These people seemed kind, unlike the smugglers, but they explained nothing, brought us no food, and answered none of our questions, no matter how often we asked. They only indicated that once we had quenched our thirst, we had to walk.

The sun was only just creeping above the horizon when we began the march that morning, Hazem and Majid struggling in exhausted bewilderment beside us, the light a dim and heavy gray. We trudged up a hill as steep as a cliff—several of us hobbling without shoes, having lost them in the surf—hauling our children, old people, luggage, and wearied bodies over the rocky and arid land. Nothing surrounded us but white dust and stone, although once in a while we came across the gnarled trunk of an olive tree, a spear of cypress, or a prickly bush. Goats stared at us and then scampered away, filling me with envy of their four legs and sure balance, their sharp and meticulous hooves. But other than the hollow clank of the bells dangling from their necks and the occasional plaintive wail of a gull, the only sounds were our laboring breath, the cries of babies, and the multilingual rain of our questions: "Where are we going? Where are you taking us? Why is there no information?"

After we'd walked for an endless hour or so, the sun winter-pale and chilly, our clothes still wet and our stomachs empty, we reached a stretch of land paved with broken concrete overrun by weeds and encircled by such high fences it made me think of a zoo. Whispers quickly spread that it was an abandoned slaughterhouse, the blood of *haram* pigs soaked into the ground beneath our feet.

At the entrance, marked only by a black kiosk and a break in the fence, we were met by three uniformed policemen. "Line up here," one shouted in accented English, jabbing a finger at the fence. So line up we did, still straining with questions. The police pushed us into the kiosk one by one, searched through our telephones and baggage, confiscated our passports if we had any, poked, peered, and questioned. Then they made us hold a number on a placard to our chests, took our photographs, and wrote that same number on the back of our hands. B32, said mine, inked in black on my skin.

Finally, they shoved all sixty-seven of us into a cinder-block hut with one glass window and bolted the door.

"Let us out!" we shouted. Some of us wrestled with the handle, others tried the window. "Why have you put us here?"

The reply came through the keyhole: "Wait and all will become clear."

But nothing became clear. "What have we done to make them treat us like this?" I moaned to Leila.

"Be thankful, Amina," is all she replied, pulling her sons to her belly. "At least we're safe from Bashar's thugs and the sea. And, *insh'Allah*, Farah and Dunia will catch another boat soon and join us."

How I have come to despise the words *be thankful, all will become clear,* and *you will understand.* The words *waiting* and *perhaps.* Even the word *insh'Allah.*

For the rest of that day and all the following night we were kept crushed together in that hut, shuddering with cold while the odors of our drying clothes, saturated with urine and sweat, grew so foul I couldn't inhale without gagging. Hazem and Majid put their heads in Leila's lap and at least managed to fall asleep, frightened and hungry though they were, but she and I sat against the wall, unable even to doze. I saw her eyes gleaming in the dark as rats scurried across the floor and over the bodies around us, and the stains of what I took to be pig blood crept into our clothes. I saw her horror, just as I felt mine.

At sunrise, a new group of police officers flung open the door and announced that we had five minutes to gather our belongings and children and step outside to form yet another line. How we scrambled! Babies crying, clothes buttoned up every which way, shoes on the wrong feet, hijabs untied, shirts hanging out, socks missing. They marched us back over the stark and craggy landscape the same way we had come, and without a word more, herded us onto the deck of a coast guard boat.

We sailed for nearly three hours, still asking questions and receiving no answers, until an island materialized in front of us, ringed by beaches and rising to a cluster of green mountains in the center: Samos. How beautiful it looked to me then. How beautiful and full of promise.

As the boat drew nearer to the port, I squeezed between my fellow passengers to see what lay ahead. I took in a wide walkway by the sea, an even wider road flanked by palm trees, and on the other side, shops and cars and flowers and cats. I stared at it, shaken out of time and logic. Here in plain sight we were being treated like prisoners, while only a few meters away women chewed on breakfast rolls, young men sipped their coffees, old men smoked and fingered counting beads just like Baba's, while church bells rang across the town. The aroma of freshly baked bread wafted over to us through the cold air, an aroma I hadn't smelled since I'd been dragged off to prison. It transported me back to the winter days when Mama would send me and Tahar to the bakery to fetch *khobz* for the family, which we would tuck under our jackets for warmth, the bread mouthwatering and hot against our bellies. The memory made my chest burn for home and my stomach convulse with hunger.

Once we'd docked, the police ordered us off the boat and into a fenced-in area, where they told us to wait with our families, if we had any, in yet another line. Finally, they packed us into a series of white vans, the windows too narrow and dark to see out of, and drove us uphill to where we are now.

"No talking!" an officer commanded as we clambered out, blinking in the sudden light. A flock of people closed around us, clamoring for news of their lost loved ones, as Leila is always doing now, but the officer shouted and shooed them away. Only once they were gone could I see the filth of my surroundings. Leila and I looked at each other in shock. Black garbage bags swarming with flies, wasps and rats teetered beside us in enormous, stinking piles as high as my head. Rivers of mud ran between rows of stained metal boxes like the one we live in now. Thousands of tents were squeezed up against the hurricane fences and into every nook and alleyway. Shreds of paper, bits of Styrofoam and empty bottles scudded past our feet. And every tent and fence we could see was draped in tattered laundry.

We had always heard that once we refugees reached Europe, we would be given a warm house, food, our rights, and our dignity. What had gone wrong?

A tall Greek in a white doctor's coat appeared then, his hair the color of ash, and instructed us to tell him if we had any medical problems, while a scrawny Egyptian translated. Three or four of the men answered, but what could we women say in front of all these strangers about dried-up nursing milk, constipation, or the rampant urinary tract infections resulting from lack of water and toilets? In my case, was I to speak of the wounds the prison guards had left on my body—the vaginal and rectal lesions, the lacerations on my breasts and back, or the absence of my menses? No. So we said nothing.

One of our fellow passengers, a young Syrian with sad, drooping eyes, tapped the translator on the shoulder to ask a question. "Don't touch me!" the translator snapped, turning on him a look of contempt.

Oh, I thought. This is who we are now.

After that, we were locked into the cage beside the police station, where we were told to find a seat on one of the benches or the concrete floor. "Why do they keep locking us up like this?" I asked Leila. "Do they think we're criminals?"

"Shush, Amina. This is not the time to make trouble."

There followed yet another interminable wait, after which an official came in and began shouting at us in rapid-fire Greek, translated by that same Egyptian who didn't like to be touched. "What's he saying?" I whispered to Leila because I could hardly understand the jargon coming out of the man's mouth. She only shushed me again, straining to grasp the words.

"I think," she replied at last, "that they're trying to make us agree to go back to Turkey."

Hearing a scuffle, I looked over and saw the police handcuffing Ali, the boy who had been forced to steer our boat, and marching him away. Later, I heard that they'd beaten him until he signed a statement in Greek confessing to being a human trafficker. This is when I learned what the other men on our boat must have known all along: that to steer a refugee boat in Greece, even if you are a refugee yourself, can send you to prison.

We passed the rest of that day and night in that police cage, the same cage where Leila now looks for Farah and Dunia every time a new boat arrives. They gave us each a bowl of rice and strangely slimy spinach and allowed us to use the row of nearby portable toilets, although there were so many of us that they soon became too foul to enter. But they handed out no blankets or coats, so Leila and I pulled the boys to us, huddled together on the muddy ground, and tried to sleep on top of our backpacks. My feet, sockless in my thin sneakers, had numbed to stone by then, while pains were shooting through my back, but at least I had the bodies of the boys to keep me warm. Most people had nobody.

Early the next morning, a voice began calling us by the numbers on our hands and sending us inside the police container beside the cage. Yet when my number, B32, was called, I couldn't move. "Go, Amina!" Leila urged, holding her shivering boys close. "Don't be afraid. These are Greek police, not *al mukhabarat*. We are in Europe!"

"But Auntie, they arrested Ali."

"Just go!"

Reluctantly, I climbed the three steps to the container door, pulled in a long breath to steady myself and edged inside. There I found myself facing a policeman and a table, on which sat some sort of machine. Ordering me to approach, the policeman—whose weak chin reminded me chillingly of Bashar al-Assad's—checked the number on my wrist and made me place all ten of my fingers on a scanner, one by one, which took some time because my hands were shaking so badly. "Go," he commanded when we were finished, pointing through the door to a row of outside tables. "Go on, go!"

At one of the tables sat a burly Greek man beside the Egyptian translator, who told me to sit on a metal chair opposite. The Greek had the red face and meaty hands of a blacksmith, the Egyptian the squinty eyes and claw fingers of a bureaucrat. "Are you comfortable?" they asked once I was seated.

"Yes, thank you."

"Would you prefer a female interviewer?"

Sensing some sort of trap, I told them no.

"Where are you from?"

"Manbij, Syria."

"What is the name of your local mosque?"

I looked at the Greek's meaty face in surprise. Why did he want to know?

"Answer, please." This was said by the Egyptian with the insolence of a man granted an authority he has neither earned nor deserved.

I did answer, after which the two men asked me a string of other such questions plainly designed to test whether I was who I said I was, even though I'd shown them the birth certificate and identification Mama had given me: "What was the name of your school? Name the main street of your town. Where did you buy bread?" They also asked whether I knew anybody in Europe or had relatives there. But most significantly, "Do you wish to claim asylum in Greece?"

I was so certain they were trying to trick me that the truth began to sound like lies in my ears. But I understood that I had to say yes to that last question or they would send me back to Turkey, and perhaps even to Syria and my brothers.

When they were finally finished with me, the Greek handed me a paper and waved me away, leaving me with no idea of what would happen next or how he had judged me. All he said was that I could take the papers to the UNHCR office next door, where I'd be given a cash card for my allowance, and that in a month or so I would also receive something called an International Protection Applicant Card, both of which I'd have to renew every month. On that second card would be typed a date for the first of the two interviews I must undergo in my quest for asylum.

"When will those interviews be?" I asked the Greek and his Egyptian.

"As we said, the dates will be on the card. Now, go."

"Go where?"

"Wherever you can."

I hesitated. "But sirs, I heard we would be given a mat and a blanket?"

"We have none left. There are too many of you."

"But where am I to keep dry and safe?"

"Wherever you can," they repeated. "Go."

When I joined Leila, who was waiting for me nearby, she told me that the Greek and his sidekick had said the same to her. So she picked up Majid, I took Hazem by the hand, and heaving our bags onto our backs, we made our way along the muddy pathways of the camp, stopping at every metal box we saw to ask where we could sleep. Not a single box had space, not a single bed was free. After more than an hour of this, Leila approached the information window, a square hole cut out of the side of yet another white metal box, and implored the official inside to find a home for us and her children. But this was as fruitless as her pleading with the smuggler had been on the beach. "No room," the official kept saying. And once again, "There are too many of you."

So we were forced to spend the first twenty-five nights on this island sleeping on the ground among the same olive trees where we meet Nafisa today, shivering under the rain and wind, with nothing but a plastic tarp Leila had found to cover us and our own clothes as a mattress. Every one of those nights, Leila and I lay awake for hours, listening to the wild boar crashing through the woods, the jackals crying up the hills, the vermin scurrying over our bags, and most frightening of all, the drunken men cursing and stumbling around us.

Only after all of us were worn thin from the cold, insomnia, insect bites, and fevers, did I finally find an empty tent crammed into a row of other tents inside the camp. We moved in, the four of us squashed together in a space made for two, while Leila gave thanks to Allah for this deliverance.

"Keep no food in your tent, my dears, or the rats will grow even bolder," our neighbor told us, poking a small, friendly face out of her tent into ours. "Here, take these bottles of water and this blanket. I have a spare. And this umbrella. You can hit the rats with it." That neighbor was Nafisa.

Long after February had turned to March, a family was at last transferred to the mainland, opening the two bunk beds we occupy now. I tried to find a place for Nafisa, too, but there were none to be had. Still, we were overjoyed to have shelter at last, and to feel halfway human again.

We also received the little white identity cards we'd been promised, three pages folded into a tiny book, stamped with the dates of our first interviews. Leila's was to take place in a few weeks, but mine wasn't until the summer—why so long, nobody would say. And when our second and official asylum interviews were to take place nobody would say either; only that they might not happen for years.

And so here we are, four months later, nothing changing from one day to the next, except for the overcrowding, which grows worse by the week. Many of the newest families in our metal box have only one bunk between them now, the parents crushed together on the narrow bottom bed, the children packed like matches on top, while the tents outside continue to multiply, squeezing one another tighter and tighter. The lines for food grow longer, the water supply shorter, the rats fatter and the toilets fouler, their walls and floors blackened and broken from overuse, leaving gaping holes for the unwary.

There are too many of us here, indeed.

14

NAFISA

This morning, Amina arrives at our tree without Leila and the children for a change, her face sheened in sweat. The air has become particularly hot and still now that July is approaching, the grass so brittle it snaps beneath our feet like glass.

Where's Leila? I ask as Amina settles beside me with a sigh beyond her years.

"Waiting to see the nurse with the boys. Majid woke up crying again last night. His ears hurt." She runs her fingers through her long hair and casts her eyes around the hill. "Auntie, are we ever going to get out of this place?"

I move off my log into a squat. These dead trees and rocks on which we sit are knobby enough to make even the hardiest of behinds long for a cushion. Enough of that, my dear, I tell her. Now, give me some news. Have you seen your boyfriend again?

She darts me a scowl. "I don't have a boyfriend, and I don't want one. I told you." Frowning, she twists her hair into a pile on top of her head and fastens it with a clip. She has magnificent hair, Amina, thick and curly and threaded with red, which is perhaps why she is always fiddling with it.

I smile at her evasion. But you did see him again, didn't you? I can see it in your face.

She pulls her knees to her chest in her usual way and wraps her arms around them. "Maybe . . . Well, yes, I did, in town." Her voice softens now. "He said something kind to Majid. But please, Auntie, don't say anything to Leila. She wouldn't approve."

I won't. But did you talk to him?

Amina leans her forehead on her knees, picking something off her tennis shoe. "I'm too afraid."

That won't do! I know you have much to overcome, little one, but try, yes? Promise me you'll open your heart and try?

She shakes her head so vehemently that her hair breaks loose of its clip and tumbles back down around her shoulders. Pinning it up once more, she looks away from me, her young face troubled.

Silence blankets us then, each lost to her own thoughts while we gaze blindly out to sea, crickets hobbling around us in the dry grass, cicadas buzzing. Amina shifts on her log, trying to stay in the tree's meager shade. "Auntie," she says eventually, "can I ask you something?"

I wait.

"I know this sounds foolish, but . . . do you think there's any chance that Mama might be able to catch a boat here and join us? Leila listed herself on that Trace the Face site. You think maybe Mama might do that, too, and find me?"

The question saps the speech from me for a long moment. Amina can be so hard-bitten that I forget she is still a child.

Ah, little Amina, I reply at last, what can I tell you? All I can say is that wherever your mother might be, I'm sure her spirit is with you.

"I don't want her spirit." Amina buries her face in her knees. "I want her."

I watch her helplessly, this lonely girl I have come to love. I wonder if my Amal yearns for me like this. Or if she is so angry that she has expelled me from her heart forever.

We cease talking then because Leila appears after all, hauling herself up the hill like an old woman, Hazem and Majid trailing after her in their usual listless manner, eyes vacant, bodies limp. They slump onto the ground while she settles on a root of our tree, greeting us with a sigh. She mops her brow. "This heat is killing me."

"Any luck with the nurse?" Amina asks.

Leila shrugs. "She gave him some more eardrops but I already know they don't work. He was in such pain last night, my little sparrow, Allah help him."

I glance over at the boys, their heads drooping, bodies inert. I would not say this aloud for fear of distressing Leila, but I think something is wrong with her children. I see Amina trying to engage them, giving them tasks, taking them for walks, working to awaken their curiosity, but left to themselves they do little but sit and stare at the dust. Even when I talk to them or try to tell them a story, they barely respond, especially Majid, who I am convinced is going deaf. Perhaps, like their mother, they are consumed by mourning for Farah and Dunia, although they never speak of them. Perhaps it is the delayed effect of losing their father, or of bombs. Or perhaps, dispossessed as they are here of books, pen and paper, toys and school, they, like prisoners, are growing more stunted by the day.

My Amal would certainly have suffered had she been deprived of school like this, so seriously did she take her studies. I often wondered at how she split herself into two such different people: the hardboiled girl who negotiated the tough streets of Sofia, and the studious and considerate daughter she was at home. "*Umi*, you look terrible," she would say when I was particularly unwell. "You need to relax." And she would put away her books, make me sit with my back against the sofa, and humming a soothing tune, knead away the tension in my shoulders while I closed my eyes and rested my head against the taut plane of her teenaged belly. Never had I believed that I could feel such contentment after the slaughter of my family, such peace. Amal, one who truly does bring hope.

But peace, of course, never lasts, and as the new millennium crept through its teens and wars all over the Middle East and Africa drove refugees westward, the clouds of hatred began to gather over Sofia, just as they were gathering everywhere else. Almost overnight, it seemed, the faces of the townspeople grew lumpen with distrust. Backs began to turn, voices to sneer, words to demean, and the more the television and newspapers screamed reports of attacks against London, Paris, and Berlin, the more local gangs took to roaming the streets looking for scapegoats. Mobs threw rocks and shouted at immigrants to leave. Thugs doused a family of Afghans with petrol and set them on fire. A pack of men calling themselves "migrant hunters" took to catching people crossing the Turkish border and tying them up. The police came to our door ever more frequently to demand our papers. And all of us in our chicken battery were ordered to the local immigration office to have our fingerprints retaken, which were to be entered into every database in the hemisphere and tracked to every country of the world. This so frightened some of my neighbors that they took to searing their fingertips and thumbs on stovetops, filling our hallways with the stench of charred flesh.

The thicker the forces of hatred grew in Sofia, the more afraid for Amal and myself I became. I recognized that this hatred sprung from ignorance, deprivation, and hearts starved of hope, but the recognition brought me no comfort and no urge to forgive. Many in the world are ill-educated and deprived without feeding on hate.

"Haters learn to hate because they're manipulated by their leaders. I saw this at home," Amina says when I express this thought aloud. "Leaders love hatred. It's their most powerful weapon."

"Hatred, along with its father, fear," Leila adds.

I lean forward and drop my voice so that her boys, or at least Hazem, cannot hear. What you say is true, my sisters. Me, the haters found when I was already grown and a mother. But my Amal they took when she was only fifteen.

Leila looks aghast, and then wary. "Are you sure it is wise to talk about this, sister?" she asks.

I ignore this.

She was on her way home from playing football with three friends when it happened. The boys were from Afghanistan, the girl from Iraq—I knew them well—all of them chatting and prancing, the sweat drying beneath their track suits, book bags bouncing against their backs. They took the same long route home they walked every day from the park where they practiced: down the cobbled side streets, through the Women's Market where I bought my fruit and rose oil, over the old stone bridge spanning the dry riverbed, and past the discount stores run by immigrants who never seemed to sleep. And finally, along the tram tracks to our quarter of concrete towers, their windows cracked and their walls stained with damp and graffiti.

I was sicker than ever by that time, my factory work draining my spirit and my Fugnido disease my looks, but I was still working, even though Amal begged me to stop. "I'll take a job so you can retire," she kept saying. "Please, *Umi*, you need to retire."

"No, my love," I told her. "You finish school. Build your bridges. Then I'll retire."

Amal did work, though, selling shoes on weekends in one of the dusty shoe shops behind Pirotska Street. I hated the idea of her crouching at the feet of others, but then all her friends had to work at one humble job or another, if they were lucky enough to find any jobs at all in that dying country. She never complained. I watched with wonder at how she balanced it all. Studying, working, exercising, fighting, laughing.

The police found their bodies in a parking lot behind an abandoned building. The two boys were dead, their young throats cut. Amal and the other girl had been used as girls are. I cannot tell you what more was done to her, sisters, as to speak of it is beyond my strength. I will only say that all her life I had dedicated myself to protecting her from the fate that had befallen me. And I had failed.

Leila murmurs. Amina remains silent.

The sun was feeble enough in that country before the haters arrived, but after my Amal was attacked it seemed to fade away altogether. The streets and houses shone black under the rain, as though the city had turned to coal. Black rain-coats, black umbrellas, black cars. Scowling faces, heavy brows, hooded eyes. Scuttle and skulk, dart and sneak. Never a direct look, never a smile.

While Amal lay sewn up in the hospital, I set out to find the haters, the men who did to her what her twelve fathers had done to me. I knew their type only too well. They are all the same, such men, whether in the guise of soldiers, rebels, smugglers, or thugs.

"Prison guards or brothers," Amina spits, the lemon back in her voice.

I tried to approach the mothers of the other children who had been with Amal that day to ask them to join me, but each had sealed herself in a tomb of grief. The police refused to do anything, caring not a mote about us refugees and im-migrants. The local citizens did nothing, either, for they shared the view of the police. And I knew what would happen to Amal were I to try to force this to a trial: cross-examination. He said, she said. She flirted, she drank, she wanted, she asked, she fought him, she didn't fight him, she cried too much, she didn't cry enough, she changed her story, she contradicted herself . . . and look at what she was wearing. Anyway, who cares, she's Black.

The haters would have suffered no consequences at all had I not acted, sisters, and so would have been free to hurt again and again. How could I have allowed that?

"Vengeance or justice, what's the difference?" Amina says, quoting me.

Exactly.

I soon discovered that the haters lived in an encampment under a highway bridge not far from us. They were workers from the countryside who had come to the city to find jobs, not knowing there were no jobs to be had. Rendered useless and humiliated, they were easy pickings for the manipulators. And so they learned to blame us.

"The strong eat the weak, the weak eat the weaker," Leila mutters.

But I was not weak, my sisters. They made a mistake there.

The haters had built their encampment out of huts fashioned from scrap wood and cardboard. One was a shop, one a bar, one a gambling den, the others for sleep. There they gathered every night to drink rotgut and rakia until their lust for violence was sufficiently fueled, went out to wreak their havoc, and then returned to celebrate their victories by drinking again until they fell unconscious.

"And that's when you acted?" Amina asks.

Yes, little one. I gathered my tools, hid them in a bag and waited in the shadows until nightfall. Then I positioned my fuse and petrol, readied my match, and watched until the drink had knocked each and every one of them out as effectively as a mallet.

Oh, the glorious leap of flames! The smoke billowing black and venomous! I stepped back and laughed, my mind heaping onto the pyre all the men of violence in this world: the criminals who had attacked Amal and killed her friends; the soldiers who had murdered Osman, my children, and my dignity; the husbands and fathers, leaders and fighters who crush the lives of women and children everywhere. I laughed until the encampment was reduced to a pile of ash. I laughed until nothing was left but their shrunken hearts littering the ground like pebbles.

My sisters turn mute again. So I wait. But then, Amina speaks.

"I don't believe you did that, Auntie. I don't believe you could."

Amina, my sweet, perhaps you are right. I did run a fuse. I did light a fire. I did burn their huts. But the haters were not as deeply asleep as I supposed and so awoke and escaped. Their homes were cinders, their skins scorched, but the steely bones of their hatred remained intact, alas, as did their pebble hearts.

This time Leila speaks. "I think you did do it, Nafisa. I think you did it exactly as you said."

Ah, my sisters. Maybe I did, maybe I didn't. Look into your own hearts and decide.

15

LEILA

Hellenic Boat Report
June 28, at 4:48 AM

A boat heading toward Samos capsized outside
Kuşadasi, Aydin province, 03.25 this morning.

The boat was carrying 13 people.

Four people were rescued: 3 men, 1 child.

Nine drowned: 7 women and 2 children.

৵

Why is it, I wonder, that so many more women drown than men? I see it all the
time in these Boat Reports. Is it because nobody taught us to swim, just as that
same nobody taught so many of us to read? Is it our clothes, the heavy skirts and
layers, or our subordinate status that drowns us in such numbers? Is it that men
push us aside to save themselves first? Or is it that we mothers die trying to save
our children? Allah knows best, of course, but I wonder.

Today, I visit all the office containers in the camp: the police, the Greek coast guard, the army, UNHCR, and beg them to tell me the identities of those seven dead women and two drowned children in the Boat Report. They cannot. Will not. Even the officials at Frontex, who rescue more refugees than anyone else, refuse to help.

At home in our city of Homs, I ran a business as a wedding photographer and volunteered as a reading teacher for orphans in my spare time. My husband, Mansour, may Allah grant him mercy, taught mathematics in our local high school. Farah was renowned as a tailor, especially among brides-to-be. Hazem, who was only three years old when the revolution broke out, watched his beloved football on TV, if the electricity was working; drew pictures of his hero, Ateef Jeneaat; and kissed me all over my face when I let him. Majid, who came into the world just as the war began, was always performing for us, even with that shadow over his head, singing the songs he invented in his songbird voice, his stocky little body bouncing on the sofa—a voice I never hear anymore now that he is growing deaf, which sends a crack through my heart. And then there was Dunia. *"Teta, why do people have toes?"*

At home we were a family. Even with Assad choking the life from us, even after Farah and I were thrust into widowhood, even with bombs shattering our city, tearing open our skies and stealing the childhoods from my sons and Dunia, we were a family.

But here my boys are treated like mongrels begging for scraps. Here my voice goes unheard and my face unseen. Here my daughter and granddaughter are worth less than the time it would take to pick up a telephone, call the hospital, and ask after the drowned.

16

AMINA

I have taken to exploring this island lately, even as its beauty fills my mouth with bitterness, for I find long walks the only way to escape my endless cycle of worries. Often, I make my way along the shore until I am surrounded by nothing but olive groves and goats. But today I climb the eastern side of Mount Thios, which is steep and rocky and rises quickly away from town, where I can look out at Turkey and toward my home beyond.

The air is cooler up here than in the camp, the company nothing but birds, insects, and lizards, whose stares, unlike those of men, reflect their own fear rather than provoking mine. The higher I climb, the freer and lighter I feel, the lightest since I ran the Manbij streets with Tahar. For a moment, I even seem to lift away from this trap of an island altogether, as though I were no longer the earthbound girl who once held the string, but the kite.

I've been climbing for some forty minutes when the sound of singing drifts over to me through the trees. It startles me at first, the voice being a man's, but the tones are so rich and sweet, I stop anyway. Cautiously, I follow the song until it leads me behind one of the prickly bushes plaguing my ankles, around the trunk of a vast cedar, and to an unexpected sight.

It's a tent, but not like any tent I've ever seen here. Rather, it looks like a miniature circus tent, its cylindrical walls stitched out of rags and blue tarpaulin, its pointed blue roof decorated with green stars. Assuming it must belong to an eccentric tourist, I hide behind the cedar, not wanting to be seen but needing to listen. And then I realize the voice is singing in Arabic, the words catching at my skin like thorns.

The heart of a woman is the only country
That I can enter without a passport,
Where no policeman
Asks for my card,
Or searches my suitcase
Full of contraband joys,
Forbidden poems
And delicious sorrows.

I close my eyes. Oh, for my own suitcase of contraband joys, my own forbidden poems! I haven't written a poem since my disastrous elegy for Tahar. In prison I was deprived of books, pen and paper altogether, and since I came here, I haven't been able to read anything without my mind drifting to the prison guards, to Tahar's death, to what might have happened to Mama after I left, to what might happen to me. I'm letting myself wither to nothing but a body void of feeling, a head empty of everything but worry.

The voice stops singing. "Who's there?" A face pokes out of the tent door: a narrow, bony face half hidden by a woolly puff of beard.

"Oh, it's you!" Sadek of the Song says, who seems as astonished to see me as I am him. "What are you doing all the way up here? And why are you hiding behind a tree?"

I blush, mortified by the thought he might think I was following him.

I . . . I was just passing by, is my feeble answer.

He examines me. "Do you often eavesdrop like this?" He offers me another of his smiles, lips a little crooked, teeth more so.

I blush again. No . . . I . . .

"I'm only teasing. What do you think of my singing? Not bad, huh?" He steps out of the tent one long leg at a time, his body unfolding like an extending tele-scope. "I not only sing, I speak five languages and juggle. What do you do, shy girl, other than look so pretty and follow me up mountains?"

I survive, I tell him with a scowl. I am disappointed. He is not only a flirt but a braggart.

"Good. That's what we're all doing. This is why I sing."

We're not surviving, we're settling, I retort. But where did that song come from? Did you write it?

"No, no, it's by an Iraqi poet. But I did put it to music." Sadek of the Song grows serious now, his eyes, a light and dancing gray under heavy lashes, leaving my face for a moment to gaze down the mountain at the camp, where more and more people lately have been making a home—collecting shelves and blankets, building chairs and beds, setting up outside ovens, shops, and businesses—as if not to seek the freedom we came here to find, but to surrender. "We are settling, you're right," he says then. "I've been here for two years already. You?"

Five months. Do you really speak all those languages?

"I do. English, French, Kurdish, Turkish, and, of course, Arabic."

No Greek?

"Not yet. I'm studying it, though. I like to study. Have you anything to teach me?"

I pause, not sure if he's teasing again. Despite his unwelcome flirtation, his eyes are still kind.

I could teach you to write poetry.

He looks pleased. "You're an unusual girl. Have you something you'd like me to teach you in return?"

I hesitate. Then I tell him, yes, I'd like him to teach me a language.

"Which? English? French?"

I examine him once more, weighing the risks.

I already speak some English, I say. No, the language I would like you to teach me is the language of escape.

He looks surprised at that, then quickly smiles and nods, as if he's understood me perfectly. But before he can respond, an announcement interrupts us, blaring out of the camp loudspeakers below and echoing up the mountain. "Amina Al-Sarhaan, Amina Al-Sarhaan, report to the Asylum Office immediately! Report to the office immediately!"

That's me! I look at him in a panic. What day is it?

"The last day of June, Amina Al-Sarhaan."

My interview!

I've been worrying about this interview for months—how could I have forgotten? Time is so elusive here, as slippery as a fish, heavy as a whale.

"Is it your first?"

Yes, I cry, turning to run down the mountain.

"Then make sure to tell them it's not safe for you in Turkey!" he calls after me.

By the time I reach the camp office, which is also in a metal box, like everything else in this camp, I am panting and sweat-soaked, my stomach on fire with anxiety. A worker is standing outside, rolling a cigarette. "Where do I go?" I ask her through my gasps. She looks me up and down, then sends me into a room with a growling air conditioner that does little more than fill the air with the smell of mildew. I stand trying to catch my breath.

Two women are there, sitting behind a desk and a computer. They look up at me. One, yellow-haired and somewhere in her fifties, her face plump and blue-eyed, introduces herself as my interviewer; the other, young, dark-haired and sleek, as my translator. They don't look threatening, but nor do they look kind. They direct me to a chair on the other side of the desk.

Wishing that I also had a desk to hide behind, I sit, already feeling in the wrong.

"Good morning," the yellow-haired one says, pouring me a plastic cup of water from a bottle, the tap water here being unsafe to drink. She knits her fingers together on the metal desk, her nails short and blunt. "Are you ready?" I tell her I am.

She glances down at a paper in front of her. "Before we begin, we wish to make it clear that this interview is according to the Safe Third Country concept. Do you understand?"

I've no idea what a Safe Third Country is, but through the translator, I tell her I do. Folding my hands on my knees in unconscious imitation, I sweep my eyes around the room, looking for instruments of interrogation: ropes, whips, wire, chains. Men.

"All right. Now, you must also know that all persons in this room are bound by confidentiality. The information you give us will not be communicated to the Syrian authorities, but may be to the Greek authorities." The interviewer pauses to scratch her nose. "The Turkish authorities may also be informed, but only of your basic statistics, not of your personal information."

What kind of confidentiality is that? I want to ask. And what business am I of Turkey's? But I remain silent.

"Now, are you ready to cooperate with the Asylum Service and truthfully state the facts of your case?"

The fire in my stomach flares again and I am unsure whether to look at the yellow-haired interviewer or at the interpreter, their faces being inscrutable. I choose the interviewer.

I am ready, yes.

"If you need clarification of a question, you may ask. And if you feel tired, you may ask for a rest. Shall we begin?"

I swallow.

Yes.

"Do you understand everything I've said so far?"

I do.

"Do you understand the interpreter well?"

She isn't Syrian, but she speaks more clearly than that Egyptian.

Yes.

"Are you in good condition for this interview?"

All conditions being relative, I tell her I am.

She follows with a repetitive set of queries about my identity, papers, nationality, and all the other information I gave when I arrived on this island. And then:

"You are single?"

Yes.

"This may sound odd, given your answer, but do you have any children?"

I stiffen. What does she take me for?

No.

"Do you have any other children in your care?"

Yes. My friend's sons. They are nine and seven years old. But they are not solely in my care. Their mother is with them.

"Where are your parents and siblings?"

One of my brothers is . . . deceased. The others, I don't know.

"Have you any family members in Greece?"

No.

"Have you any family member dependent on you?"

Mama in her *heart.*

No.

"Are you yourself dependent on any family members?"

Mama in my *heart.*

No.

"So you're entirely alone here?"

Yes. Except for the friend I came with, the mother of the boys.

The interviewer looks at the interpreter, scribbles on a piece of paper, turns a page. What is she writing? Have I said something wrong?

"Where were you born?"

Manbij, a city just northwest of Aleppo.

"Have you lived anywhere else, other than Manbij?"

Only the detention center.

"Detention center?"

The military prison where I spent three years.

"What was your last official address in your home country?"

I don't know the address, madam. It was a secret military detention center.

"No, I mean your family address."

I give her the address of my parent's home.

"What was the charge against you when you were arrested?"

Terrorism. For writing a poem.

"Who arrested you?"

Al mukhabarat al jaouea. A branch of Assad's intelligence agency.

"Were you given a trial or any judicial procedure?"

Nobody gets trials under Assad, I tell her. Not real ones, anyway.

"Now, let's talk about your education. What is the highest level of education you completed?"

I was in ninth grade when Daesh—what you call ISIS—closed our schools.

"Did you work in your home country?"

I was a schoolgirl. Then I was a prisoner. Now I am a refugee.

Pause. The women shuffle papers. Does this mean that they are pleased or displeased with my answer? What must one say, anyhow, to pass this test, if a test it is? I wish now that I'd had more time to ask Sadek for advice.

"We will move now to a discussion of your health. Do you have any health problems? Keep in mind that I mean both physical and mental health."

I examine this interviewer, whose face is like a teacher's: patient, heavy around the chin, a little bored, her yellow hair cut in a curtain across her brow like a girl's, the ends curling neatly under her jaw. She wears a wedding ring. I wonder if she has children.

"Answer the question, please."

Sorry?

"Are you in good health?"

I look down at my hands.

They . . . my hands . . . shake sometimes.

"Anything else?"

Yes. My eyesight. For distances? It's not good anymore. The cell I lived in for most of my imprisonment was. It was like a tomb. No window. No light. For three years, I saw so little . . . The sun dazes me still. And my digestion . . .

I stop.

"Yes?"

I have . . . bad dreams. Or I wake paralyzed. I am afraid of sleep.

"Anything else?"

I rub my eyes before I can answer.

I have pain. In my ankles, madam. And my wrists and shoulders from. When they hung me from. And . . .

I fall silent.

"Have you seen a doctor in Syria or Greece for these problems?" The voice has, at least, turned soft.

I shake my head.

"Please answer in words for the documentation."

The term *documentation* sends a shiver through me. I watch the interviewer as she writes down what I presume are my words. I want to ask who will read this writing, who will decide my fate—her? A board of anonymous judges? Or will they throw my name in a lottery pot, my fate as unconnected to my history as if I had no history at all?

"Have you seen a doctor?" the woman repeats.

I had no chance to go to one in Syria, madam. Nor here. I've tried. But there's only one doctor for thousands of people. I wait for hours. By the time it's my turn, he's always gone. My friend has also tried many times to see the doctor for her son, but they, too, get nothing but lines and waiting. It's criminal that your camp has only one doctor!

The woman ignores this. "Are you taking medications?"

No.

"Do you have any medical documents that would confirm your health problems?"

How could I when I can't see a doctor?

"We will change the topic now. We're going to ask you about your experience in Turkey. When did you leave Syria?"

I pull in a tired breath and rub my eyes.

On the third of February this year.

"Which countries did you pass through before arriving in Greece?"

Only Turkey.

"How did you cross the border from Syria to Turkey?"

In a van. And then on foot.

"Did you experience any problems while crossing the border from Syria?"

The groping hand. The vomit in the pocket. The airlessness. Leila's life savings disappearing into greedy hands.

Not really.

"Did you succeed in crossing the border the first time you tried?"

Yes.

"On what date did you arrive in Turkey?"

The same day I left Syria. My home is near the border.

"How long did you spend in Turkey before you arrived in Greece?"

About two weeks.

"Had you ever been in Turkey prior to this journey?"

No. But my father and elder brothers used to go sometimes for business.

"Please explain in your own words for which reasons you left Turkey."

I said before. We only crossed. We never intended to stay. Syrians cannot get refugee status in Turkey, madam. We can't get citizenship, either.

"Did you come into contact with Turkish authorities at any point?"

We were afraid we would be caught by the police or the coast guard. But no.

"How did you travel from Turkey to Greece?"

By rubber boat. We were sixty-seven persons with luggage. The boat was made for twelve.

"Did you travel alone or did others come with you?"

I came with the same friend I mentioned before. And her sons.

"Did everyone on board make it safely?"

No. My friend's daughter and granddaughter were kept back by the smugglers. Turkish smugglers. We think they were kidnapped.

"Was this your first attempt to cross to Greece?"

Yes.

"What date did you arrive on Samos?"

The twenty-first of February, 2018.

"Now we will ask you some standard questions, which you might find redundant as I need to make your case very clear to the Greek Asylum Service. I ask you to reply to each question: First, did you apply for International Protection or residence in Turkey?"

I wonder how Sadek of the Song answered this question. I sense in it a trick.

No. As I said, we have no right to do that.

"Please explain why you didn't apply for International Protection in Turkey."

Or maybe this one is the trick.

Madam, as I explained, I could not.

"Did you work in Turkey?"

How could I in two weeks? Anyway, it is almost impossible for Syrian women to find work there. And it's dangerous for all refugee women.

"Do you have family members, relatives, or acquaintances living in Turkey?"

I know nobody there. Except my friend's daughter and granddaughter who were seized by the smugglers. If they are still there.

"Do you think you can return to Turkey?"

Are these women listening to anything I say at all?

No. I would prefer to die in my own country.

"Please explain why you think you cannot return to Turkey."

I bite my lip, trying to hold on to my patience.

Because of exploitation, I answer.

"What do you mean by 'exploitation'?"

We can't work legally in Turkey, madam, we have no rights. And refugee women are sexually attacked there. Kidnapped. Forced to be prostitutes . . . It's on the internet all the time!

I am shouting now.

Pause.

"Is there anything else remarkable about the treatment of refugees in Turkey?"

For women, it's sexual exploitation and trafficking, as I said. For men, it's the fear of being caught and forced into the military either by the regime or Daesh. Syrian secret service and Daesh recruiters are all over Turkey, madam, looking for men to capture and send back. Everyone knows this.

"Can you explain more about why you feel Turkey is unsafe?"

Turkey is cruel to refugees, madam. A boy in the camp here was beaten and set on fire by Turkish hooligans just for sleeping in an abandoned house. And a girl here told me her cousin died during a simple appendix operation there. When her family saw his corpse, it had no organs in it. I know many people who worked for months in Turkey, digging ditches or cleaning toilets and roads, but when they asked for their pay, they were fired and left with nothing. You know, madam, when Turks fled to Syria in the war of 1912, we were not so unwelcoming. The same when it came to the people of Palestine and Lebanon and Iraq. We did not herd them into camps or prisons . . . we opened our homes and took them in. We did not call them refugees or migrants but friends and guests, welcome to share our food and drink and clothes. But who returns the favor today? Who takes in a Syrian and feeds and clothes her?

The women look uncomfortable. I've said too much. Mama was always telling me I say too much.

"We'll have a break soon. There are not many questions left."

I've been here for more than an hour. What more could they want of me?

"Is there anything specific or personal that you are afraid of in Turkey?" the Greek asks next.

I look at her in disbelief. Am I talking to a tree?

Yes. I'm afraid for my life.

"Is there anything else you would like to say about why Turkey is unsafe for Syrian refugees?"

No, madam. I'm too tired.

"Would you like a rest?"

No, thank you. Please ask your next question.

"All right. Now we'll address the topic of your vulnerability. I'm coming back to your health situation. Would you say that you have any psychological issues due to the conflict in Syria?"

I try to tamp down the new anger rising within me. Madam, I tell her, much of my city was bombed. My friend's house. I saw her body in the rubble. Her head had been. It had been smashed. Her mother's. Her legs were gone. This, madam, is hard to forget.

"Did you witness any other such incidents firsthand?"

I saw death all the time. In the prison and outside.

"You are referring to when you were detained by government forces in Syria? Could you please tell me in more detail what happened?"

Do I have to?

"This is important for your case. You may ask for a break whenever you need one."

I glance at the dark-haired woman who has been translating all these questions for me. The name on her badge is Gania. Perhaps she is Libyan.

"Shall we continue?"

I inhale again and hold the air for a long time, as if it were not air, but strength.

I was arrested three years ago, madam.

"You were what age?"

Sixteen.

"Continue."

When we arrived at the prison, they pushed me into a room. I couldn't see—I was blindfolded. They took off my clothes. Handcuffed my hands behind my back . . . Hung me. From a chain in the ceiling . . . Men kept pulling me down to beat me with a stick on. My breasts and stomach, ordering me to confess. They. Made me sign blank pieces of paper. Later they wrote confessions on the paper. They also.

. . .

"Yes?"

They also hung me by my feet. Shocked me. With electricity. When I lost consciousness they. They threw cold water over me.

"How long did this treatment go on?"

The entire three years. On and off. Other times . . . they burned me with cigarettes. Hung me. By my hair . . . All around me women were screaming and dying. Sometimes we had to sleep next to corpses. Before they were taken away the next morning.

My eyes are closed now and I am rocking in my chair.

"I'm sorry to ask this, but we do need to know. Were you also sexually assaulted?"

A long pause. I turn and vomit on the floor—it comes too fast to warn them.

The Libyan offers me my untouched glass of water. I take it, drink. "I'm sorry," she says, "but we need you to answer in words."

Yes.

The sound barely crawls from my throat.

"And?"

I was in a cell with maybe. Sixty girls and women. But one of the. One of the guards chose me. Many times he chose me. Please . . . can we stop?

I am allowed a break. Someone comes in with a mop to clean up my confession. They give me a second glass of water.

"Are you ready to continue?" the Greek woman says.

No. But I say yes.

"Have you made an appointment with the psychologist?"

I look down at my lap until I can find words again.

I've tried, madam. It's the same story as with the doctor. Every time I go, I'm told to come back in three hours. I wait. Go again. Same thing.

"As well as the incidents you mentioned happening to you, did you witness the torture and death of others?"

I raise my head and look at her.

I have already told you yes. But everyone in Syria has witnessed death.

"Has this had an effect on you?"

I stare at these women, the Greek with her teacher's boredom, the Libyan looking drained.

If you saw a teenage girl die of torture in front of your eyes, madam, would that have an effect on you? If you saw your own brother dead of a hundred bullets, would that have an effect on you? If you saw your friend's house bombed to ash, her head crushed to pulp, would that have an effect on you?

"We are not challenging that it's affecting you. We only need to know how."

I've answered that question.

"We need to be clear for your asylum case."

I close my eyes.

I can't sleep. I have bad dreams. My body hurts. My heart is dead. I cannot cry. I am afraid day and night. Isn't that enough?

"We'll take a break now and then return for a readback. Is there anything you would like to add?"

No, I whisper.

When they finally finish with me, I stumble back to our metal box, lie on my bunk bed, and do not get up for ten hours.

BOOK THREE

JULY 22, 2018

17

KOSMOS

"*Kyria* Hilma, you must listen to me. We have to take the child to the hospital. Now."

Hilma is sitting in one of my deck chairs, glaring at me angrily, her arms around the little girl she rescued, who is huddled into her lap. I moved the two of them out of the wind and into the sun to absorb as much warmth as they can, but even though Hilma is in dry clothes now, the day is hot and the child wrapped in thick towels and even a blanket, they are both still shivering. The girl looks pitifully fragile, her face peeking out frightened and big-eyed, her hair straggling over her thin shoulders—a tiny brown flower shocked and battered by the sea.

"I know we do, you don't need to keep saying that," my guest snaps, cuddling the girl closer. "Just not yet."

"Then I'll call the police." I've been telling the woman this for hours now, our argument going around and around like a carousel, but I repeat myself anyway. "If we don't report that you found her, we'll get into very big trouble."

She looks at me sharply. "And I've told you to keep the police out of this. She needs nourishment and clothes and more rest before we expose her to any new traumas. Cops are too scary."

I throw up my hands. I don't exactly know why, but this *Amerikanikh*, with her gamine face, skinny legs and wide bottom, has me ensnared. So I've fetched them both warm mountain tea made from our local ironwort plant, the gentlest drink in the world; I've fetched them soup and I've fetched them bread. And all the while I've been checking the time. Hilma found the child at about eight this morning, it's now eleven and we still haven't contacted any authorities, which, given that under Greek law even offering a refugee a five-minute ride in your car can open you to charges of human trafficking, could get us—or at least me—clapped into jail.

Leaving Hilma to coax the child to take more soup, I drive as quickly as I can to my local supermarket to find some little girl clothes. My wife Eleni used to be in charge of all the shopping for our daughter, Sophia, when she was small, so I've no idea what I'm doing, but with the help of an eager if overly nosy salesgirl, I choose stretchy jeans, a red T-shirt, a thick blue sweater, white socks, and tiny blue shoes. We need to dress the child as warmly as possible.

Earlier, Hilma sent me down to the beach to fetch the mask and snorkel she left there, along with the girl's dresses and leggings. The clothes looked so forlorn, scattered in tiny wet heaps over the stones, but I gathered them up anyway and carried them back to the house, along with her sodden life jacket. And even though the dresses were too tattered ever to wear again, I washed them carefully and hung them out to dry behind my house: little blue, yellow and red frocks embroidered prettily around the hems by some loving mother or grandma, I assume, remnants of a family the child may well have lost forever. The dresses reminded me of the outfits Eleni used to sew for Sophia when she was in her princess phase. Now Sophia's a lawyer who flies in from Sydney with her husband to visit me every other year, rushes about like a tourist spending money, and flies away again. "Come see us, *Bampas*," she says, waving a hand in the air like a princess herself, but she never sends an invitation, just as she never helped me when her mother was dying. You give your children everything to make them happy, everything you never had yourself, only to find out when it's too late that all you've done is teach them to be selfish.

"Now, *Kyria* Hilma," I say firmly when I come back with the new clothes. "We must dress her and take her to the hospital. No more delays."

She looks away from me and hugs the girl even closer. The child still hasn't said a word, but she does cling to Hilma, who is gently rubbing her back, kissing her head.

"But Kosmos, I'm scared about what the hospital will do with her once they've made sure she's ok." Hilma looks up at me with somber eyes—strikingly pretty eyes, I might add, the blue of an early evening sky just before sunset. "They might send her to that horrible camp. Or lock her up in a detention center. I think she'd be better off if we didn't take her to the hospital at all."

Not again. "Miss Hilma, I've told you. We have to take her."

"Why, what's the point?"

My guest and I then proceed to have a fight. I argue for reason, she for madness. Perhaps it's American arrogance, perhaps sheer pigheadedness—who knows? But she is certainly being irrational.

"And what if her parents drowned when her boat went down?" she goes on. "That would make her an orphan. You know what happens to orphaned refugees in your country? Child trafficking, forced prostitution, cruelty, drugs."

"Where do you read such rot?" I shout. "We Greeks adore children, we don't traffic them! And we are not cruel to refugees. My own wife and I helped many Syrians and Afghans when they started coming here three years ago, and so did our neighbors. We brought them food—some of us even gave them beds, at least before our whole island became clogged with them and all those Africans. And what makes you so sure her parents are drowned? Refugees are rescued off capsized boats all the time."

"Don't be so naïve, Kosmos, of course the girl's parents could have drowned. And of course the hospital will send her to some terrible institution or other, where god knows what will be done to her. It's what happens to unprotected children all over the world, including in my own country."

"That's because you have that *poutsa* president with the fake hair, and a long history of racism. It's not the same for us."

Hilma gives me a look that could freeze a fish on a fire. "You know something? Only last year, there was an effort here to find families willing to foster a refugee child who arrived here without parents. You know how many volunteered? In the whole of Greece? Thirty-seven. Tens of thousands of orphaned refugees and only thirty-seven families agreed to take even one. So much for your famous Greek hospitality."

"But this only happens because we're poor! Most people can't afford to take in extra children. You know how many people in Greece don't even have jobs anymore?"

The *Amerikanikh* snorts. "That's nothing to do with it. And by the way, you're wrong about what happens to the children nobody takes. There is child sex trafficking in Greece, just as there is prostitution and drug running. I heard about it on the BBC. You need to inform yourself better, Kosmos, before you preach at me."

"You have no right to say such things! What kind of moral superiority can you claim when your people voted for that fascist clown and shoot one another all the time? Your country is barbaric!"

"Stop shouting, you're scaring her."

The girl still isn't talking, but she does cringe and huddle closer into Hilma, which makes me sorry.

I crouch and look into her little oval face. She is very sweet. Such wide eyes, such a tiny bud of a mouth. Now that her hair is dry and brushed, it looks sleek and shiny and so black it's almost blue. But what she might look like if she smiled, I don't know.

"I'm sorry, sweet flower," I say in Greek, knowing she won't understand the words but hoping she will the tone. I reach out to caress her shoulder, but she shrinks away.

"Don't touch her!" Hilma glares at me.

Rising to my feet with a sigh, I gaze down at them. A little Madonna and Child I have here in my deck chair, Hilma so sanctimonious as she clasps the girl to her chest.

I try a different tack. "Miss Hilma, let's stop this fighting and going in circles, it's a waste of time. Rescuing this girl was very brave and I admire you for it. But now you have to be brave in a new way. She has to be seen by a doctor because who knows how long she spent in the sea and hypothermia can damage internal organs—her kidneys might fail, or her heart. She's probably severely dehydrated, might even be in shock. And we really do have to report her to the police. What if her mother or father did survive and are looking for her, God help them? Have you thought of that?"

"Of course I have. But I still think it unlikely."

"*Kyria*, they could be pining for her right now. Just as she must be for them."

My stubborn guest falls silent for a long time at that, looking down at the little girl's face. "I wonder what your name is," she says quietly, stroking her cheek. "I'll learn how to ask you in Arabic. Maybe teach you some English, too."

I refrain from pointing out that we don't know whether Arabic is the girl's language. It could be Pashto or Dari, Farsi or Kurdish . . .

The girl nestles into her. "*Teta*," she whispers, the very first word she's spoken, her tiny voice as hoarse and bubbly as though still soaked in the sea. I don't know what this means but it seems to be her word for Hilma, who smiles at her tenderly.

"I'm Granny," she says, touching her own chest. Then she touches the girl's chest, too. "What's your name?" But the child only shakes her head, her long black hair swinging over her little shoulders, her face crumpling. And for the first time she begins to cry, passionately but without a sound, the tears flooding her cheeks as if they'll never stop.

Hilma pulls her close and murmurs to her, stroking her head, humming a tune, rocking her in her arms, just as I did Yiannis and Sophia when they were small. But it makes no difference.

"Kosmos," Hilma says over the girl's sobs, "I need to keep this little girl safe. I need to protect her from any more trauma, not just for now, but always."

Inwardly, I close my eyes in exasperation. "We'll do our best," is all I reply. "Now please, *Kyria* Hilma, we have to go."

She hesitates a long moment, the weeping child still clinging to her. But then she does finally stand, the girl's arms entwined around her neck. "Ok. But promise you won't let them separate us at the hospital. See how she holds onto me? She's been through too much already."

I concede, knowing I lack the authority to promise anything at all, and put them in the back seat of my car.

"Drive sensibly," Hilma commands, buckling the two of them in and covering the child with a blanket. "Both hands on the wheel. Eyes on the road. No insane passing and no radio. And by the way, I agree. My country is barbaric."

18

LEILA

Hellenic Boat Report
July 22, at 4:00 AM

Early this morning, 04.00, a rubber boat carrying approximately 83 people capsized outside Dikili, Turkcy. Boat was heading toward Samos.

Number of people rescued: 77.

The survivors were all adults.

Search continues for 6 people who are missing: 3 women, 3 children.

৯

Lights scanning the black water. Mothers' screams lost in the wind. A frantic splashing caught in a beam. A hand claws. A body flails. A head sinks.

The sea has taken its quota.

Clutching my phone, I stumble back to our container and collapse onto my bed. Hazem and Majid are sitting on the floor beside me, dropping pennies into an empty soup can they found on the beach. They should be running outside and playing, not counting coins like avaricious grandfathers. But I cannot move. Cannot help them. I am in pieces, my body in one place, my heart in another, my foreboding in a third.

"*Teta*, answer my riddle: 'A bowl within a bowl floating in the sea. White from within and brown is its skin.' What is it?"

"The ship we are to sail away in, my little love?"

"No, silly! A coconut!"

Of all the capsized boats, why am I so certain that Farah and Dunia were on this one? Why, Allah help me, do I know?

19

AMINA

Mama used to say that the longer you watch a pot of rice, the slower it will cook. Yet I can't stop counting the days. Twenty-three have passed since my interview with no word of whether I'm to be sent back to Turkey or allowed to stay, and I am tormented by the thought that this is because I said something wrong. Perhaps I should never have scolded the yellow-haired Greek for having only one doctor in the camp; never have talked about forced prostitution. Or maybe it was my mention of the word "terrorist" that doomed me, if doomed I am. I spend all day now, and most of my sleepless nights, combing over every word of my answers in my mind, looking for my mistakes.

Meanwhile, Sadek of the Song may not yet have found me escape but he has taken to visting me every day with one excuse or another—sometimes to accompany me and the boys to the beach, sometimes to show us a new litter of kittens he found behind a bush, sometimes to help us carry our shopping, even though we don't need help. Leila is as disapproving as I predicted, but, as usual, she is too preoccupied with her Boat Reports to bother about me for long.

"Little hedgehog," Sadek said over the heads of the boys the other day—a name he gave me because, he says, I'm so prickly—"I know a place I think you'll like. You can take an English class there, or Greek, if you want. They have poetry writing classes, too."

Leila will never let me go, I told him. You know I can't walk around with you alone.

"Tell her it's for your education. I bet that'll work."

And it does, because when he arrives to take me to this place early this morning—the day after the most violent storm I have seen here yet—she waves us away without fuss. "Go learn what you can," she tells me. "You might as well squeeze something worthwhile out of this hellhole."

Sadek leads me to a white cube of a building not far below the camp, a charity center run by volunteers who've come to Samos from the wealthy countries of the world to offer what comfort they can. I knew about it before but never dared enter because everyone says it's packed with men. And, indeed, when Sadek first leads me inside, the odor of sweat and beard is so dense that I reel back as if I've been slapped.

"Don't be afraid, hedgehog," he murmurs, beckoning me forward. "There's no danger here."

Dozens of young men fill the room, drinking tea, staring into their phones, talking, sleeping on sofas, playing chess, their thighs taut, necks strained, jaws flexing. I glance up at him, afraid indeed.

"Come, you'll be fine," he says, and he ushers me through them all and up a metal staircase, my flesh shrinking as I feel their eyes tracking my every move.

The stairs take us to a square white room under the roof, where the ceiling is so low that Sadek has to stoop as he walks. On the far side, we find a child-sized table and two low shelves of books. Oh, look! I exclaim, bending to read their spines. Poetry!

For the next hour, he and I kneel beside the shelves and search through every volume we can find in Arabic or English for poems that speak to us. I find poems about broken hearts and betrayal, the moon, the stars, flowers, and God, none of which thrill me as they used to. But then I discover a book called *Liberty Walks Naked* by Maram al-Masri, a poet of my own people who now lives in exile. I settle on the floor to read it.

Sadek, I say after a time, this woman has written a poem for Syrian women in prison—a poem for me. Listen:

What do you do, my sisters,
when your breasts swell
and harden with pain?

When suffering
tears
your belly? . . .

What do you do, my sisters,
when rage rises behind your eyes?

Oh, I want to write like that!

"Then do it. Nothing to stop you here." Sadek pulls some loose sheets of paper off another shelf, a pen from his pocket, and hands them to me. "But remember, you promised to teach me how to write poetry, too." So we crouch at the table in little metal chairs, his long legs poking up like a cricket's, each of us chewing on a pen. "Where do I begin?" He looks at me anxiously.

From inside. Write nothing that's not true and honest.

"Then I'll write about you."

Don't be silly. Write about what matters.

"You matter."

Strangely, I don't seem to mind Sadek's courting. I thought I would fear and despise men forever after the prison, but when he touches me, a finger on my wrist, a hand on my elbow, or looks into my face with his dancing gray eyes, I'm not filled with the terror I expected, but with warmth.

"Now," he says, "write a poem for me. I want to see how it's done."

I can't. I'm too out of practice.

"Just try."

I refuse a few more times, afraid to open that tender, wounded part of me I need to write a poem. Afraid, too, of the punishment I have learned a poem can bring. But at last Sadek persuades me. So, without much faith in myself, try I do, taking inspiration from one of the al-Masri poems in my hand.

Let me plump your pillow, little moon,
let me fix you a meal.
You work so hard.
Here, give your Mama a kiss.

You will excel, my darling.
Outshine all your rivals,
wax where they wane.
Prove yourself to your father.

"Everything in my house stinks of women and decay,"
your father likes to say. "Even my own teeth."

And when, little moon, you come home
with your diploma and new blue coat—the coat I sold my gold bangles to buy—I
shall shower you with flowers,
And your father will be sorry.

She left the next day, my daughter, with her bag and her books,
her papers and her dream-filled eyes.
Waved goodbye from the bus with a saucy twist of her wrist,
her fingers still as plump as a child's.

The coat came home a week later,
dark with blood,
one of those fingers in its pocket.

Sadek says nothing for a long time. But finally he asks, his voice quiet, "What will you call it?" Before I can answer, a tall European girl with dangling hair the color of sand walks up and greets him in loud, cheerful English. He springs to his feet in clear delight, wraps his arms all the way around her and gives her a long, tight hug, while I watch in confusion. He's never hugged me like that— he's never hugged me at all. After they finally release each other, she turns her freckled face in my direction and offers me her hand to shake. She's dressed in what look like pajamas, loose pink trousers and an oversized white T-shirt, her eyes such a light blue they're almost no color at all. She looks so like a doll, I expect her eyelids to click when she blinks.

"I'm Lily—I teach the English writing classes here," she says chirpily. "What's your name?"

I return her shake and quickly retrieve my hand, trying to dredge up enough of my schoolgirl English to answer with proper courtesy. Before I can, Sadek answers for me. "This is my friend, Amina. She's the brilliant poet I told you about. And she can speak some English—when she wants." He grins at me.

"Ah yes, Sadek told me you're interested in my class." The girl bathes me in her own wide smile. "We're starting right now. Want to give it a try?"

I glance at Sadek, confused. "Go on," he says. "It won't bite."

And so, somewhat dazed, I follow this Lily into a small white classroom bright with sun. Eight people—five women, three men—are sitting around a table as white as the walls. They all look up at Lily eagerly. She is, I suppose, pretty.

"Good morning, everyone," she says and turns to me. "This is Amina. Take a seat, please." I hesitate, unsure what she means—am I supposed to carry a seat somewhere? But when she waves at an empty chair, I understand, so slip between a slender young African woman in a bright yellow hijab and a short flat-faced youth who appears to be blind in one eye.

Three of my fellow students, I discover, are Syrian like me, the rest from five different countries. The half-blind youth is from Afghanistan; the woman in yellow from Somalia; another, older woman from the Democratic Republic of the Congo; and the two men, both young and bearded, from Iraq and Palestine respectively. Speaking in our various levels of English, we begin by talking about how last night's storm poured so much rain on us for so long that many people's tents were washed into the valley, along with all their belongings, while others' mattresses floated in the mud like boats. We **also talk** about what our seasons are like in our home countries compared to those in Greece. But we do not talk about our pasts, as Nafisa, Leila and I do, because we have no wish to pry open wounds, and because we are strangers to one another and therefore guarded.

Lily suggests that we practice our English by reading and discussing an ancient Greek myth and then writing down what we think it means. The myth is about a princess called Cassandra and how, when she was licked by the temple snakes of the sun god Apollo, she was given the gift of prophecy. "It'll be good to know the ancient stories of Greece, now that you live here," Lily says. "So let's begin by . . ."

"Speaking of snakes, one slithered into my tent during the storm last night," the Congolese woman interrupts. "It was chasing a rat." And out of nowhere, we are laughing. First the woman who said it. Then the Somali. Then me—and finally everyone. We laugh loud and long and helplessly, until we are wiping our eyes and gasping. We laugh at snakes and rats and rain and mud, at bedbugs and scabies, at statelessness and loss, at death and heartbreak, even as we know our tears are not those of true laughter but of the sorrow pressing against the thin casing of our skins. Even Lily laughs, although it is not a joke that applies to her.

After the class is over, I find Sadek downstairs amid the men and their miasma of smells, sipping a glass of tea and playing chess with a friend. Sadek is taking lessons in this building, too, not English but the Greek he told me he's eager to learn. He also volunteers here, teaching guitar to children, which is why, I presume, Lily knows him well enough to hug him like that, so close and for so very long. But I see a lightness in him when he does this work—a satisfaction and a purpose. Had he been granted a normal life, instead of being chased away from home only to be caught in the vacuum of uselessness that swallows us here, he might have been not a clown, but a teacher.

"Come, little hedgehog," he says when I appear, "let's get out of here. I need some air."

I feel nervous walking with him alone like this. I'm still afraid, and the gossip in this camp is as vicious as it was among my neighbors at home. So, as we make our way across the town and up to an area of winding back alleyways and ancient houses where we refugees rarely venture, I try to cover my agitation by talking. I tell him about the class, the laughter and the other students, although I don't say anything about Lily. And I tell him about Cassandra's curse: that no matter how true or wise her prophecies, she would never be listened to and never believed.

So many women carry that curse, I say, thinking of how my brothers treated Mama. The world refuses to hear us, no matter how wise we might be. We tell men to stop killing; they won't listen. We tell them to save the young from war; they don't hear. We tell them not to fight; they call us ignorant. We tell them not to poison the planet; they count their money. And look at the world now.

"I will always listen to you, little hedgehog," he replies. And with a quick look around, he stops and pulls me into his long arms for the first time.

I shove him away with a cry.

"Shush, Amina, I won't hurt you." Gently as possible, he takes my hand and pulls me to him again, wrapping his arms slowly around me. "There, you see? It's all right."

For a moment I struggle, the terror in me rising wild and blind. But his murmurs and caresses stay me at last, my muscles gradually releasing against his warm body, my trembling subsiding, until I'm nestled close, my head only as high as his ribs. Resting his hand on the back of my head, he cradles me against him, his touch as tender as a mother's.

I wish I could find my tears again now. I wish I could melt and slip between his ribs for safety. I wish I could let go of all that has happened and stay here forever.

Sadek, I say after a time, I don't want this to end but we have to get back. Leila will be worried.

"You're right, little hedgehog," he says, and with a last, lingering hug, lets me go.

When we do return to the camp, though, both of us dreamy and happy, we are greeted by a scene of mayhem. Some sixty or so people are standing by the police cage, wet and shivering under blankets, clearly having just been rescued from a capsized boat. The usual throng is pressing around them, clamoring for news of relatives and home, and the usual police officers are shouting and trying to shoo them away. I've seen this scene many times before but it never fails to fill my heart with pity.

I look around for Leila, as she always rushes to scenes such as this, but to my surprise she's not here. So I force my way up to the newcomers as she would do, searching every woman's face for Farah's, every child's for Dunia's.

How telling the faces of these people are, the whites of their eyes stung red, their lips blistered and cracked. A mother is doubled over, sobbing; a father tearing at his hair. I wonder how long they floated in the water before they were found—four, six, eight hours? Longer? It can take days for a ship or helicopter to spot a capsized boat, which may look huge and overwhelming when you're floundering beside it, but is a mere speck in the vastness of a sea.

I look and look . . . and then, Allah help me, I see her! Or think I do—she's turned away from me, so I can't be sure. Tiny and frail, she is standing apart from the others in an overlarge abaya, a silver space blanket around her shoulders, long hair exposed, tangled and dripping. Could it be?

Farah? I call, running to her. Farah, is it you?

Slowly, she turns to face me.

It *is* you! I cry. You're alive! Thank God you're alive! Leila will be overjoyed! Yes, they're here, your mother and brothers—I'll take you to them now. Oh, Farah, how glad I am to see you!

I throw my arms around her, my heart alight, the clammy sea seeping from her clothes into mine. But she is so unresponsive, so limp in my arms, that soon I let go and step back. Her face holds no joy, not even relief. Rather, her normally full cheeks are sapped of color, her mouth slack, eyes blank.

Where's Dunia? I ask.

But even as I say it, I know.

20

KOSMOS

The little fish will not stop sobbing. The entire way to the hospital, she sobs until it's all I can do not to sob along with her. Hilma is almost in tears herself, her efforts to soothe the child still going nowhere. I'm so distracted by watching them in my rear-view mirror that I almost run down a motorcyclist.

"Jesus!" Hilma yelps. "I told you to be careful! You're not driving a fucking horse!" I manage to ignore this, but by the time I park, every nerve in my body is ready to snap.

"Ok, this is the plan," my impossible guest says as she releases the girl from her seatbelt. "You go in ahead of us, explain how I found her, and I'll carry her in behind you and try to keep her calm. But you mustn't forget your promise not to let them separate us. Got it?"

"Yes, *Kyria*, I've got it."

But, of course, the minute we walk in and I tell the nurses who this child is and how we found her, all our plans explode. The receptionist shrieks and presses a button, a nurse snatches the child from Hilma, two cops snatch Hilma herself, and a third snatches me, bundling me down a flight of stairs to a room in the basement, Hilma's curses and the child's cries trailing me all the way.

The room where the cop takes me looks exactly like I've always imagined a police interrogation room to look: windowless, concrete, gray, and furnished with one metal table, his chair and mine, and a glaring lamp burning down on my head as if to laser my brain. He orders me to sit, takes his own seat on the other side of the table and leans back, crossing his arms over his bulging chest. He has the overfed, muscle-pumped look of most cops here in Samos. Why they all have to be so upholstered in fat I don't know, although I suppose the muscles make sense. His face is wide and pink, with a tube of a nose that closely resembles a cucumber and two pinpoint gray eyes.

Another equally corpulent cop comes in to stand behind me, blocking the door, in case, I presume, I try to bolt. I guess I should be grateful not to be handcuffed. This is what I get for overstepping my boundaries as a host. Fuck Airbnb.

The first cop interrogates me, not for ten minutes or even thirty, but for an entire hour. The police here can be sons of bitches when they want to be and they clearly want to be now. The point, of course, is to assess whether I'm a pimp, a professional child trafficker, a perverted kidnapper of little girls, or merely some hapless sap in the clutches of a mad tourist woman. God, I'm a fool.

Meanwhile, Christ only knows what said tourist woman is going through herself, with her lack of Greek and messianic complex. I fully expect to have to bail her out of jail. If, that is, I'm not in jail myself.

I keep asking the cops to check if the child is all right, but they ignore this. Instead, cucumber-nose subjects me to a long stretch of routine questions regarding my identification papers, origins, job or lack of one, Airbnb business, property ownership, connections, children, dead wife, and whether I know anything about the various rings of human traffickers, smugglers, and other lowlifes on the island. Only then does he get down to business.

"Now." He folds his hands over his beach-ball stomach. "Explain exactly how this child was found."

Explain I do.

"And how many hours did you keep her in your house before driving her here?"

"Three or so."

"You are aware that keeping a child like that is against the law?"

"I am."

"So why didn't you call us as soon as you found her?"

"The kid was too upset, Officer—she'd just spent Christ knows how long in the sea, maybe all night. And we were afraid she was suffering from hypothermia."

"Then why didn't you take her to the hospital or call an ambulance right away?"

"We thought she'd been traumatized enough. And we wanted to calm her and warm her up first." Even I can hear how implausible this sounds. "Can you please ask the nurses if she's all right?"

He ignores this again. "Are you not aware that you could be charged with kidnapping, possibly even trafficking, for keeping an unaccompanied minor in your house for five hours without informing us?"

"Three hours, Officer."

"Answer the question."

"Yes, I'm aware. But if I'd wanted to kidnap her, I wouldn't have driven her here just now, would I?"

And on and on. I refrain from blaming the *Amerikanikh*, as I hope she's refraining from blaming me: honor between thieves.

After the hour is up, during which I urgently need to piss—a curse on my old man's prostate—the cop by the door ushers me to a toilet not a minute too soon, stands watching me as if he suspects even my penis of being stolen goods, and then he and cucumber-nose announce, to my surprise, that I can go home.

Upstairs, I find Hilma free of the police as well, but creating a scene in the reception area, predictably enough. "I have to see her now!" she screams at a nurse, who looks at her with all the sympathy of a Medusa. "I need to see the child this minute! I won't leave until you let me see her!" And to my horror, she yells, "*Malaka*!"

"Miss Hilma, please, stop." I put my arm around her. "This won't help."

She flings herself against my chest, sobbing. "She must be so scared all alone. Why won't they let me be with her? She's only a tiny girl!"

"Because, my friend, you're not her mother. You're not even a relative." I fold my arms around her and hold her shaking frame. I feel sorry for her, I do. She clearly has some kind of problem.

"What will happen to her, Kosmos?" she finally says, pulling back and wiping her wrecked face.

"I don't know, but I'll ask."

By now not only Medusa but all the hospital staff are glaring at Hilma like Gorgons. Any minute, they'll call the cops again and have us thrown out. So I apologize profusely, explain that Hilma is unstable and in shock, thanking Jesus and the Virgin Mary, too, that she can't understand me, and beg the Gorgons to at least tell us what they'll do with the child once she's released.

Finally, one of them agrees to throw us a crumb. "She'll be taken to a shelter for unaccompanied minors. That's where we send all the small refugee children who arrive here alone, as well as all the girls."

"See?" Hilma cries when I translate. "What did I tell you? They'll stick her in some hellhole!"

"Where is this shelter?" I ask the Gorgon, trying to keep a semblance of calm. "And will we be allowed to visit?"

The Gorgon shakes her head. "The location is secret. For the protection of the children. Now I must ask you to leave, or I'll have to call the police again."

So leave we do.

All the way home, Hilma screams at me. "Why didn't you listen to me!" she keeps yelling. "See what we've done? We've thrown the child to the wolves! I told you! This is a disaster!" And then she begins to cry. "Oh, Kosmos, that poor little girl!"

21

NAFISA

Amal, my love, I have found the perfect place up on the mountain to hide and live while I wait for you. On one side sprouts a bush of thyme the size of a sheep, its peppery-sweet fragrance permeating the air, and on the other squats a great boulder that guards me like a faithful dog. I've had enough of my reeking flap of a tent, tattered plastic bags blowing around me like the cries of the dead. Enough of people pressed up against me, too.

Amina and Leila have not yet discovered me here, which surprises me—perhaps something has happened to distract them down at the camp. But they will come eventually, of that I am sure, and when they do, they will try to persuade me to return.

No, dear sisters, I shall tell them, I prefer to live here amongst the dust and leaves, the earth my mattress and the sky my quilt. Leave me be; I am content.

Ah, Amal, how deathly still you lay in that crisp, white bed the last time I saw you. Tubes snaking from your nose and stomach, your body so battered I could not bear to look. But you managed to clasp my hand and move your eyes to mine, remember? "Stay with me, *Umi*," you whispered. "Please stay."

Stay with you I did, as long as I dared, my forehead resting on your palm. But the smoke was still rising from the haters' encampment and I no more wanted you to see me hunted down than I wanted you to know the history of your twelve fathers. If you were to survive, I told myself, I needed to survive, too, so that one day I could return to fetch you and we could run across the world together.

And so—I dare not confess this to Amina or Leila—I waited until you had fallen asleep, and then slipped under your pillow an envelope containing the keys to our chicken battery, the money I had saved for you and a note:

Never fear for me, my sweet girl; only know that I will always love you. I'll put you in danger if I stay, and having failed you once, I can't risk doing so again. But you will recover, you will be strong. And you will build your bridges.

I kissed your warm, smooth forehead, tore my heart from my breast, and left it quivering beside you. Only later did I see that the warp of my reasoning, the cost of my anger, had led me to do the one thing I vowed never to do: abandon you.

At home, I threw away my telephone so the police could not track me, packed my medicines and necessities into a small backpack, hid some cash in my waistband, dressed in sturdy shoes and trousers, and waited for night to fall. Afraid to board a nearby bus for fear of being recognized and arrested, I made my way on foot for some two hours through the streets of Sofia to Vitosha, the mountain that lies south of the city like a sleeping giant, where I planned to hide until I could make my way to the border. The walk was dark and dangerous, with stray dogs chasing me and drunks lurching out of alleyways spewing obscenities. But once I reached the mountain, I was able to leave these hazards and weave my way up through brambles and briars until I was out of sight.

In my backpack, I had bundled a wedge of hard cheese, black bread, and an onion, and these I ate sparingly and only when my strength faltered, but I allowed myself no rest until the lights of Sofia were blocked by trees and I could find somewhere hidden and dry in which to sleep. Eventually, deep in the densest part of the woods, I settled on a triangular-shaped crevice between two slabs of rock leaning against each other like playing cards. After testing them to make sure they wouldn't collapse and crush me, I used a stick to sweep the ground of ants, spiders, and the poisonous salamanders scuttling around my feet, made a pillow of my pack and lay curled tight until I heard your voice, Amal, low and sweet, singing to me through the trees. You sang the lullabies I had sung to you in your infancy, your voice slipping around tree trunks, skimming over branches, sighing between the leaves, soothing me into slumber.

After descending the far side of the mountain, I walked for a week through fields and woods, avoiding every sign of humanity I could and putting as much distance between myself and Sofia as possible. And then one night, as I was asleep in the middle of a forest, I was awoken by voices—not dream voices like yours, my beloved, but men and women together, whispering. Creeping from my hiding place, I peered through the trees and saw a small group hurrying along a path in single file. Their leader was robust and soldier-like, while they were bedraggled and half-starved, so I guessed they were refugees following a smuggler. Eager to find safety in numbers, I stepped out. "Wait, please," I called quietly in Bulgarian, holding up my hands to show I had no weapon. "May I join you?"

The smuggler swiveled around, a pistol poking out of his jacket, while the others stopped and looked at me, their eyes blurred with exhaustion. "No," he snapped. "Go away."

"Please? I'm by myself and can pay."

"I told you, leave!"

A man stepped forward then—about forty-five, only a little older than I was, with the cast of illness in his wan face and an unruly, gray-flecked beard. He was so thin I could make out his ribs even under his shirt, as if his clothes hid not a body but a cage. "If you force her to go, she might turn us in," he said to the smuggler in English. "It would be safer to keep her with us."

"How do I know you're not with anyone else?" the smuggler growled at me.

"I swear to you I'm on my own. If you see anyone with me, you have my permission to shoot them."

"We've no time to waste," he said then, but he seemed to be relenting. "Give me your money and hurry. From now on, we stop for no one."

I handed him half of what I had, knowing it was a risk to keep any of it back. But he only scowled again, scraped his eyes over my body and pocketed the cash. "March!" he ordered, so march we did.

With us were three families, or what remained of families, all of whom I guessed were Arabs, from what I could see of their features in the dark. The man who had spoken on my behalf was holding the hands of two small girls, the eldest about eight, her sister five or six. Behind them was a woman of thirty or so with her much older husband, their faces scored by sorrow, each stooped under the weight of the toddler they carried on their backs. And bringing up the rear were a boy of about eighteen and his little brother, who was perhaps twelve, each with the sunken cheeks of the starved. None of these people had a single bag between them.

The smuggler made us walk fast, no matter how dark and root-webbed the trail, explaining that we needed to reach a certain point before daybreak to avoid being caught by the police. If we grew faint with hunger, he made us eat while moving, while those of us who needed to relieve ourselves had to do so openly by the side of the path and run to catch up, there being no time to seek privacy.

"Brother, I thank you for what you did for me back there," I whispered in Arabic to the father of the girls as we rushed along the path, the moon flickering through the forest canopy, "but what are you all doing so far from the border, and why do none of you have any luggage?"

"We were robbed, God help us," he answered. "We paid to be driven across to Serbia, but our crook of a smuggler forced us out here and took off with all our belongings. So now we have to walk."

The Serbian border was some hundred kilometers from where we stood, over plains, the Balkan Mountains, and peaks of snow and ice. This was where I planned to go—after all, I was used to long treks—but none of my companions looked nearly strong or warmly dressed enough for such a journey. "But who is this man leading you?" I asked.

"He was partners with our smuggler till the bastard robbed us and kicked him out as well. He's not as bad as he seems. At least he's stuck with us." The man glanced at me, his face gray and drawn above his beard but his eyes gentle. "But what are you doing here all alone, sister? Is your husband dead? Forgive me . . . I've forgotten how not to be blunt."

"Yes, my husband has long been with Allah. I am here to save my daughter." I still believed that in the blindness of my anger and fear.

"Good luck to you then, and may your husband rest in peace." The man drew his girls closer. "These are my children, Zahra and Maryam. My name is Mahir. May I ask yours?"

I stroked the girls' heads, their oval faces looking up at me with the same empty stare my own daughters wore after witnessing what those soldiers did to me and their father and brothers. Zahra and Maryam were both dressed in a pink sweatshirt and leggings, their feet in dirty red sneakers, their hair straggling around their shoulders. "Hello, little ones," I said. "I am Amal."

I thought that if I took your name, my daughter, I could keep you with me. That each time somebody called me this, they would be calling you to me, too.

"I'm glad we found you, Amal." Mahir glanced at me with a wan smile. "We came from Iraq and hope, *insh'Allah*, to make it to Germany." He broke into a cough so long and deep I could hear his lungs straining, as if they were bound in wire. Zahra and Maryam watched him intently, their brows furrowed.

"Shut up back there!" the smuggler snapped. "Save your breath for walking. Fools."

We walked for days. Through woods and forests; across grassy plains, where we were often chased by packs of wild dogs; and around the outskirts of red-roofed villages, hiding as best we could from train tracks, roads, and eyes. Every evening and night we walked, sleeping during the daylight hours in abandoned farmhouses or barns, or under trees deep in the dark of forests. My sturdy shoes were now worn to rags; my feet blistered and swollen to twice their normal size; my skin inflamed by the bites of insects; my illness worsening by the day. But whatever I suffered, the others suffered more. I may have been unwell, but I was not starved, I was not old, and I was not a child.

The smuggler, a young Bulgarian by the name of Simeon who had the build of an athlete and a face knotted with muscle, allowed us so little rest that soon the smallest of the children, with their tiny soft feet, were collapsing onto the ground in tears of exhaustion and pain. So I took one of the toddlers on my back to give their elderly father a rest, while Mahir carried Maryam, Zahra bravely walking beside them, whispering stories to distract her younger sister from crying. Mahir and I whispered as well, whenever Simeon marched too far ahead to hear. Walking while mute is so much longer and lonelier than it is with talk.

"My wife and I were doctors at home," Mahir told me during one of these conversations. "We trained in Baghdad after America's second war against us was over and then, last year, we moved to a village to practice."

"I've always admired doctors, brother, in particular women doctors."

"I feel the same, although, alas, not everyone shares our view, especially not ISIS. I'll spare you the details, but a group of their fighters came to our house one night, beat me unconscious, and murdered my wife, may Allah protect her, right in front of our daughters."

I caressed the girls' heads. I did not mention my own murdered Osman, my own murdered daughters and sons. I only whispered, "Yes, this is the way of all such men."

"I cannot describe what it was like to awake and find my beloved Hibah as I did, our daughters weeping over her corpse," Mahir went on. "I can only say that to save our lives, I had to bury her right there in our garden as quickly as I could and then run with Zahra and Maryam to a cousin's to hide. The next day, I withdrew all our money from the bank, hired that smuggler who stole every penny, and you know the rest."

Mahir had been speaking in spurts between bouts of coughing, his face and lips ashy with pain, but now his cough grew worse and I saw blood in his beard. I wondered if the beating he had been given had split his ribs and perforated his lungs, or if he was riddled with disease.

"Don't talk anymore, brother," I told him. "Rest your voice. I'll help with the children."

We had been walking for enough days by then to have reached the western mountains, which we had to cross in the daylight, despite its dangers, nightfall bringing the risk of falling off invisible cliffs or down the dark throats of chasms. This was the most trying stretch of our journey, for the path took us over towering crags slick with snow, patches of ice, frozen lakes, and gigantic piles of stone slabs, while the air was as frigid as if we had climbed entirely out of summer into winter. "Hurry, you slowpokes, or we'll miss our connection!" Simeon kept hissing. In his impatience, he even took one of the toddlers onto his shoulders himself for a time. When we passed several small mounds in the ground, he told us they were the graves of earlier refugees who had been as slow as we were.

Mahir, too, had to take little Maryam on his back again, as weak as he was, for she could no longer walk at all, her feet sliced and peeling. She cried, but silently. Children can be so much older than we think.

"And what is your story, sister, if you wish to say?" he whispered to me one bitter morning as we descended into a forested valley between peaks, shivering under a pelting rain.

I told him only what I could bear to speak of aloud, which was not much.

"How we humans like to make one another suffer," he said when I finished, his voice fainter than ever. "I can only hope that once we reach safety, *insh'Allah*, we'll be able to help each other instead. Which brings me, Amal, to a request."

Each time he uttered your name, my love, prickles ran down my arms and I looked about quickly. I could not stop sensing you close by or expecting to see you step out from behind a tree.

"You only need to ask," I replied, already knowing what he wanted, but at that moment he doubled over and collapsed, spilling Maryam off his back. She was unhurt, only shocked, but she forgot even to cry at the sight of what was happening to her father. Mahir was in convulsions. His limbs shook, his back arched and his eyes rolled into his head. He fell unconscious before any of us could react, only to awake a minute later in his most extreme fit of coughing yet. Blood spat from his mouth, mingling with the mud saturating his clothes and beard.

Simeon stood over him. "Get up!" he said, although not in his usual harsh tone. "I'm sorry you're sick, but I've told you—if we don't speed up here, we'll all be fucked. *Get up!*"

Mahir tried but he could not even sit, let alone stand and walk. His daughters were crying now, pulling at his arms. I, too, bent to lift him, as did the old husband and the emaciated teenager and his little brother. But Mahir only collapsed again, as if his muscles had turned to water.

"We'll have to leave him," Simeon announced. Grasping Mahir under the arms, he dragged him to a pine tree, took out a coil of rope and bound his hands behind his back, tied his feet, and strapped him tightly to the trunk, ignoring our cries of protest. Mahir moaned and coughed, his beard and shirt running with rain and blood, but he had no strength to resist. Simeon then crouched beside him, pulled a roll of tape from his pack, and prepared to seal his mouth shut.

"Stop!" we begged. "You'll suffocate him!"

"Sorry, no choice. If I leave him here to cough and scream for help, the cops'll find us all." He tore off a piece of tape with his teeth.

"But he'll die here! He'll suffocate or get eaten by wolves! Let him go and we'll carry him. Please!"

Simeon looked us over—two women, the old man, the teenager, and five children. "Carry him? How? You can hardly carry yourselves."

"But if you leave him, it'll be murder! And what about his daughters?"

"Listen, you idiots," Simeon replied. "Don't you know what the cops here do to people like you if they catch you? They steal your phones and your money, beat you up and throw you in jail, and then send you back to where you came from. So make your choice. If we take him, he'll stop you getting anywhere and you'll be fucked. If I leave him here able to scream, you'll be fucked, too. But if I gag him, you might just have a chance to cross the border."

"I won't scream, I swear. Release me, I beg you," Mahir gasped.

"Your coughs alone will attract attention," Simeon told him. "If you survive here and I find you on my way back, I'll do my best to get you to a hospital."

Mahir and I looked at each other, his eyes desperate. How I wished I could promise to stay with him and protect him, but what could I do against his illness, the police, wolves, or the ruffians who roved these forests looking for people like us to rob and rape? And if I stayed, who would care for his girls?

Hearing no further objections, Simeon bound the tape over Mahir's mouth and tightened the knots holding him to the tree. "Now get going," he said to us, "or I'll leave you all here." I looked at Mahir, my heart burning, while Zahra and Maryam clung to his legs and sobbed. He gazed at them, unable to give them even a comforting word or caress, and then raised his wide, dark eyes to me, the shadows around them as blue as plums.

I knelt beside him. "My answer is yes, Mahir," I whispered. "I shall look after your daughters and never let them out of my sight. This I swear. And brother, my name is not Amal. That's my daughter's. My name is Nafisa."

ॐ

We ended up running for months, Zahra, Maryam, and I, hoping, as Mahir had, to cross a border and eventually make our way to Germany. When Simeon failed to take us into Serbia after all, getting himself arrested instead, we hid until Maryam's feet had healed, and having lost the rest of the group, set off on our own, trying again and again to cross into Serbia, and then north into Romania, only to be turned back every time. We ran through forests and over mountains, swam rivers, hid in the backs of trucks, and clung to the tops of trains. We walked for days on end and slept in the woods at night. Once in a while, we found refuge and work for a few weeks, picking fruit from a field or moving rocks to clear a road. But inevitably someone would grow suspicious of this unlikely African woman with two Arab children, raise an alarm and we would have to run again. For some of those months we ran with other refugees, usually led by a smuggler who had extorted money from them, or sex. Most of the time, we ran alone. But no matter how far and hard we ran, we were stopped at every border. For half a year we ran like this, and by the end of it we had gone nowhere at all.

Not long after that, we were betrayed. The usual story—a snitch and a bribe, a lie and a trap. We had traveled so many hundreds of kilometers by that time that I could barely keep track of where we were. Amal, my love, you were right to imagine how grateful we refugees would be to have bridges of stars over which to travel the world, their sparkles lighting the way. But somewhere in the southwest of Bulgaria, I found another ragtag group of refugees who had pooled their savings to hire a smuggler. "He will take us across the border to Macedonia, and from there to Albania and western Europe," they told me. "Pay what you can."

Instead, he led us into a gulley, where we were ambushed by the border enforcers—those same keepers I see here in the camp, with their prison-bar eyes and lipless smiles. Two of our band tried to run, only to be shot in the back. The rest of us were handcuffed, tossed into a truck, and driven into the darkness.

At the police station, I was given no lawyer and no say. My arson, my maybe-murder, was never discovered. But Mahir's orphans were taken and put who knows where, crying out for me as they were dragged away, as I cried for them. Then I was driven to the dumping ground of Turkey, robbed of all my belongings and thrown over the border. I never saw Zahra and Maryam again.

And now, here I am, a year and a half later, lying on a bed of pine needles and earth, telling my story to you, Amal, and to the stars, because I, a woman who loses children the way others lose sleep, am too ashamed to tell it to anyone else.

22

KOSMOS

I haven't mentioned this yet, but during this entire ordeal of a morning, from the moment Hilma staggered out from her downstairs apartment clutching a half-drowned child to when I finally extracted her from the hospital, she has been a bedraggled mess. Her hair, normally tightly coiled in a neat crop and tipped with silver, is clumpy and misshapen with saltwater. She's wearing a mishmash of clothes she must have grabbed without looking: navy shorts; a stained green T-shirt; sandals from two different pairs, one black, one brown. Her lovely eyes are bloodshot, her thin mouth and little chin trembling. And she looks as exhausted as anyone would who just pulled a waterlogged child out of the sea.

"Come," I say as soon as I park outside my house. And helping her out of the car, I usher her up to my terrace, sit her down and pour her a large ouzo. "Now, Miss Hilma," I tell her firmly, "take a big breath and drink. Then we can talk this over like adults."

"Kosmos, I want to adopt her."

So, the madness isn't over yet. "But you don't even know whether she's an orphan," I reply with the little patience I have left. "Anyway, you can't. For one thing, you're not Greek, you're not even a resident, and we don't allow foreign adoptions here. For another, and I'm sorry for saying this, but you're too old. You have to be under sixty to adopt."

"I am under sixty, thank you very much. I'm fifty-eight."

"Oh. Excuse me. Still, you remain not Greek."

"Then I'll buy a house and become a resident. I met an American once who became a Greek resident by buying a house here. Do you know any that are for sale?"

"No need for that. You can marry me." I grin and lift my glass.

She scowls. "Kosmos, this is no time for joking. And how do you know all this about adoptions, anyway? Are you making it up?"

"Of course not!" This truly offends me. It's none of her business, but I know because my poor Eleni had so many miscarriages before our children finally arrived that we thought we would have to adopt if we were to have a family at all. But all I say is, "*Entaxei*, I will stop joking. But please, *Kyria*, be sensible."

"But I can't just let her go! It'd be like saving her from the sea only to throw her back in. Don't you see?" Hilma looks at me, so tired and miserable, I can't help but feel for her.

"Yes, my friend, I do see. I'll keep asking for news of her, I promise. Maybe I'll be able to persuade someone at the shelter to let you visit her. But we mustn't lose sight of the fact that what we want for her is to find her parents and be happy, yes?"

Hilma presses her lips into a tight line. "Happy? How? Even if they're alive, how could she be happy when she'll be a refugee? What kind of a future can she have here living in one camp or another all her childhood—who knows if she'll ever even go to school? What kind of a future can anyone have who starts life like that? No, she'd be better off with me."

"That's a terrible thing to say."

"I know. But it's true."

"A child needs her parents. That's more important than status."

"Easy for you to say. You're not a refugee."

Actually, I am. A Cypriot, exiled from home forty-four years ago, when Turkey invaded and robbed my family of our land and everything else we owned. But it's not my job to lecture Hilma about my past or her assumptions. So I continue the argument at hand. "Nor, lady American, are you."

She stares at the ground a long while. Then she sighs. "I need to change."

"Go change. And then come up and join me for lunch. I'll cook you the fresh fish I bought this morning while you were doing your own fishing, I'll give you the best Samian wine, we'll celebrate the fact that you saved a life today, and we can make peace between us. Do you accept?"

She gazes at me, this mess of a woman—a woman I realize now has been emanating loneliness the entire time she's been here—and shrugs in resignation. "Kosmos, you are incorrigible. But if you insist, I accept."

23

AMINA

Farah is nothing like the fierce little woman I met five months ago who cursed that smuggler so roundly on the beach. She is cowed and shrunken now, skin sallow, eyes flat and dull. Even when Sadek and I bring her back to my metal box after she's been registered and we have reported Dunia missing, she barely notices her mother and brothers' cries of welcome and relief, and seems oblivious to our roommates poking their heads out of their gray blanket curtains to congratulate her on surviving. She only sits on my bottom bunk, clasps her arms across her stomach and collapses over her knees.

We stand helplessly around her, Hazem and Majid watching her hunched back in fright, her clothes still wet from the sea, body shivering. The other families tactfully withdraw while Leila tries to comfort her, although she is weeping herself. "*Allah ysaàddna*, why so merciful and yet so cruel?" she keeps sobbing. "Why give with one hand only to take with the other?"

Unable to bear this scene a minute longer, I tell Leila that Sadek and I will go back to the office to ask again about Dunia. Maybe they've found her by now, *insh'Allah*, I say. We'll take the boys with us. You stay here with Farah. And please, don't give up hope.

Even I am saying it now. *Insh'Allah*.

So I join Sadek, who is waiting for me outside, and with Hazem on one side of me, Majid on the other, both somber and silent, their small hands sticky and hot in mine, we hurry to the camp information office to join the line at the window. Here, as everyone knows, is the hub of all hope and no help. But we wait for it anyhow.

More than eighty frantic new arrivals are already here, most of them survivors from Farah's boat; the only people who might have seen what happened to Dunia. But because they're still in shock and desperate for answers, I can't make any of them listen.

Please, I keep calling over the crowd of heads, did anyone see what happened to the little girl on your boat?

Like Cassandra, I'm ignored.

Have mercy! Tell me if you saw the child!

Sadek tries calling out too, but nobody shows any sign of hearing us. All they do is press forward, elbowing and shoving one another to get to the window. I try again.

Please, somebody answer me! Doesn't anyone remember the little girl Dunia?

Only then does one of them react, a young man near the front. "I do," he calls to me over the crowd. His face is as round as an owl's, his eyes even rounder, their expression soft and sorrowful. His beard is nothing but a small vertical stripe in the middle of his chin, which makes him look both comical and kind. I fight my way to him, pulling the boys behind me, Sadek following. "*Salaam aleichum*," the young man greets us when we reach him. "We had five children on board, Dunia included."

You knew her? I ask, my heart lifting. Did you see what happened to her? Is she alive?

My words trip over one another in my eagerness, but he understands. "I did know her, yes." He shakes his head. "I don't know how to say this." His round eyes fill, and when he speaks again, his voice quivers. "When we fell into the sea,

I tried to catch her, I swear, I tried and tried. But . . . she was swept too far away to reach, may Allah bring her peace. I am so sorry. I'm so very sorry."

But how do you know she was Dunia? Maybe it was a different child!

He looks at me more mournfully than ever. "During our time in Turkey, I came to know Dunia and her mother well. They're like my own family." And again, "I'm so sorry. I truly loved . . . I truly loved that little girl."

My eyelids fall shut.

What time did the boat capsize? I whisper.

"About four this morning. May I ask, are you related to them?"

If Dunia fell into the sea at four this morning, that means she has already been missing for nine hours.

I force my eyes open. No, I'm not a relative, I tell him, I'm a friend of Farah's mother. A close friend. We traveled here together from Syria.

The boy looks out at the crowd. "Where is Farah? I don't see her."

Here, but grieving.

"I'm so sorry," he repeats once again, his eyes overflowing now. "Dunia was a child full of light."

I thank him as best I can, wishing he hadn't used the past tense; wishing, too, that Hazem had not heard his words—this little niece he and Majid loved as a sister. "Is that man talking about Dunia?" he asks, Majid watching in puzzlement. "Did he say Dunia drowned, Auntie Amina?" Hazem begins to cry.

I bend to hug him. Hush, little man, I tell him, we don't know what happened yet. All we can do is hope and perhaps it will help her. Will you hope with me? Hazem nods solemnly, so Majid does as well, but already I regret my words. I've no right to burden these children with a task like this; no right to make them responsible in any way.

Having lost our place in line, we have to stand at the very end again, every person in front of us engaging in long and frantic arguments with the visibly weary man in the window. The line moves so slowly that each minute seems to crawl backward, and all the while Sadek and I keep calling out our pleas: "We have a missing child to ask about—please let me ahead! Every second that passes is another wasted chance to find her! Please, let us move through! *Please!*"

But again, we are not heard. We might as well be shouting at graves.

The information official, a graying, heavyset man with a face coarsened by too many sunburns, does seem to be trying his best, a rare Greek around here who speaks Arabic. But he has nothing to give us. When a pregnant woman cries that if she has to sleep among rats and excrement in this heat after surviving a boat wreck, the stress will cause her to miscarry, he shrugs regretfully and says, "But we have no more room." When a sickly old man explains that he can't sleep on the ground because he has a bone disease, the officer shakes his head in sympathy and says, "But we have no more beds." When a mother wails that her children are allergic to the insects in the woods, the officer clucks his tongue and says, "But we have no more containers." And after every answer he adds the sentence we hear all the time: "There are too many of you."

As another hour of this creeps by, I can't stop picturing Dunia all alone and terrified in that vast black sea. Is she floating? Has she sunk? Did she cry out for her Mama and *Teta* until her voice gave out? Did she freeze to death or die of thirst? How can the world do this to a child?

At long last, our turn arrives and we rush to the window, where the official insists in an exhausted voice that we tell him all the same things we told the police before: Farah's name, Dunia's name, Leila's name. Dunia's olive-shaped face, her nutmeg eyes, her height and age and origins. The name of Hassan, the father she has never known.

The official writes it all down. "The police will be told," he says, his voice flat and weary, the creases in his overcooked face deepening with fatigue. "The hospital will be alerted."

But we already did alert the police and hospital! I tell him. I'm only asking if any of them has found out anything new.

"We've heard nothing. We'll keep checking, though." But I can see already that he thinks it hopeless. "Can she swim?" he asks just as I am about to walk away.

Of course not, I tell him. She's only five. But she did have a life jacket and she does have determination. She is a child who could kick a demon from its bed.

Yet even as I say this, I am aware that if Dunia hasn't been rescued by now, she is lying at the bottom of the sea.

BOOK FOUR

AUGUST

24

FARAH

There is a man in this camp of whom I'm afraid. He was on the capsized boat with Dunia and me, and before that, in the basements where we were trapped in Turkey. I'm too ashamed to say anything of this to Mother or Amina, but he controlled me there, where I had no choice, and now he's trying to control me here, even as I am in agony over Dunia.

Ya Allah, why are you making my daughter suffer so? First imprisoned with me in Turkey and then so tiny and alone in the sea. Have you taken her from me forever, Allah, or have you allowed her to be rescued? Will you ever let me know? My body is eaten out with the need to have her back. Yet all the while this man follows me, lacerating me with his eyes.

In the beginning, I thought him kind. On the night we were prevented from boarding the boat with my mother and brothers, I was certain we would be sold to traffickers, raped, killed, or all three. Why else would the smugglers keep us back like that, us and the twenty or so other people stranded on the beach, most of whom were women without husbands, like me, or children without parents? So when this stranger, a towering Damascene by the name of Haider Akil, stepped forward to shield me and Dunia from the smugglers' groping hands, I thought that you, Allah, had sent him to save us.

As soon as the boat was out of sight, the smugglers rounded us up and drove us to what they called a safe house, where, they said, we could stay until another boat could be found. "But why did you stop us from boarding that first one?" we cried.

"You were too many. You would have drowned." True though this might have been, we knew it was a lie.

The "safe house" was nothing but an abandoned farm somewhere outside of Izmir, and the minute we arrived, four armed men we had never seen before locked us in its basement, confirming our fears that we were indeed no longer in the hands of smugglers but of traffickers.

For weeks we were trapped in that basement, eating what scraps they threw at us, urinating and defecating in a bucket in the corner with nothing but our skirts to hide us and not so much as a window to light our days. Over time, all the young women but me were taken away, never to be seen again, while the three parentless children also disappeared to fates I can't bear to think of. Why the traffickers didn't release Haider and the other two men among us—one a grandfather named *Ammo* Salman, the other a war-shattered boy called Kareem—I never understood. My only guess was that the traffickers were afraid the men would report them to the police.

Throughout all this, Haider continued to protect me and Dunia, for which I thanked you, Allah, every night in my prayers. Many times, I begged him to help the other women and children too, but he only said that if he tried to protect everyone, the traffickers would overwhelm him and he would fail. "I can only do so much, one man against four with guns. But if I make it difficult for them to take you, they'll be more likely to move to easier targets." His answer chilled me but I had no power to change it. And when Kareem tried to stop the traffickers from taking one of the children, the traffickers broke three of his ribs, as if to illustrate Haider's point.

I did everything I could to shield Dunia from what was happening around us: the women gagged, hooded, and dragged out in the black of night, the children terrified and kicking in the traffickers' arms. I tucked her away in a far corner on a pile of straw and told her the fairy tales her father used to whisper to my belly when she was still inside my womb, sang her the songs Mother used to sing, taught her to write numbers and letters with her finger on my palm. Kareem helped me once he had recovered from his beating; a twenty-year-old with a moon face and round, shocked eyes, who had deserted Assad's army so that he would no longer have to kill. He told her more of the riddles she loved, invented games that made her laugh. After all, he was barely out of childhood himself.

Kareem is in this camp now. But he has not come to find me.

"Mama, why are we here?" Dunia kept asking, huddling up against my side. "Why are we living in the dark like potatoes? And where are *Teta* and Majid and Hazem and the lady who likes riddles?"

Where indeed?

Every so often the traffickers would rouse us in the middle of the night, hurry us into a van or truck, and drive us to another basement, storeroom, or barn. But in the end, it was always the same. The dark and hunger. The fear and disappearing women. The stink and chains and locked door. And all the while, Haider screening me like a wall.

Perhaps I'm naïve, because it took me many days to recognize the brutality that lurked beneath his veneer of kindness. Rather, I felt sorry for him, thanks to the tales he told me of his past, the most pitiful of which was unrequited love.

"Her name was Yasmin," he whispered one night in our basement cell, "a girl who lived two houses down from my family, with a laugh like the tinkling of bells. From the age of ten I yearned for her, built dreams of our marriage, our lovemaking, our future. For year after year, I pined."

Even then I thought that Haider suffered from an excess of romanticism and self-pity, but I couldn't help but feel for the boy he had been.

"I struggled long and hard to find the courage to confess my feelings for Yasmin to my father and persuade him to help me by asking for her hand," Haider continued. "I was mortally afraid he would mock me or refuse me flat, for even by the age of twelve, I was already overlarge, with the muscles of a grown man, legs like stilts, and a face nobody liked to look at for long. But I was also the most intelligent boy in my school and had the personality of a leader. I believed that if only my precious love's parents would allow me a moment alone with her, my wit, height, and precocious strength would win her for my bride. All I had to do was wait until I turned thirteen.

"The morning of that birthday, I chose my best shirt and freshest trousers, combed and oiled my hair, shaved—yes, even then I needed to shave—and practiced my confession in the mirror so I would sound neither like a pleading child nor a braggart. Trembling and sweating, I knocked on my father's study door. He ran his eyes over me when I entered, leaning back from his desk. 'What's the matter with you?' he said. 'You look as if you've swallowed a cockroach.'

"'Baba.' I admit my voice squeaked. 'Baba, I wish you to ask Yasmin's father for her hand in marriage. I love her.'

"'You're ridiculous. Go away.'

"'But Baba, Yasmin is virtuous, her parents are no less rich than we are, and her father's a judge.'

"'It is not her qualities I'm worried about.'

"Over the next two years, I begged with him again and again to ask for Yasmin's hand, meanwhile finding any excuse I could to hover about her house, trying to catch her eye, certain that her inability to notice me was a manifestation of her purity. I left her presents, I left my father presents, I left her parents presents. I dreamt, I sighed, I groaned. No other girl was visible.

"Finally, when I was fifteen, my father relented, although his face was grim. 'You should have set your sights lower.' And with these ominous words he put on his visiting clothes and knocked on their door.

"He returned twenty minutes later, cheeks flaming, walked up to me and slapped my face."

Yes, it took time for me to understand that this and all the other stories Haider told me were designed to seduce my sympathies and blind me to his malevolence, just as it took me time to recognize that he must have paid the traffickers to let him keep me for himself. Yet, even once I'd realized all this, I felt power-less to do anything about it. I wanted desperately to tell him to leave me alone, that I could look after myself, as I had ever since my husband Hassan had been killed. But I knew that, in reality, I could do no such thing. Not while we were under the traffickers' control, not with Dunia to keep safe, and not while I felt that you, Allah, had deserted me. So I let Haider guard us, and when he began to speak as if he owned me, I hid my humiliation and smiled.

The others thought me his mistress. He told them as much—I heard him—and because he had the shoulders and hands of a giant, they found it safer to believe than challenge him. He told them worse things about me, too: that I'd per-suaded him to protect me and Dunia at the sacrifice of the other women and children, attributing his own arguments to me, and that I'd offered my body as payment. With these lies, he ensured that if I ever reached out to our remaining companions to help me escape him, they would look at me and spit.

Kareem was the only one among them who knew the truth. He knew I despised Haider and would never make such a devil's bargain. And he knew I was deter-mined to be true to the memory of Hassan. The only reason Haider didn't force himself on me was because Kareem was always watching. Even Haider couldn't rape under Kareem's haunted eyes.

The night of our release didn't arrive until we had been living like vermin un-derground for five months, by which time only seven of our original number remained: the three men, Dunia and myself, and a pair of women too old to sell, *Oum* Aziz, a stringy widow of sixty, who, like me, had been separated from her family on the beach; and *Oum* Mahmud, an apple-faced grandmother of ten who refused to explain how she had ended up alone. But come our release did, the traffickers presumably eager to get rid of us now that they'd taken all they could. "Out!" they shouted, bursting into our basement without warning. "We've found you a boat! No talking!"

"They're making us go out in this?" wailed *Oum* Aziz, for the wind was scream-ing through the trees and the clouds were so thick not a star could be seen—a night the traffickers had no doubt chosen because they knew the police and coast guard would stay safely ashore. "But they're sending us to our doom!"

"Better that than one more hour in this living grave," Kareem muttered. I was only grateful that the traffickers hadn't chosen to murder us with guns rather than the sea.

They drove us to a beach in the dark, just as they had the night I lost Mother and my brothers, where they forced us with some eighty-three other people into a rubber dinghy meant for twenty. Dunia still had her pink backpack, the dresses my mother had made her wear, and the life jacket I'd bought for her before we were kidnapped on the beach. I had nothing.

Cries and shouts, bags lost in the dark, children shrieking, screams and rough commands. A lurch, a drenching wave, and out we were launched into the storm, our boat lying so low in the water that the sea's surface glistened only a finger's length from where we sat. The boat jumped and tumbled over the waves, thunder exploding in the distance, the wind knocking into us like a charging bull. We seized hold of one another and fell into a heap, desperately trying to keep from pitching overboard.

I looked around for the smuggler who was steering the outboard motor in the back, thinking to implore him to be more careful, but he'd vanished. Instead, one of the passengers had hold of it, looking as terrified as I felt myself.

With clouds covering the moon, we couldn't tell where the sea ended and the sky began, so had to rely on people who owned working phones to find which way to go. We dipped and rolled and bucked and dipped again, the waves stampeding around us, leaving us soaked and quaking. Up and down we went, the rubber twisting and flapping until, with a great crack, the flimsy plywood plank that made the floor splintered in two, causing the boat to fold in the middle and spring back up, spewing water bottles, telephones and luggage overboard, the passengers screaming. Holding Dunia tightly to my chest, I clung to a rope attached to the boat's edge. Haider laid his enormous body over us, his weight saving and suffocating us at the same time.

On we heaved through the night, people vomiting and crying out your name, Allah, all of us in terror for our lives. Only after we had endured this for some three or four hours did the storm calm at long last and the wind die down, our nerves and stomachs settling with it. The clouds parted to allow a glimpse of stars. Kareem gave Dunia his remaining bread. I gave her my drinking water, my thirst so fierce I felt delirious, even as I was soaked and shivering, as if my head were in a desert and my body in snow.

Just as the quieter waters were beginning to soothe our spirits and raise our hopes of a safe landing, it happened. I don't know why. Perhaps two waves converging on us from opposite directions. Perhaps a razor-finned fish. Perhaps merely our collective weight overwhelming the dinghy's flimsiness. But with no warning at all, something made the boat snap in half like a cracker, deflate, and sink.

"Dunia!" I screamed, clutching her to me as we plunged into the black water. Realizing I was dragging her down with me as I sank, I let go and she bobbed up again, gagging and spluttering. Kareem reached for her too, managing to grasp a strap on her life jacket and thrust it at me.

"Mama! Mama!" Her voice as faint as a kitten's mewl against the wind, her face already invisible in the dark.

I flailed and kicked to stay afloat, looking for something to hold onto—to hold her to—while others gasped and choked and floundered around me; none of us able to swim. I saw the life jacket of one young man fill with water and drag him under; a ring of death around his neck. I saw a woman reach for her little son and sink just as she touched him.

"Take this." Haider thrust an oar in my direction. Gripping the strap of Dunia's life jacket with one hand, I clung to the oar as best I could with the other. But just at that moment, a huge wave ripped Dunia out of my grasp and spun her away.

"Dunia!" I screamed. "Dunia!"

Kareem called her too, thrashing through the water to try to catch her. But we could no longer see or even hear her, not even the faintest cry. The sea had whirled her out of sight, its thunder deafening us, its salt blinding. All we could do was shout her name into the darkness, our voices as ineffectual as if we were whispering into the throat of a lion.

❧

Now I move through this camp as if I've been struck blind, caught halfway between the living and the dead. And all the while Haider watches my every move, trails my every footstep, hissing at me as I pass. "You belong to me. You owe me your life. And if you refuse me, I'll find a way to make you pay."

I don't belong to you or any man, I tell him. Leave me alone or I'll report you to the police! I'm not afraid of you!

But, of course, Allah, I am.

25

NAFISA

How content I have grown up here on my mountain, the soil beneath me as soft as any feather bed, the grass a fragrant pillow. Why my sisters have not found me, I don't know, but in truth, I no longer much care. I can look after myself. When I need nourishment, I make my way down to the town for supplies. When I need shelter from the wind and rain, I have my rock, my bush, and my umbrella. Otherwise, I am happy to spend my time watching the stars and waiting for the day when I can leave this place, Amal, and find you.

I'm getting to know the animals up here—they keep me entertained. The drab little nightingale who serenades me to sleep every night from a nearby pine, boasting of romantic conquests and territorial triumphs. The scorpions like tiny dragons, spearing their enemies with lethal accuracy. The Samos jays in their bold blues and reds, wagging their patchwork tails as they tell me of their quarrels. The blackbirds who study me sideways before bursting into their jubilant songs. The golden jackals with their sail-like ears and delicate fox faces, wailing together at dusk like heartbroken women.

Do you remember the rook you kept in Sofia, my love? The one who grew to know and guard you? Every day she would perch on the windowsill and wait for you to come home from school, when you would feed her the sesame seeds and pine nuts you had picked off the crusts of our bread while she eyed you with her head cocked, just as the blackbirds eye me here. She came when you were seven and stayed until the winter you turned eleven. You cried through the night when she disappeared.

I wonder how you are faring, my sweet. May the spirits of your brothers and sisters watch over you, and the spirit of Osman, too. I only hope that their strength is enough to help you withstand what I did to you.

When we find each other again, my daughter, I pray that you will have relinquished your anger at me as Amina is relinquishing hers at her mother. Love, after all, is stronger than anger. I pray, too, that your tears over my abandonment were not as anguished as mine were at leaving you. But if they were, my Amal, if I made you suffer as much as I fear, I swear that when we meet again, I shall beg your forgiveness, unravel all the hurt I have caused until you are soothed, and with the grace of Allah, stay and protect you for the rest of my life.

26

AMINA

Farah refuses to leave our metal box. I try to drag her out, tell her she needs fresh air and sunshine to keep up her health, but she only pushes me away without a word. I've given her my bed and now sleep above her, the boys squeezed into the narrow bunk over their mother, but she only lies all day with her face pressed into her pillow. Not even Leila can get her to move.

Leila is trying to be stalwart through all this, although I hear her praying when she thinks I can't, and the prayer is always the same: "Merciful Allah, I am ever grateful for the return of my daughter. But why, after all we have suffered, did you have to take our Dunia away?"

Even the boys refuse to be distracted. "Where's Dunia?" Majid keeps asking, his little point of a face crumpling with worry. "Isn't she ever coming?" says Hazem, staring at Farah in fright. None of us has an answer.

One, two, three days pass like this, empty of news, each of us unwillingly but helplessly relinquishing our hopes for Dunia. And every one of these days, Sadek and I wait for hours at the Frontex, UNHCR, police, and information windows over and over to ask if she has been found, even though we never learn anything new. It has reached the point where as soon as the officials see us coming, they close their windows in our faces.

"Amina?" Leila whispers to me on the third morning, holding me back before I can join Sadek outside. "I need to ask you a question."

I look at her.

Her cheeks flush inside her tight black hijab. "I don't want you to think that Farah and I aren't grateful for Sadek's help. But be careful, little one. He seems a decent young man, but what do we really know of him?"

I know he grew up in Raqqa, Auntie, and that he was at Damascus University before the war interrupted. He's a good person, I swear.

"But we don't know anybody from Raqqa, Amina, so how can we tell if this is true? We don't even know who his family is. Remember, it's not only your reputation at stake here but ours, and people are already whispering."

I trust him, Auntie, I reply, trying not to get angry, so you should too. And who cares what other people say?

But her gaze has already wandered back to Farah.

"Little hedgehog," Sadek said to me only yesterday, resting his kind eyes on mine. "You are the light of my heart."

And you, Sadek, I replied, looking back up at him, are the light of mine.

On the fourth day of this no-news, I'm startled out of an uneasy sleep at dawn by the sound of him calling from outside our metal box. "Amina! Farah! Quick, come!"

Jumping down from my bunk, I run to open the door a crack, while Farah and Leila cover themselves hastily and follow. Shush, Sadek, I whisper, you'll wake everybody up. What is it?

"They've found a child!" He waves his long arms around, too excited to lower his voice at all. "A little girl saved from the sea! I overheard the camp manager talking about it. The girl was rescued the morning your boat capsized, Farah. She must be Dunia!"

At this, Farah lets out such a shriek that she rouses not only everyone near us, but all the rest of our neighbors, too. *"Alhamdulillah!"* Farah cries. "Where is she? Is she all right? Is she safe? Take me to her now!"

We dress quickly and rush with Sadek through the metal boxes and tents, litter and laundry, Farah striding in front of us, her head held high for the first time since she arrived.

When we reach the police office window, we are told, of course, to wait. So wait we do. For ten minutes, thirty, forty—for most of an hour we wait, while the policeman inside chats to someone behind him, browses through his cell phone, fiddles with papers, and sips his coffee. Farah tears at her fingernails with her teeth and walks in ever-tighter circles. Hazem sits on the ground and picks a scab on his knee. Majid pulls at his ears. Leila and I glare at the police officer, swatting away the flies feasting on our faces and necks. And Sadek tries and fails to get his attention.

At long last, the officer pushes away his cup and leans into the window. "What do you want?" he asks in English. It's all I can do not to spit in his eyes.

We explain who we are and that we have registered Dunia as missing. Now she has been found, we say, we need to fetch her this instant. "Where is she, Officer? Please tell us where we can find her," Farah implores, Sadek turning her Arabic into a mixture of Greek and English.

The policeman pinches mouth into a knot. "It's against the law for us to disclose the whereabouts of unaccompanied minors or expose them to un-identified adults."

Sadek translates.

"What do you mean, 'unidentified'?" Farah exclaims. "I'm her mother!"

"What makes you so certain this child is yours?" the policeman asks next.

"Because of when she was found. I only need to see her to know."

Sadek translates again.

"You can't see her without proof," the officer replies.

Sadek translates this too.

"What kind of proof?" Farah is growing frantic now.

"Her birth certificate. Your birth certificate. Your marriage certificate. Your identification papers. Her identification papers. You know, the usual."

We stare at this hulk of a man inside his protective window, his square face grooved, his eyes a murky hazel, his receding hair flattened with gel. He looks as though he might be kind in other circumstances. "But all my papers were lost in the sea," Farah tells him, her voice dropping.

Sadek translates yet again.

"Then you better find a lawyer and go to court. The judge'll decide."

"Decide what?"

"Decide if you can see her and whether the child will be safe with the claiming adult."

"'Safe'? In what way? How much safer could she be than with her own mother?"

"We are mandated to protect children against traffickers and neglectful or abusive parents."

"But this is madness!" Farah cries. "My daughter was taken from me by the storm. What has neglect and abuse got to do with it?"

"The law is the law. You'll have to press your claim in court. It's the only way."

"When? Can we do it now?"

The policeman looks at her with at least a modicum of sympathy. "Of course not. Our courts are backlogged and our judges overloaded, so even if you can find a lawyer, and that's very expensive, you'll still have to wait weeks or maybe months for a court date." And then he says it: "I'm sorry, but there are just too many of you."

Sadek translates once more while the officer squints over our heads at the people waiting behind us—quite a crowd by now. "We should go," Sadek says to Farah gently. "The man's getting impatient with us, which won't help. We'll find out if the child is Dunia, somehow. I promise."

"*Ya* Allah!" She is clawing her face now. "With rules like this, how do children and parents ever reunite? Let's go to the hospital. Maybe they'll tell us more than this pig-face will." And in an instant, she is running down the hill, the rest of us rushing after her, Hazem and Majid in tow.

When we reach the hospital, damp with sweat and breathing heavily, Sadek approaches the receptionist with one of his broad, friendly smiles—the smile of the circus—and explains our mission in a mix of English and his rudimentary Greek. A pink-faced nurse standing nearby responds sympathetically and tells us that there was a little girl here who had been rescued from the sea, but that she left several days ago for a shelter, the location of which nobody is allowed to disclose. The receptionist, however, a burly woman with a large bosom and short black hair, threatens us with the police unless we leave immediately. "Go!" she shouts, pointing at the door. "Get out!"

"Where is your mercy?" Farah responds in her tenth-grade English. "It is my daughter I look for."

"If you want mercy, go back to your own country."

Leila pulls Farah outside, the rest of us hurrying after. "Ignore her, my love, or we'll all get into trouble," she says.

"But why was she so rude?" Farah breaks into sobs. "How are we ever to rely on such people when they have coals for hearts?"

Over the next three days, Farah turns manic. No longer afraid to leave her bed, she now stands in front of the police container every morning in her black hijab and abaya, screaming curses and raking her cheeks until Leila or I pull her away. "Thieves!" she shouts, her face bleeding. "Child snatchers! Sons of dogs! Shoe-faces! Allah curse your mother-whore and father-pimp, too!"

"Shush, Farah, or you'll get arrested." But nothing we say will quiet her curses or stop her hurting herself.

Meanwhile, Sadek and I spend every minute we can waiting for one official after another so we can ask where Dunia is, when we can see her, and whether she's safe. But, just as before, each time we are told nothing and have to return with this same nothing to Farah and Leila. Even when we go to the charity center to seek help from one of their free European lawyers, most of whom have the same sort of open face and chirpy manner as Lily, they explain that they are trained to advise on asylum cases, not to retrieve lost children. All they can offer is a sympathy as useless as Farah's tears.

Lily is no help, either. "I'm sorry you're going through this, though I'm sure the shelter is fine," she says, sending one of her wide smiles to Sadek. "But we volunteers aren't allowed to know where it is, either. Amina, when are you coming back to class?"

27

HILMA

"Kyria Khilma," Kosmos says this afternoon as he trots down the flagstone steps from his upper terrace with an armful of fresh towels. "Why is it you have stopped talking about your little fish? First you speak like a madwoman about adopting her, now you say nothing." He narrows his pebbly blue eyes at me. "What plot is it that you are plotting?"

I take the towels from his gnarly arms. "I was in shock when I said those things. I know better now. I'm trying to forget."

His eyes turn from suspicion to skepticism. "Where, then, you go all day in your little clown car?"

"That, Mr. Constantinides, is none of your business."

We've taken to squabbling like an old married couple. It's very odd.

But in fact, Kosmos is right. I am plotting. Because if the child is indeed an orphan, and I'm certain she is, I am determined to rescue her. So I'm shopping for a house near a decent school, preferably on a beach; somewhere pretty with a lovely big room for her and a studio for me. I've filled out the application for the permanent residency and home ownership that would qualify me to adopt. I've written to my attorney at home to send me the various papers I also need, including clearance from Homeland Security, of all things. I've alerted my bank and taken on a real estate agent. And I've hired a lawyer right here in Samos.

I shall keep all this a secret from Kosmos, of course, given how obvious it is that he would disapprove. But once I have a home and all my papers, I'll be able to offer my little fish everything she would never find as either an orphan or a refugee. After all, didn't she call me grandma? I looked up *Teta* and that's what it means. And what do I have left in New York anymore to pull me back? Here, I can start again. We both can.

I found the lawyer online; not, perhaps, the wisest way to choose such a person, but the only way available to an outsider like me. Despina Metaxas is her name—villainous sounding but perfect for her chosen career. She told me on the telephone that she's never heard of an American trying to adopt an orphaned refugee in Greece but that she welcomes the challenge. She also said she believes I have a good chance if the little fish has no surviving relatives because placing her in an orphanage or finding her a foster home is expensive for the government and the government is poor. "It is good you are helping Greece like this," she said to me before she hung up. Helping Greece isn't exactly what I had in mind, but I let that go.

Meanwhile, I can't stop worrying about what the poor child must be suffering in that shelter. She's been in there for twelve days now and who knows what it's like—kind or cruel, loving or cold. Is it like those detention centers we have now at home, where immigrant children are locked up for months in cages and not even allowed to touch one another? Or is it like a sweet nursery school, with cuddly teachers and teddy bears? I've no idea because for all his promises, Kosmos has failed to find out anything at all about her or the shelter, let alone obtain permission for me to visit. Given what I've seen of how the Greek government treats refugees at that camp, though, I fear the worst.

In the evenings now, when I sit alone on the terrace after a day of house hunting, looking out at the view, I no longer think about the Aegean blues, Nick, Theo and Megan, or even Linnette. I think only of how, when I held my little fish on the way to the hospital, my heart ignited with a powerful need to give her a home. I need to keep her safe. I need to keep us both safe. She will save me, this little fish from the sea. Just as I saved her.

❧

My first impression of Despina is not auspicious. Not only is she nowhere to be seen when I arrive at her Vathi office at our agreed time—Greeks, it seems, make a point of being late—but when a colleague shows me into her room to wait for her, I find it bizarrely empty, without so much as a single diploma on its walls or a curtain at its windows. Its only furniture is a gray metal desk and two equally gray metal chairs, unless you count the rattling and noticeably filthy fan standing in the corner, swinging its head from side to side like a demented elephant. For a moment, the suspicion needles through me that this room, its desk, chairs, and even the fan have all been rented as a front—that Despina is a swindler and I her mark. Why else would the place look so naked? Unless this, like the dysfunctional plumbing, is a result of Greek austerity.

When she does eventually deign to arrive, an entire half hour late but with no apology, her appearance disconcerts me almost as much as her office. Trim and hard-looking, with a narrow face and short blow-dried hair the color of hay, she's wearing so much makeup it looks about to slide off, while her body is squeezed into a tight pink shirt and even tighter white jeans. I drop my eyes over her, stopping at the hot pink toenails crushed together inside her white stiletto sandals. This is nothing like any outfit I've ever seen on a lawyer in New York. What have I waded into?

Her manner, however, is nothing if not professional. "*Kalispera, Kyria* Khilma," she says in the same guttural accents as Kosmos and every other Greek I've met, shaking my hand firmly. "Please, sit." Sitting herself, she pulls a slim file out of her briefcase and places it on the surface of the desk, which is as nude as the room. "Now," she continues without further preamble, folding her beringed hands on top of the file, her long nails polished the same pink as her toes, "I'm afraid I have news that might alter your case."

"Afraid? Why?" I move to the edge of my metal chair, heart already hammering.

She opens the file, avoiding my eyes. "The child, it seems, may have surviving family after all. Or at least a woman who claims to be her mother. She has petitioned to take the girl back."

My stomach balls into a fist. "Who . . . where is this woman?"

"In the camp."

"Has she seen the child?"

"No. This isn't allowed." Despina turns a page.

"Then how does she know the girl is hers? Couldn't she be the mother of some other girl who fell off a boat?"

Despina looks up at me, her hazel eyes ringed by eyeliner as thick and shiny as vinyl. "Unlikely, Miss Khilma, because the date you found the girl corresponds with the date this woman's boat sank and when she reported a missing daughter."

"There weren't any other children missing?" I can only hope I don't sound as desperate to Despina as I do to myself.

"Yes, two. But they were both boys. Sadly, one, a baby, has never been found. The other was already dead when they pulled him from the sea."

I gaze down at my lap. The room has grown furnace-hot, despite the lugubrious fan, my legs sweating under my khaki capris, the metal of my chair burning. I should be happy for my little fish. But I'm not.

"I suppose I haven't a chance then. I suppose I better give up."

Despina drums her long fingernails on the desktop. "Not necessarily."

I raise my head. "What do you mean?"

She smiles, her teeth even and white behind her immaculate pink lipstick. "I mean we still have several eggs in our stew."

I blink. Her English is impressive but there are occasional slips. "And those are?"

"Well, my assistant and I have been making inquiries among the other survivors of the boat wreck. Looking for witnesses, Miss Khilma, who might be able to help us determine the facts of the case, and one of these witnesses has cast doubt on the woman's claim."

"What kind of doubt?" I wish this damn Despina would stop stringing me along like this.

She sits back and crosses her arms in clear satisfaction. "Most of the survivors told us that they don't know the claimant because there were at least eighty people on the boat, almost all strangers to one another. But one man had something to say that I think will make you see your chances differently." She pauses, looking pleased with herself.

"What was it?" I want to slap her now.

"He told us that the claimant is a fraud. He said he knew the real mother in Turkey and that she drowned when the boat broke."

"So she did drown! I knew it! But then who is this woman claiming her?"

"This is what we and the judge have to determine."

"Judge?"

"Yes, this must go to court, of course."

"Do you think that man you spoke to is telling the truth?"

Despina splays out her hands in the international shrug. "It is hard to tell. These asylum seekers lie all the time if they think it will get them something. But I'll make further inquiries because if it is true, you obviously have a much stronger case for adopting her."

"But why would anyone try to claim a child who isn't theirs?"

"Who knows? She might be a relative, in which case she must be investigated to make sure she is safe for the child. She might be deluded, or she might be a trafficker pretending to be a relative, as our witness suggested. Child trafficking is a well-known problem for refugees, Miss Khilma. This is why we bring these cases to court in the first place."

I try to soak this all in. "Do you have any other eggs?"

"Indeed we do. First is the fact that to retrieve the child, the claimant must produce identification papers proving that she is the mother—birth and marriage certificates and so on." Despina leans forward and plants her elbows on the desk. "She has no papers. They were all lost at sea."

"But can't the court just test the mother and child's DNA?"

Despina nods, which, it takes me a moment to remember, means no. "The test is too expensive for the court, Miss Khilma. Anyway, it's against the law to test a child without parental permission."

"And even if she is the parent, she can't prove it, so can't give permission?"

"Exactly."

I shift on my chair, suddenly hotter than ever. "But why don't they just bring the woman and child together to see if the girl knows her?"

"Because, as I said, this is forbidden before the judge hears the case."

"That's crazy!"

"It's for the protection of the children, Miss Khilma. Traffickers—any adults, in fact—can frighten children into saying anything."

I'm unsure of this logic but all I say is, "And the other . . . eggs?"

"The claimant must also prove to the court that she is fit as a mother. It's not easy for a person with no home, no income, no property, no passport, and no husband to prove she is fit to raise a child."

"No husband?"

"Correct. We've been told the claimant is a widow."

Theo is shouting something at me now. I brush him aside. "But what can 'fit' even mean for a refugee? Doesn't the court only mean not neglectful or abusive?"

"The law is always open to interpretation, Miss Khilma." Despina sits up and gives her shirt a quick tug to smooth it out. "In your favor is that you are rich, Christian, and married, if you will excuse my being so blunt."

Rich I could debate, as in New York terms I'm not. In Samian terms, though, perhaps I am. As for the Christian and married parts, I let those pass too, Theo shouting all the louder.

"Also in your favor," Despina continues, "is that the justice system on this island tends to work like this: If you're a refugee, you're guilty. If you're not Greek, you're probably guilty too. But if you are rich, Greek or not, you are innocent."

"But this isn't about guilt or innocence, it's about giving a child a future," I almost say but don't. "When will this hearing happen?" I say instead. "I want to get the poor girl out of that dreadful shelter as soon as possible. It must be terrible for her in there."

Despina stands and drops the file into a sleek pink briefcase. "Have a little more faith in our system, Miss Khilma. We may not be your United States of America but the shelter is just fine." I blush, thinking again of the refugee children we're locking up at home. "As for when the court date might be, I'll ask the judge. I'm having lunch with him tomorrow." And with that she shakes my hand and all but pushes me out the door.

28

KOSMOS

I've been thinking a great deal about my wife Eleni lately. My deceased wife, that is. Of what she would have done in this circumstance, what she would have me do. I can't even imagine the pain we would have felt had Sophia or Yiannis been lost at sea and then found again, only to be stolen away from us, possibly forever. The thought makes the blood bubble up in my veins. But whether Eleni would approve of my tactics with this crazy *Amerikanikh* I'm not so sure. For one, I seem to have become a stalker. For another, I've taken up lying.

So it is that when Hilma sneaks out of my house this morning, dressed not in her usual sports attire but a pretty white summer frock and matching sandals, and drives off in her ridiculous bubble of a car, I jump into my own vehicle and follow at a discreet distance. Her driving, I might mention, is a crime. She creeps along so slowly, her little body hunched over the wheel, her curlicue hair like a swarm of bees around her head, that she forces otherwise sensible drivers to take insane risks just to pass her. Tourists really should be banned from driving in Samos. They should be mandated to take taxis.

Her first stop is in Vathi, where she pulls up in front of a real estate office to pick up a fellow who, I can tell with one glance, is a shark. I see his coiffed hair from the back when he ducks into her car, his buffed nails clutching the dashboard.

So she really is shopping for homes. God help that child.

Her second destination is a hideous concrete condominium in the resort town of Kokkari. Once a picturesque pink and white fishing village, Kokkari has been ruined by German and Scandinavian package companies who like to build cheap holiday rentals and hotels, ship tourists in by the hundreds on cruisers and grab all their money for themselves, funneling barely a penny back to poor, shaky old Samos. Kokkari also has the worst restaurants on the island, lined up like parked cars along the beach, all eagerly frequented by the same suckers those companies ship in. Why Hilma would even consider buying a home here reveals a bad taste of which I would never have suspected her. I park under a tree by a church and hide among the sun-and-alcohol-dazed tourists staggering down the street from bar to bar, every one of them burned lobster pink and reeking of sun lotion. She emerges from the condo shaking her head.

The next home to which the shark directs her, after a long and winding drive through vineyards, farms, and forests up the west side of Mount Kourvounis, is in Platanos, one of the oldest villages on Samos and near where I used to teach. Just off the village square, prettily cobbled and shaded by the giant *plátano*—the plane trees that give the village its name—sits a fountain that claims to grant immortality with every sip of its mountain spring waters. Why anyone would want such a curse I can't imagine, but Hilma might be interested to learn about this village because it has its own history pertaining to refugees. When Samos went through the desertification she seems to know so much about, the hardy citizens of Platanos were the only people who refused to flee—or so it's believed—making them the only true native Samians left, everyone else being Johnny-come-latelies. In other words, everybody on this island, aside from an ostensible few in this village, is descended, if not from a refugee, from an immigrant.

I park uphill by a graveyard and hide behind a *plátano* overlooking the house Hilma is inspecting. This one is a find: an old-style stone house with a stunning view over the vineyard-laced valley below and a pantile roof in genuine terra-cotta, not the plastic crap so many are using these days. It even has a traditional clay pigeon affixed to its cornice. Add a few potted plants, an orange tree and a garden, and, were I a rich tourist like her rather than an unemployed history teacher, I'd be tempted to buy it myself.

Hilma takes her time with this one, emerging with a smile and a nod at the shark.

I must put a stop to this madness. The question is how.

Once I've followed her home, after detouring to a grocery shop to cover my tracks, I stand in the shadows of my terrace looking down on this unpredictable woman who has so disrupted my life. She's sitting at an outdoor table on the lower terrace, still in her pretty white frock, typing away on a laptop, up to God only knows what.

"Kosmos, stop being a creep," she says, startling me. Pushing away from the table, she stands and turns around to glare up at me. "What do you want?"

"A drink with you," I reply, stalling.

"No. I'm busy."

"By the way," I say, "isn't tomorrow your last day here? I believe you only booked until the end of the week."

She looks shocked. "Shit, is it? I lost track." Hilma's foul mouth never fails to startle me.

"My next guests won't arrive for a few weeks yet. You can stay if you want." I don't actually have any next guests, but I don't want to give her the idea she can mess up my life forever.

She hesitates. "Not if you keep creeping me out like this. No more spying on me. *Dax?*"

How did she suddenly turn this into her doing me a favor? "*Dax*. You pay me through Airbnb, though. No cash."

"Fine. Now, I need to work."

"What work?"

She hesitates again. "Filling out forms. Boring, but it has to be done. Not that it's any of your business." I can picture only too well what forms those must be: residency permit, tax, visa extension, real estate application, adoption papers. She's hired another shark, too, that lawyer Despina Metaxas, well-known around here for her lacerating cross-examinations and for cozying up to our judges—another of my stalker discoveries and an alarming one.

"Hilma, please, you can't work all day. You're supposed to be on holiday. Come up, have a drink, and we can talk about how to find your fish."

She sighs with exaggerated irritation, plods up the stone steps to my terrace and plops her little body down on a chair with a scowl. This offends me—nobody should plod in my beautiful house, let alone scowl. Why I find her so attractive after all this bad behavior beats me. "Wine or ouzo, fisherman lady?"

"Enough with that joke." She scowls again. "Wine. I can't stand that horrible ouzo stuff."

"Ah, I see we have dispensed with manners now."

"Sorry. I didn't mean that. It's just too licoricey."

I pour her the wine. "Now, Hilma," I say, settling further into mendacity. "I think I've found a way to persuade a friend of mine who works at Metadrasi— that's the Greek NGO that's sheltering the child—to let you visit her, given that you were the person who saved her. But I'll only make this effort if you promise not to meddle with her family."

She fixes me with her wonderful eyes. "I don't understand you. Your English is falling apart. You said something about metal?"

It's true that my English words don't always come out the way they sound in my head. I try again, more slowly.

"What do you know about her family?" She glares at me, her little mouth pinched.

"I know she has a refugee mother who wants her back."

"Where did you hear that?"

I lean forward and pat Hilma's knee. "This is a small island. We talk. And I have friends who work in the camp. Everybody here knows what you're doing."

"Kosmos, it's really none of your or 'everybody's' business what I do, and you should know better than to listen to rumors. And take your hand off me. Anyway, the identity of that supposed mother is in serious question."

I sit back. "What do you mean?"

"I mean my lawyer told me that another passenger from the boat says the real mother drowned."

For a moment I'm speechless. "Then who is the woman who has petitioned to take her back? A relative?"

"The passenger said she's a fraud, maybe a trafficker."

"Surely you don't believe that?"

"Why shouldn't I? I told you there were child traffickers in Greece."

"Is this something your lawyer persuaded you to believe?"

"Kosmos, stop."

I stare at her, desperately searching for a new tactic.

"Hilma, I don't wish to fight. Why don't you let me help you with those forms you're filling out. Are they in Greek?" I look at her innocently.

She knocks back the rest of her wine, puts the glass down and stands. "I'll teach you an American saying: MYOB. Look it up." And she stomps down the stairs.

29

AMINA

Now that August has us in its grip, this camp has become like a soup pot stewing over an ever-hotter flame. Thirty-five, thirty-nine, forty-three degrees. Sadek says even his circus tent has become unbearable. The heat not only brings out the stench of rotting food, but sewage and sweat, forcing me to walk around with a handkerchief clamped to my face. In Manbij the summers were hot and dusty too, but there we were not crammed up against one another like beans in a stew, nor were we deprived of sanitation and water, not even during the war.

The heat is also fraying our patience, making it almost impossible to push through a day without someone's temper erupting. It happened again only last night, when a cluster of young men broke into a fight—something to do with a few Christian Africans playing music too loud during the Friday prayers of a few Muslim Arabs—and before anyone understood what was happening, the police stormed in wielding sticks and shields as if it were a riot of hundreds, not a skirmish between eight.

And where is Nafisa through all this? We so need her advice. But she hasn't shown up at her tent or under our olive tree for days now, and Leila and I have been too consumed by our search for Dunia to look for her.

Last night, after my usual long struggle with sleep, I spun into a dream about Nafisa. She and I were burying Dunia somewhere in a garden, hiding her tiny bones under the earth. "She looks so tranquil," Nafisa said, bending to tuck the soil around her like a blanket. "I wish I could rest that peacefully." She raised her head to look at me. Her face had turned into a skull.

"Allah save us!" Leila exclaims when I describe the dream to her this morning. "Don't you know that the Prophet Muhammad, peace be upon him, said never to tell bad dreams or they might come true? Come, we better go look for Nafisa right now."

So, while the night crickets are giving way to daytime cicadas and before the sky grows too hot to bear, we leave the boys in the breakfast line with Farah and clamber up behind the camp, serenaded by the morning melodies of blackbirds and the hunting cries of falcons.

Nafisa is nowhere near our tree, or near Sadek's tent, either, so we keep climbing over the rocks and thornbushes that hold up the sandy soil of the mountain. "Do you really think she could have walked all the way up here?" Leila asks me, panting.

I do, Auntie. She's always loved the top of the mountain. There's a spot she told me about. I think I know where to find her.

We climb so high that the wild olive trees above the camp, with their canopies of silvery leaves and thick contorted trunks, give way to stunted scrub pines and sometimes to a patch of no trees at all and therefore no shade. Leila is wheezing by now and I'm soaked in sweat, my shirt and jeans weighing me down like sodden blankets. I know Nafisa's disease comes and goes, leaving her wrung-out on some days while not seeming to affect her on others, but how she found the strength to walk this far under a sun this pitiless I can't imagine.

"Little one, I need to catch my breath," Leila gasps after a time, her face red and damp, so we stop to sit on a rock and gaze out at the sea below, a vast field of crystalline blue glittering all the way to the horizon. "Think of how many dead lie under those waves, Amina." Her old theme. She pulls off her white hijab and stuffs it in her pocket, exposing her cropped hair to the breeze. "That's why I refuse to eat the fish here. They've fed on the bodies of our children."

I hadn't thought of that.

Up we clamber for another twenty minutes, following the path I remember, until, after a further half hour along the mountain crest, we catch sight of a shape lying half hidden behind a bush of thyme. We stop, reach for each other's hands and stare.

Perhaps it's only an animal, I say at last.

"Perhaps," Leila whispers. With this we find the courage to move again, push past the bush and approach.

It is not an animal.

Nafisa is on her back, wrapped in a long cloth, her head resting on a hillock of grass, as if she's in bed. Her eyes are closed and her face more at peace yet also more sunken than I have ever seen it. Beside her, an umbrella is propped up on sticks, providing a sliver of shade, and underneath that a plastic bag of fruit and granola bars and a bottle of water.

Auntie? I crouch and touch her gently. Auntie, wake up!

For a long time she doesn't respond—long enough to frighten us all over again. But at last she lifts her eyelids as slowly as though they're weighted down by stones. She gazes at us in confusion for some moments before her expression clears. "You see my new home here, sisters?" she says as if we've been talking all along. Her voice is raw with the rustiness of one who hasn't spoken for days. "Isn't it beautiful?"

We both tell her it is but I am horrified. No woman in sound mind would choose to sleep up here alone like this without protection from jackals, spiders, snakes, and, most of all, men.

Can you stand, Auntie? I ask. Why don't you come down to the camp with us for a shower and a meal?

She sits up and brushes the pine needles and dust off her lap. "No, little one, I'm much happier here. Don't worry yourself about me. Now, tell me what's kept you away from me all this time. Has something happened?"

Leila and I look at each other.

"Come, speak to me," Nafisa says again. "I want to hear all your news."

So we squat on the ground beside her and tell her about the arrival of Farah, the rescue of the child we're sure is Dunia, the way we are being kept from seeing her, and the fact that we have to go to court, even though nobody will name a date when this is to happen.

"Allah is indeed great and generous to have returned Farah to you," Nafisa responds with a smile. "And what joy to know that Dunia is alive as well!"

"Yes, but . . ." Leila's voice trembles. "Now it only feels as though she drowned twice."

Nafisa clucks her tongue. "Don't say such things, sister. Never let the keepers defeat you. Fight to get your Dunia back. Allah will light the way."

Leila only rubs her bare head and sighs. "Nafisa, what are you doing here?" she says then. "You should come down with us to your tent and see the doctor."

"No, thank you. You should go now, my dears. I need to sleep."

We try for some time to persuade her to come back to the camp with us, but she will not be moved.

Would you like us to bring you more food and water, at least? I ask in resignation.

"If you wish. Now, go get Dunia back and don't give up till you do."

30

HILMA

I think I've found my little fish a home. It's on the northwestern half of the island, the half Kosmos calls the quiet side, by a beach named Potami. If ever I saw a house with the power to heal, it's this one.

The house is old and rambling, made of the same traditional stone as Kosmos's, saturated in minerals that shimmer silver and gold. It has a large back garden planted with lemon trees and bushes of pink and white oleander, a front terrace wide enough for a family-size table and chairs, and it sits on a little cliff right above the beach looking directly westward over the waves. If all works out as I hope, my little fish and I will be able to dine outside every summer night here, watching the sun turn into a fiery red ball as it rolls into the sea. That same ball of fire Kosmos promised me back when we were still friends.

I plan to teach her to swim from this beach, once she has recovered from her trauma in the sea, because it has a wide stretch of shallow water just right for a little girl. I've seen both Greek and tourist families frolicking in it, so once I'm settled I shall make friends among the English speakers until my Greek is good enough to make friends among the Greeks.

On that beach, we will hunt for the best cobalt sea glass and luminous greens, the most perfect purse of a shell or sunset of a scallop. And when we find them, I'll show my little fish how to hear the music of the sea in a shell and how sea glass can send prisms of shifting color all over the house. Perhaps we will even paint those prisms together, tiny rainbows sprinkling our walls and mirrors and floors. I'll give her so much care and tenderness that she will forget the tragedy of the boat and her family, and learn instead to love me.

The house is near the town of Karlovassi, which is bigger than Vathi, with better shops and schools, no refugee camp, and the possibility of a civilized life. I only have to sign a few papers, persuade the owners to accept my offer, get through the hearing, and wait.

I still haven't been allowed to see her, though, Despina's efforts having been no more successful than Kosmos's. "Metadrasi will not permit it," she says with disgust when I visit her stark office today. Despina is good at disgust, almost as good as she is at playing cat and mouse with my hopes. "But have patience, Miss Khilma. They will."

Then she tells me more news. None of her inquiries among the other survivors of the boat wreck has turned up a single soul who will vouch for the woman who claims to be the mother. The only witness remains the man who says she's an impostor.

"And you truly find his story plausible?" I ask again.

"I do, Miss Khilma. Why else will nobody testify for her? It is our job to protect children from people like her."

"Can you arrange for me to meet this witness? I'd like to hear what he has to say."

Despina, whose clothes are just as clingy as before, looks thoughtful. "All right," she says eventually. "Why not? Good idea. I'll ask my contact at the camp to send him down here for you." She checks her watch. "Let's break for lunch . . . come back at sixteen hours? I should be able to get him here by then."

"Does he speak any English? I might need a translator."

"I have no idea. He speaks no Greek, I know that." She gives me one of her vulpine smiles. "Don't worry, Miss Khilma, we will find the truth. I am certain we shall prevail."

She spreads her fingers over her naked desk and smiles. This time her nails are painted a triumphant scarlet.

⅘

Having filled the long afternoon siesta with a swim and a lunch of Greek salad as big as a sunhat, my heart clattering the entire time, I fetch up at Despina's office again at four in the afternoon, half expecting it to be as shuttered and asleep as everywhere else in Vathi. But no, it's open, so in I go, entering her stark room to find it virtually filled with a man so large he could fit three of me into his shirt and two more into his pants. He's sitting in front of Despina's desk but immediately jumps up to offer me his chair, backing awkwardly into a corner. He's not fat, only rounded in the belly, but he brings to mind bulls and walls, while his beard looks as though a great black tumbleweed stuck itself to his face.

"Good afternoon," he says in English—Despina looks impressed. "I am called Haider Akil. Pleased I am to meet you, madam. Sit."

I feel diminished enough standing beside this Samson without having to shrink even smaller by sitting. But sit I do. The brow on him, a jutting plane of bone, and the directness in his marble-green eyes do not, somehow, invite resistance. Despina tells him he can find himself another chair in the adjacent room, if he would oblige by bringing it in. My guess is she doesn't like him looming over her any more than I do.

"Now," she says once he's seated beside me, lacing her manicured fingers on the desk in her habitual manner, "Miss Khilma here, she would like to hear what you intend to say in court on her behalf. Do you understand me?"

I immediately take umbrage at her tone. She's speaking to this man—a Syrian, I presume—as if he were a half-wit child. But he responds with nothing but courtesy.

"I understand, yes." He turns his anvil of a head in my direction. His hands, which are gripping his thick knees, are covered in the same curly black hairs that comprise his beard and are large enough to crush a neck with almost no effort at all, which makes me wonder what he did in the war. Speaking in simple if awkward English, he tells me that he knew my little fish and her mother in Turkey, and that, sadly, on the boat, he witnessed the mother drown. "I tried to save her, madam," he adds earnestly. "But, alas, the storm was too strong. But this is how I know this other woman, she is lying."

"And you're sure she isn't a relative of the girl—an aunt or a grandmother?" I ask him. My hopes are rising higher than ever now, a lightness fizzing through my veins.

He laughs. "She is too young, madam. No grandmother. No relative, no. She is . . ." He twirls his finger at his temple and rolls his eyes. "So sad." He shakes his head sorrowfully.

"You're saying the claimant is mentally unstable?" Despina interjects. When this meets with a blank stare she adds, "You are saying the woman is insane?"

He nods solemnly. "Poor lady, yes. Her mind, it is gone. Perhaps it is because of our war. And maybe she thinks, yes, that the child is hers. But I tell you this— the child, she is in danger with this lady. I fear for her, *wallah*, I do."

After leaving this Haider fellow in Despina's office, I drive back to Kosmos's house with more optimism than I've felt in years. Enough to brave seeking him out, even though he's taken to avoiding me. Not easy when we're the only people in the place.

I find him sweeping his deck against the wind in his usual Sisyphean manner, so I greet him in cheery tones, hoping both to make amends for my earlier rudeness and to win him over. Despite our differences, I would like to have him on my side—to help me negotiate the contract for my house and act as a character witness for me in court, if nothing else. But when I ask him to join me for a drink, he looks at me as if I'm a talking snake, jumps in his car and drives away.

So I write him a note.

"*Kosmos, I know you don't agree with what I'm doing. But I was right when I told you that the woman claiming to be the mother is an impostor. The real mother did drown off that boat—our little fish truly is an orphan. I met a man who was with her on the boat and he swore as much. He also said the woman trying to claim her is insane. So I'm not taking a child from a refugee mother, I'm saving her. Don't you see?*"

I push the note under his kitchen door, retreat downstairs to my terrace, pour myself a glass of Samian plonk, whack the cicada tree, and wait.

31

KOSMOS

There's a lot of talk these days about how screwed up my country is. Not only because the economy has turned us into the beggar orphan of Europe, forcing us to borrow money off our old enemy Germany, but because of the death of our ancient and glorious ways. Are we not, after all, the people who invented democracy and philosophy and, arguably, literature and astrology, too? And are we not the seat of theater, builders of the Acropolis, and home of the world's greatest ancient poet? And now the best we can do is bend over so that Germany can bugger us yet again? Our fathers, Sophocles, Plato and Homer, must be yowling in their tombs.

Perhaps the saddest casualty of all this defeat and degradation is our tradition of hospitality. *Philoxenia*, we call it, the love of strangers. *Philoxenia* dictates that any visitor who comes along should be wined, dined, and plied with gifts in case he is a god in disguise. I can imagine my snake-tongued guest arguing that this isn't generosity at all but only insurance, and that my country's treatment of refugees contradicts all I say, but still, as that pretty teacher we met outside *Panaghia tou Patamiou* explained, it truly is deep in the nature of a Greek to be generous. In some villages you can even find an ancient statue of a throne in the central square, on which a weary traveler is supposed to sit while the villagers heap food, wineskins, and presents around him; maybe even a daughter or sister for good measure.

If we began this *philoxenia* business under the Olympians, we kept it up when they were supplanted by the single god of Jews and then of Christians, continuing it even under the strangleholds of the Ottoman Empire, the Greek Orthodox Church, both world wars, the German occupation, our own civil war, and seven years of military dictatorship, not to mention manifold economic depressions. Our Church even appropriated the idea to the extent of trumpeting this passage from Luke 3:11: *Ο έχων δύο χιτώνας μεταδότω τω μη έχοντι, και ο έχων βρώματα ομοίως ποιείτω.* Which basically means that if you have two shirts and some fellow has none, for Christ's sake give him one. Same with food, while you're at it.

Yes, *philoxenia* survived all these upheavals of history, even the Germans, but one: tourists.

This morning I do some research on my own particular tourist. Being a total incompetent at the internet—Airbnb is the most I can manage—I commandeer my depressed, unemployed and probably drug-addled son to help. "Look up this lady for me," I ask him, "if you're not too busy." This last remark is a jab; we both know perfectly well that Yiannis is never busy at anything. "Her name is Hilma Allen. She was once an artist. Now she's trying to fuck up somebody's life."

I've been reading over Hilma's note and I'm sure not a word of it is true, whatever that other passenger says. I have no idea what the man's motives are, but why Hilma so readily believes him I can't understand. What worries me most, though, is that her lawyer, that Despina woman, is playing along. Whether she's doing it for the cash or simply to win a case, I don't know. But I do know this puts the little girl's chances of reuniting with her mother, or at least with her relatives, in true danger. After all, what power does a refugee have up against money and the law?

In no time at all, Yiannis sends me a series of what he calls links. "Click on these, *Bampas*," he writes. "Pretty interesting stuff."

She's a good painter, Hilma—her website is impressive. Abstracts, mostly. A phase of bright colored dots like those you see when banged on the head. An earlier period of black-and-white squiggles, simple but oddly compelling. And a stretch of portraits, the one exception to her abstracts, all of which depict either a small girl with ringlets haloing her head, which sounds corny but isn't, or a gawky boy with a big nose and a tangle of curly hair. Most of the paintings, though, are sweeps of colors and shapes that don't speak in narrative but rather in relation of shape to shape, color to color, space to line, nothing like a *liveloula* or a cicada among them; nothing, aside from the children, that is figurative at all. I should not, I realize, have forced Hilma to draw.

The reviews are good too. Impressive. *Art in America*, the *New York Times*, *Artforum*, a feature in the *New Yorker* magazine. Even some mentions in the French papers, and Italian, too. I examine a picture of Hilma snapped at a gallery opening. Slinky in a long black dress, those blue eyes as vibrant as if a light is hiding inside them, something silver flashing in the dense curls of her hair. How lovely she was before age and whatever else it is soured her. How lovely, in truth, she still is.

I click on the next link Yiannis sends, something he told me he had to dig awhile to find. I wish he had warned me how dangerous a highlighted word can be on the computer; a true Pandora's box.

Headlines. From newspapers, from online magazines, from tabloids. I read them with horror, with pity, with revulsion. And then with horror again.

32

AMINA

The inside of Sadek's circus tent is like a sultan's palace. It's only as wide as he is tall, but the circular floor is carpeted in blue and red blankets, the sides draped with shimmering purple veils, while a lantern of stained glass spins slowly from the point of the ceiling. His bed, which fills the back half of the tent, is draped with a cloth of multicolored patches. And best of all, a little table stands next to it, piled with books.

Where did you get all these things? I ask when he brings me inside for the first time. You truly are a magician.

"Oh, I picked them up here and there. Some I got from the Chinese shop, some I made myself." He gestures to the bed. "Sit and be comfortable, little hedgehog. I'll brew us some tea."

I settle down as he telescopes into a squat and lights the one-ring gas cylinder he uses as a stove while I admire the compact home he's made of this tent. On one side is his kitchen: two plastic shelves of dishes, tea, and spices; a Styrofoam box to serve as a fridge; a tub and towels for washing up; three plastic drawers to hold his rice and lentils; and above that, a hanging cloth lined with pockets, the type most people use to store shoes but in which he has tucked oranges, bananas, and packets of sugar. The other side of the tent is his bathroom: a tub, a bucket, a series of water bottles, bags, and jugs. Over his bed dangles a basket-shaped mosquito net, ready to be let down into a gossamer canopy. And on his little table of books stands an Aladdin's lamp.

I thought you weren't settling, I tell him with a smile.

He shrugs, looking a little abashed, and hands me a glass of mint tea. "Some of us choose to suffer through our time here, others to make the best of it. Don't you think we've gone through enough without adding to our misery ourselves?"

But how did you get all this up the mountain? Your mattress alone must weigh as much as two of you. And why did you come so high?

"To get away from the rats and heat. My friends helped me carry it all. And I've been here two years, remember. Plenty of time to build a home." He joins me on the bed and pulls me to him, nestling me against his bony plate of a chest. We sip our tea, strong, hot, and sugary.

Sadek, I say after a pause, you do want to leave this place, though, right?

"Of course I do. Every day I spend here it gets harder to breathe."

I look at him. He trimmed his beard yesterday, so now I can see more of his face. As narrow and angular as it is, it looks sweeter than ever.

Then why haven't you kept your promise? I ask.

"Which promise?"

Don't you remember the promises we exchanged the first time we talked?

"Of course I do. You promised to teach me how to write poetry and so you have, although I wish you'd write more of your own. Lily told me the other day that her students are writing poems now and she asked why you don't come to class. She says she misses you."

Hah. It is you she wants to see more of, not me.

Sadek looks astonished. "You can be very silly for one so wise, Amina. The only light in my life is you."

Truly?

He takes the tea glass out of my hands, puts it on the table beside him, and draws me closer, nestling me into his scent of soap and beard. "Truly, *oyouni*. Only you. But tell me, where are your new poems?"

Lost in the search for Dunia. At least for now.

I pull Sadek's hand into my lap and play with his long fingers. His skin is a light almond brown, his nails broad and clean. But what about your promise? I say again. You promised to teach me the language of escape. But you haven't.

He moves his other hand down my back, sending a delicious tremble through me. "That's because you already know it."

How, when I'm still here?

"It's in your eyes, Amina. In your refusal to succumb."

Not good enough, I tell him. There's only one language of escape and that's the one Nafisa seems to be courting.

Sadek pulls away in shock. "You mustn't say such things, hedgehog! That isn't escape, that's defeat." He examines my face a moment, then breaks into a slow smile. "If you stay with me, we'll learn the language of escape together until it takes us across the world." He caresses my cheek. "What do you think?"

Sadek's mind is so like Tahar's. A weaver of impossible stories, a believer in un-attainable dreams. But perhaps Sadek's songs and stories will indeed carry him across the world one day, or at least off this island, and his dreams will not be so unattainable after all. I, on the other hand, seem destined to always drag myself close to the earth, as blind and plodding as a mole.

He moves closer to me and, gently taking my face in his hands, touches his lips to mine, holding them there just long enough for me to feel the tenderness in them and to taste his breath. "Tell me what you want and when, my heart," he whispers. "I won't hurry you. I don't want you to ever be afraid or feel that you must do something only to please me."

I've never told Sadek what the guards did to me in prison, but then I don't have to; he comes out of the same war as I do. So we end the night simply by holding each other on his bed and talking as lovers talk. I tell him about Tahar, Baba, and Mama, how I miss them but don't miss my other brothers. He tells me about his childhood in Raqqa, how he had to run from his classes at university because Bashar's soldiers were beating and arresting students, and about the death of his parents and two little sisters under a bomb. But we also talk of our hopes and dreams and of all we admire in each other. And, eventually, we talk of our love.

Now we go to his little palace whenever I can make an excuse to Leila, taking separate routes to evade the spying eyes around us. And there, with care and patience, Sadek teaches me a new kind of poem: a poem of silken skin and gentle caresses, of passion, softness and surrender; a poem I thought the prison guards had stolen from me forever. Never before did I know that a hand on my hair would not lead to a blow. That the opening of my legs could feel like a promise, or the entering of my body a gift. That I could lie in the arms of a man and feel not suffocated, but safe.

My one request, I tell him, is to always keep a lamp burning while we are in your tent. I have to see your face. I need to know it is you.

੨☙

Leila is probably aware of what Sadek and I are doing, even though I tell her that I'm taking lessons with Lily or off on some errand, but she is too occupied with the fight for Dunia to take the time to examine my lies. Sadek and I are still trying to help, too, waiting in those lines day after day to ask if the date of the hearing has been set, or whether anyone will let Farah visit Dunia in the shelter. The answer is always no. But this afternoon, after yet another week of nos, we at last hear something different.

"I have no news," the information officer barks as usual the minute he sees us, reaching to snap his window closed. But before we turn away, he adds, "Oh, wait, I do have a message. There's a man, a Greek, who wants to speak to you. He'll meet you down at the charity center . . ." He glances at his watch. "Now."

"Who is it?" Sadek asks, as surprised as I am. The officer knows nothing more, however, so we hurry out of the camp and run down the hill to the center, people staring. Nobody runs in this heat but rather shuffles or plods as if weighed down by a sack of onions. But run we do, past the firehouse and church and through the dusty white streets, shadeless under the sun.

When we reach the charity center, we pause to steady our breathing, open the glass front door and step inside, greeted by the usual crush of boys and their odors. The Greek is standing right there—we can tell who he is right away because he is old and white while most of us here are young and brown. Squarely built, he's not much taller than I am, so he has to crane his neck to look up at Sadek.

"You speak English?" he says when we greet him, his accent so full of spit and tongue I can hardly understand him. His filmy blue eyes shift from one of us to the other. We both say yes, although Sadek says it with more confidence.

"And you are the family of the lost little girl?"

"We are the family's friends," Sadek replies, ever honest. I would not have answered until I knew who this man is and what he wants.

The Greek looks confused—who knows what he's been told. But he tells us his name, Kosmos Constantinides, and holds out a thick and calloused hand covered in white hairs. Sadek shakes it and so I do the same, relieved that this man is not one of those locals who refuses to touch us, even while taking our money.

"Is there somewhere private we can talk?" the Greek asks, eyeing the mass of men in the room while Sadek translates. "Would you come with me for coffee?" This last sentence I understand on my own.

Tell him first he must explain who he is, I say to Sadek.

They speak. "Hedgehog, this is most amazing. This man says he is a friend of the woman who rescued Dunia."

What woman?

"An American tourist. He says she was out swimming when she found Dunia floating half dead in the sea and pulled her to safety."

This is not at all what I had imagined. I thought she'd been saved by a fisherman or the coast guard, the people who usually rescue those of us who fall into the sea. Not a tourist taking a swim.

"This woman, she did a good deed," Sadek tells the Greek earnestly.

He wobbles his head, looking uncomfortable. "*Páme*," he says, and moves down the street.

We walk in baffled silence behind him, past shops full of pastries we can't afford and cafés full of idle old men, while cars and motorscooters sputter by and people stare at us. The Greek may be short and old but he walks fast, his arms under his short-sleeved shirt ropey with muscles and his legs as knotted as a mountain climber's. What he wants with us, though, I have no idea.

He leads us to the square with the lion statue, where he chooses a table at a fancy outdoor café, the sort of place that would never serve me or Sadek were we alone. I need to use the bathroom, which I imagine as large, perfumed, and clean, such as I haven't set foot in since I left home, but am too afraid of being shooed away. So I sit and cross my legs instead, glancing at the Frontex and Greek coast guard boats anchored along the jetty. Now, rather than standing new and wide-eyed aboard one of those boats, I am one of the people at whom I stared.

The Greek neglects to ask us what we would like to drink, instead ordering us each a coffee as if he were a father buying his children treats. The coffee, black and bitter, is brought by a young blond girl who avoids our eyes and addresses only him. She slaps the drinks down, fills a glass of water for the Greek but not us, and stalks off. I slide my coffee over to Sadek, its odor bringing back my hours buried in that van, the driver's filthy fingers probing under my skirt, the vomit I put in his pocket.

Sadek, I say, ask this man how he found us and what he wants.

Sadek does, and the Greek begins to speak. He speaks for a long time, his voice hoarse and phlegmy, while I struggle to follow. I spent six years learning English at school but my comprehension is not as advanced as I thought, at least not when this man speaks it. I can understand Lily perfectly well. But then, she is not Greek.

I nudge Sadek's leg. What's he saying?

Sadek says something to the man, then turns to me. "He says he found us through one of the officers he knows at the camp. But it's very strange, hedgehog. He says this woman who rescued Dunia now wants to keep her! That she's found a lawyer and is buying a house and that she plans to petition in court to adopt her."

You mean she wants to steal her from Farah? I thought she was a good person!

"He says she is, only unbalanced. So he told me that he's hired a lawyer for us—a Greek lawyer—to fight her. And that he will pay."

I look over at the man, his face crumpled, his eyes that peculiar milky blue.

But why would he do this? We don't even know him.

Sadek shrugs. "I suppose he wants to do a good deed too."

I absorb all this for a moment, appraising this mysterious Greek again.

Ask him if he can get the date of the hearing set soon, I say. Tell him the wait is killing Farah and cruel to Dunia. Oh, and tell him thank you.

Sadek and the Greek converse again while I wait for Sadek to remember to translate. It's often like this with men. They talk to one another while we women listen, then forget we are here.

"He says he'll try," Sadek finally tells me. "He agrees that the sooner the hearing is held the better, not only for Dunia and Farah, but so that the tourist woman won't have time to get her house and permits."

I stand, eager to run back to the camp and tell Farah and Leila about this—they so badly need good news. But first I have one more thing to say.

Tell him, Sadek, that when the hearing is held he must make the lawyer bring Dunia to court. Tell him without this, we will fail.

33

FARAH

Every night I dream of drowning. Of blue and bloated bodies. Hands flailing as they sink. Of my little one battered again and again by the waves. Yet when I awake crying out her name, it's only to find myself in this new nightmare. Dunia still locked up somewhere I can't reach her. Haider still hissing his threats. Allah still ignoring my prayers.

I wonder what she dreams about, my little Dunia, alone and surrounded by strangers speaking a stranger's tongue. Does she dream of the waves snatching her away from me? The hours she floated alone in that murderous sea? Does she believe me dead? Does she believe us all dead? And what kind of place is she being kept in? Is she able to eat and sleep? Is she able to laugh? Is anyone near her giving her any comfort at all?

My body folds over my knees.

If only Hassan were alive and here in this camp with me, we could fight for Dunia together. He would no more allow a man to plague me as Haider does than he would allow a woman, even a rich one with a future, a passport, a house and a nation, to take away our daughter. "We might have lost everything, *ya rohi*," he would say, "but we still have our love, our family, our history, and our faith. These are the richest gifts a parent can give a child, even a child in a refugee camp."

My sweet Hassan. He was only twenty when we married, I eighteen. How thrilled he was when I became pregnant. Nothing gave him more pleasure than to lie with me in bed, stroking my belly and telling his childhood tales to the creature within. Hassan, so gentle and thoughtful, his kind brown eyes the exact shade of Dunia's.

How unsuspecting we were in those days before the war, how naïve. Waking every morning to stretch like cats in the sun. Hassan teaching mathematics at our local high school, I at my work as a tailor, our families gathering over *kibbeh* and Friday prayers. We knew Bashar al-Assad was dangerous, of course, that his goons ruled the police and army and that those who crossed them would pay as Amina paid or with their lives. But we also knew—or thought we knew—that as long as we minded our own business, we could live as we wished: planning our futures, saving our money, taking pleasure in meals and walks, picnics and work, lovemaking and family.

Is this why you have punished us like this, Allah? Did you find us arrogant? For how wrong we turned out to be. Everything we had thought immovable could be moved, everything we had thought solid crumbled to dust. The sky that used to bring sunshine and rain instead brought fire and shrapnel. The earth that used to nurture trees and flowers collapsed into craters full of bones. And our city of Homs, once considered such a backwater it was the butt of jokes, was now Assad's prime target, convinced as he was that we were the seat of the opposition. He bombed our streets to rubble, our houses to carcasses, our souks to graves, our history to ash. Smashed our mosques to starve our hearts, our schools to starve our minds, our bakeries to starve our bodies. And as if that were not enough, he made prisoners of us, too, besieging us with shells and missiles, tanks and roadblocks, soldiers and snipers, all to strangle us into submission.

So came the day when my father, a gentle, quiet man who loved his family more than he loved his own life, announced that he would go out to beg some rice from a friend. "I can ignore my own hunger," he told us, caressing Majid and Hazem. "But I cannot bear the hunger of my children."

"Please, Mansour, don't." Mother seized his arm and turned her wasted face up to his. "You'll be killed if you go outside!"

"Leila." He lifted her hand away gently. "No father can stand by and watch his family starve." And, as frail and bent as he had become, he folded a bag into his pocket and shuffled out into war.

Assad's soldiers stopped him on his way home and forced him to dump his hard-won rice to the ground. They kicked his shrunken stomach and gray head, tied his hands behind his back and dragged him to a nearby square, along with the many others they had torn from the hearts of their houses that day: toddlers in bare feet and diapers, elderly men adjusting their glasses, little girls clutching dolls, mothers wiping babies. All were herded into that square like goats and made to crowd together so the soldiers could puncture them with bullets until their bodies fell, twitching and writhing, into a lake of blood.

We know of this from Hassan's cousin, who played dead under those bodies until the soldiers grew tired of shooting and drove away. When he arrived at our house, his eyes black with all he had seen, his clothes stiff with gore and his hands shaking, he huddled on the floor in a corner and told us about it: Father's death, the children, the women. "One young mother kept fumbling at her coat, trying to protect her baby's round little head with it even after the shooting began." His voice cracked.

War leaves no time for mourning. We packed up our grief for Father with my brothers' tears and our few belongings and fled Homs for Mother's city of Aleppo, where we moved in with her parents in the hope we would be safer. But, of course, we were not safer. Only a month later, Hassan was caught by a sniper's bullet on his way to find us water.

When I learned of his murder, my world emptied of color, my body of needs. I would watch my hand sewing a shirt and wonder whose hand it was, observe my feet step one in front of the other as if they were the feet of strangers. My heart would beat as though squeezed by an outside hand; likewise with the air entering and leaving my lungs. But inside, I was as inert as Hassan's corpse.

Mother was much the same. Both of us widowed and staggering through the days in our separate darknesses, much as we do now over Dunia. The house around us echoed with the voices of Baba and Hassan, who always seemed to be in the next room but never were. I felt as old as Noah; as old as though I had lived past my own death. And yet the months passed, as months will, my belly growing, the baby stirring inside her secret sphere, innocent of the fact that she was about to be born into a world without peace or even a father to protect her. I went into labor just as winter crept in, the pains blending with the roar of grief within me and the shriek of shells without.

The labor was long and agonizing but uncomplicated, so Mother was able to deliver me at home, rather than risk navigating the deadly streets to a hospital. And when little Dunia struggled out of me, her patch of a face no bigger than my palm, skin as soft as a breath, the tiny bundle of her as helpless as a newly hatched chick, we knew we had to flee to a safer place yet again.

Three days later, Mother and I gathered what remained of our family and left once more, this time for Manbij, where her brother owned a house and where, before the war, we used to go for walks and picnics in the countryside. My grandfather drove us there in his car, winding cautiously through tiny back roads of dirt and dust to avoid the *mukhabarat*, landmines and snipers, and bribing our way through the numerous checkpoints on the way, some manned by government forces, some by Russian-backed militias, others by Iranians or Iraqis—so many foreigners dressed up like fighters and waving guns at us, so many outsiders reveling in their moment of power. Before the war the drive would have taken forty-five minutes; now it took six hours.

"*Jiddo*, stay with us," we entreated my grandfather once we arrived. "Fetch Nana and come live with us in Manbij. Aleppo is impossible now."

"No, no, my dears. Nana and I are too old to start again. We belong at home with our memories. But Leila, you have your children to think of; and you, little Farah, your new baby, and for them a future must be saved."

With tears in his eyes, he embraced us and left to join my grandmother. We never saw either of them again.

My uncle's dusky pink house, three floors high and ancient, had once been grand, with a wing for each branch of the family and a tiled inner courtyard filled with fruit trees, a fountain, and flowers. But the war's deprivations, along with my uncle's flight to Jordan when the revolution began, had left the house vulnerable to deterioration and looters, so now the courtyard was crumbling and matted with weeds, the fountain cracked, half the roof caved in, and most of the furniture stolen. Even the fruit trees were uprooted or dead. Still, it had a basement to shelter us from bombs and half a roof to protect us from storms, so we made of it a home. A human can make a home of anything when necessary—a ruin, a tent, a shack, a boat, a gutter, a hole. We can make a meal of almost anything as well: stale bread crumbled into flour to be baked again, weeds and grasses stewed into soup, rice divided so many ways it yields everyone a bite. I have seen people feast on grasshoppers, on fish as small as a fingernail, even on grubs.

But war sniffs one out the way a wolf does a lamb, and just as in Homs and Aleppo, soldiers and militias were soon fighting over Manbij, too, bombarding us with bullets and mortars and *barameel*, those barrel bombs that shred a human body to pieces with nails, ball bearings and scraps of metal (why, Allah, do humans invent such things?). Assad and Russia versus the Free Syrian Army versus Daesh versus Kurds and Americans versus Turks versus Iranians—I stopped even caring whose side I was supposed to be on. To me all killers are the same.

Mother darted out for air; a shot grazed her shoulder.

I crept outside to gather weeds for our supper; a shell detonated nearby, showering me in stinking powder.

Hazem ran out the door to join a friend; a sniper shot the friend dead.

Majid pressed his face against the window to watch a cat hunting a grasshopper; an explosion sent him flying backward. His ears bled for days.

And everywhere, refuse. Not only the flattened remains of people's homes, but heaps of rags and bottles, cans and boxes, furniture and excrement, Styrofoam and dead rats filled every corner and gutter, while empty plastic bags somersaulted down the streets where nobody dared to walk. War's rubbish. The more of us die, the more it multiplies. First into bundles. Then mounds. Walls. Hills. And ultimately, into mountains.

We survived all this for five years, thanks to Mother's enterprise and the placement of my uncle's house on the edge of town. But eventually the day arrived when I'd had enough. "Mother," I said, "Dunia needs fresh milk, greens that aren't weeds and air that's free of shrapnel. She needs to be able to play outside without fear of being shot, as do my brothers. It's time for us to leave."

Mother hated to abandon her precious Syria, a land she loved as I didn't—after all, she had known many years of peace there, while nearly a third of my life had been swallowed by war. But she also knew I was right. So she made the arrangements, we joined up with Amina, packed, and fled, little suspecting that instead of the freedom and safety we thought we would find, there awaited a man who would try to steal my body and a woman who would try to steal my child.

34

AMINA

The day the mystifying Greek, Kosmos, takes us to meet his lawyer happens to be Wednesday, market day in Vathi, so as Farah, Sadek, and I make our way down through the town, we are constantly jostled off the pavement by a parade of local women in housedresses. A few smile at us as we pass, so we smile back, eyeing their baskets stuffed with the vegetables, fruit, and lamb we crave but can't afford. Most of the other women pretend we're invisible. But some cross the road to avoid us, covering their mouths. What are they afraid of? Contamination? Conversation? Do they think we will beg? Or is it shame that sends them scuttling away like this?

Down one street is a small market square where farmers park their battered vans and open the backs to display their wares: crates of oranges as bright as toys, mushrooms the size of babies' heads, jars of amber honey, bouquets of wild thyme, and spreads of the fish Leila believes feed on our drowned children. One toothless old man splits open a watermelon as we pass, its ruby interior glistering with the promise of sweet juices. My mouth waters. I have not tasted watermelon for years.

Kosmos told us that the lawyer's first name is Larisa, her last Diamandis, which I assume means diamonds, a name I trust will bring Farah and Leila the luck they so need. But why he's made us his business, he has still not explained. Sadek's guess is that he has done us some evil for which he wishes to compensate. Mine is that he's trying to butter up God with a good deed. Farah's hope is so strong that she simply believes that Allah has finally taken pity on her and sent her a man of pure heart.

She is jittery with that hope today, her eyes brighter than they've been since the day she arrived. I keep forgetting that she's only twenty-five, grief and worry having worn her down so. "Hurry," she says, pulling nervously at her beige hijab, "we don't want to miss the Greek." But there he is, waiting for us under the traffic light as he promised—the only traffic light, it so happens, in all of Vathi. He's walking in circles, smoking an unfiltered cigarette, a strand of tobacco stuck to his bottom lip, the tufts of his silvery hair rising and falling in the hot wind. The day is already sweltering, yet he's dressed in dark blue trousers and a long-sleeved shirt in pale green, circles of sweat visible under his arms. Only his feet acknowledge that it's summer; thick, hairy feet in leather sandals.

"*Kalimera!*" he calls when he sees us, one of the few Greek words we all know. And after a quick shake of Sadek's long-fingered hand, he barks out *akoloúthisé*," in a voice that clearly means we should follow him, and leads us down the street.

The lawyer's office turns out to be in a narrow white building squeezed between a taverna and a pharmacy, its doors and windows unmarked by either a name or number—we never would have found it without Kosmos. We ring the bell and a woman opens the door; a tall, stork-like person with sleek brown hair pulled into a bun and the pouty face of a model. Greeting us with perfunctory handshakes, she explains that she is Larisa Diamandis herself, leads us inside a small white office, nearly empty of furniture, and asks us to wait while she sends a young man to find us chairs. We stand in awkward silence and I am suddenly afraid that she might be able to smell the camp on us, the lack of hot water, the garbage and sewage. I've taken nothing but cold showers for months.

While we wait, she sits behind a desk and busies herself with papers, which gives me a moment to study her. She's dressed in a white sleeveless blouse, a tight black skirt that stops just above her knees, and black high-heeled sandals. She looks no more than five years older than I am, which sends a wrench of envy through me. Had I not been caught in the claws of history, I, too, might have been degreed and professional by her age, with a career, fancy clothes and, who knows, perhaps even an office.

Once her assistant—if that's who the young man is—returns with some folding metal chairs, Larisa joins us to sit in front of her desk, the four of us facing her like children at school. Crossing her legs, which are long, tan and naked, her toenails painted dark bronze, she tucks a loose strand of hair behind her small pink ear and says, "My English, it is not very good, but it is better than my Arabic."

Realizing this is supposed to be a joke, we try to smile.

She then asks each of us to tell her our names and explain our relationship to Dunia. Kosmos tries to help Larisa with her English, while Sadek translates the parts Farah and I can't understand, but this only results in all of us speaking at once in our various tongues, causing such confusion we have to start again.

"Farah, your mother isn't here?" Larisa asks once we've untangled our introductions and fallen quiet.

"Here in Samos? Yes, she's up at the camp with my brothers."

"She should have come with you today and brought her marriage and birth certificates. Tell her to bring them to court the day of the hearing." Larisa turns to me. "Amina, I understand that you came to Samos with Farah's mother and brothers?"

I did, I reply in English, my hands fiddling with each other in my lap. I cannot shake the feeling that we are constantly being tested on this island, although for what and why we will never be allowed to know.

"And you met Farah and her daughter before you left Syria?"

I glance at Sadek for help with this one. He translates and I answer.

"And what happened after that?" Larisa plucks a notebook and pen off the desk behind her. "I ask even though I know the answer because you might have to explain this to the judge and I want you to practice." Sadek translates again.

You mean I might be a witness? I ask her.

"Of course. A key witness, in fact, because you're the only person outside the family we have so far who can vouch for Farah's claim that she's the girl's mother."

Excuse me, Larisa, but what Farah says is not a claim. It's the truth.

She shrugs. I don't believe lawyers are interested in truths. They are only interested in arguments.

After I tell the story, Larisa gives us a task. We are to track down every person in the camp who knew Farah in Turkey and ask her or him to come to court. The same with anyone from the boat who might remember her. All these people have to do, Larisa says, is testify that they know Farah to be Dunia's mother. "The more people you can find to say this the better. As you have no documents, Farah, we have to rely on witnesses instead. When you find these witnesses, tell them to come here so I can help them prepare their testimony."

"Only five people are left who were with me in Turkey," Farah replies uneasily. "And I do not think they will be willing to help."

"Five is more than enough." Larisa gives her a bright smile. "And if you explain the situation to them, of course they'll be happy to help." She scribbles her telephone number on a page of her notebook and hands it to us, even though neither Farah nor I own a telephone. "Call me whenever you find a witness."

"But can't I see my daughter now?" Farah asks, moving to the edge of her chair.

Larisa looks startled. "Oh. No, I'm afraid not. That's out of my hands."

"But I thought we were coming today because you could arrange this." Farah's voice is rising. "It's been three weeks since I lost her—I must see her now!"

Larisa glances at Kosmos. "I'm sorry but the law won't allow this."

"*Ya* Allah, why are you all so determined to keep me from my child?" Farah moans. "What about a photograph? Surely somebody can take a picture of her for me. I need to see if she's all right!"

Sadek puts this into English but Larisa only shakes her head. "It's illegal in Greece to photograph unaccompanied minors without permission from the public prosecutor."

"But she's only unaccompanied because you won't let me be with her!"

"I'm sorry, Farah. We are trying to fix this, believe me."

"Then at least give her a picture of me, please! Has anyone even told her that I and her grandmother are here waiting for her—that we're alive and safe?"

"This isn't allowed either, I'm afraid." Larisa tugs her skirt nearer to her knees. "Not until the court determines that you are the mother."

When Sadek translates this last statement, Farah lets out such a scream that we all jump in our chairs. "Torturers!" she shouts in Arabic. "Sons of whores, you're all torturing my child!"

Shush, Farah. I lay a hand on her shoulder. Screaming won't help. We need this woman on our side. Can you calm yourself, please?

Larisa is standing now, a strained smile on her face. "I know this is difficult, but we will find a way to solve it, I'm sure. Now, go gather your witnesses and we can plan from there."

"Have you a court date yet, Miss Larisa?" Sadek asks as we rise to leave, his voice placating.

"Not yet, no." At this, Kosmos speaks up at last, saying something rapid and forceful in his own language. The lawyer replies equally rapidly, looking at her watch. Our time is clearly up.

Outside, we walk back to the traffic lights in silence, Farah quivering with fury. Kosmos shakes Sadek's hand again, looking pleased with himself but explaining nothing. I watch his small, square form striding away from us toward the seafront with the confident swagger I see on so many Greek men; the confidence of a man who possesses liberty.

Why's he doing all this for us? I ask Sadek yet again. But Sadek knows no more about Kosmos now than he did when we first met him.

As we make our way back up through the narrow streets to the camp, Farah still cursing, we pass an Orthodox priest, fat and ancient in his black robes and cakebox hat, sitting like a great toad in a café chair; his beard, square and white, spread over his chest. He eyes us from under straggly gray eyebrows. Vathi is full of such priests and their churches, yet not one that I know of has helped us refugees in any way. We have no mosque or imams to offer us solace, either, aside from a few self-proclaimed ones in the camp I do not trust. We have only ourselves.

I turn to Farah and ask which of her fellow passengers we should approach first. We should do it now, I tell her, because the sooner we find witnesses, the sooner the court date might come and the sooner you can have Dunia back.

She looks down at her child-sized feet, as dusty as mine in their scuffed white sneakers. "They've been through so much, these people," she mumbles. "I can't ask them to do more. Anyway, I don't know how to find them."

I stop in the street and stare at her. Farah, what do you mean? We can find them just by asking around. Come, let's do it now.

She only shakes her head, her eyes still on the ground.

I fear for her reason, to tell the truth. She screams day and night about Dunia being stolen, curses the police and rants outside their office, claws at her cheeks and bites her fingernails, but now that she can finally do something to win her daughter back, she shrinks into a shell. I might be a mole but she has become a snail.

I can't draw another word out of her after that, so once we reach our container, I pull Leila outside and tell her what happened. She looks at me aghast and runs back inside.

"Farah, *benti*, what's come over you?" Taking her by the shoulders, Leila stoops to look into her eyes—even Leila, small as she is, is the taller. "Where's my lioness? Where's my Farah who fights for her daughter and so boldly berates the police every day?"

Farah pulls in a breath and sinks onto her bunk, once more folding over until her head rests on her knees. For a long moment she remains hunched like this, silent and still, while Leila and I look down at her in bewilderment. But at last she shakes herself and stands, plucking off her hijab and rewrapping it tightly around her head. "All right, I'll try. But don't raise your hopes. Fetch Sadek. I'm ready."

The first person she leads us to is a boy named Kareem, who she says was her dearest friend in Turkey and kinder than all the others. We find him easily enough by asking our fellow camp dwellers where he lives—it seems many people know him—and when we do, I recognize him as the owl-eyed boy who told me he'd tried to save Dunia from the sea. He lives in the woods outside the camp's northern fence, an area of dust, rocks, litter, and tree roots that people have taken to calling the Jungle.

We find him crouched in front of a tent—a squat blue hump held together with black duct tape—trying to mend the soles of his sneakers, which are peeling off and riddled with holes. He stands when we arrive, his eyes sliding to Sadek, but instead of expressing joy at the sight of Farah, he edges away. Even when she greets him with affection and tells him that Dunia is not drowned, only imprisoned, he looks afraid. This is not the way a dear friend behaves, let alone someone who wept when he told me of his fear for Dunia's life. What could have happened?

Farah grows so distressed at his behavior that she loses her words, fixing her gaze once more on the ground. So I take over. *Salaam aleichum* brother Kareem, I say, I'm glad to see you again, and I explain Farah's predicament. Will you please testify for her when the time comes—tell the court that she's Dunia's mother? It's all we need to reunite them.

He turns his saucer eyes away from us. He's so young, this boy, as gangly as a calf, yet his face for the moment looks old. "I'm not sure. Maybe." And without another word he hurries away through the tents, leaving us standing in the dust.

What's he afraid of? I ask Farah. Is he scared of the authorities, is that it?

She shakes her head, darts a fearful look over my shoulder and lowers her gaze again. I turn to see what frightened her. A colossus of a man is standing under an olive tree not far away, glaring at her. His shoulders are as thick as logs.

Sadek, I whisper, stepping backward, my prison memories rising in me again.

Sadek turns and sees him too. And then my brave poet, Sadek of the Song, does what only Sadek would do. He smiles one of his circus smiles, walks a little toward the man and says, "Peace be with you, brother, I hope you are well today, but my family is having a private moment. I'm sure you understand."

Sadek might be tall but he's as narrow as a bulrush, his muscles stringy and his shoulders mere bone, especially in contrast to this mountain of a man. And yet the man hovers uncertainly, shoots another threatening look at Farah, turns and lumbers away. *Inside the roar of every lion quivers the heart of a sheep*, as Mama used to say.

Is he what's scaring Kareem? I ask Farah once the man is gone.

She nods and rakes her face again.

Why? Who is he?

But this she will not answer.

It goes the same with the three other possible witnesses she finds: a shriveled grandfather named *Ammo* Salman and two women, *Oum* Aziz and *Oum* Mahmud, the first as long and spindly as a rake, the second round and crinkled as an old peach. They were all imprisoned in Turkey with Farah, they all know that she is Dunia's mother, yet not one of them will agree to testify for her, not even the women, who I assumed would be sympathetic, being mothers themselves. All they do is glance at Farah with disdain and turn away.

I would have thought that people who had lived trapped together for months, who had survived a storm and near-drowning while clinging to one another at sea—who had known irresistible little Dunia—would be more courageous than this.

Every day in this bitter place I learn a new lesson about human nature. Nafisa once told me that suffering can bring out a deep well of generosity in people. But whatever generosity might linger here seems to have withered and blown away. Is this what being a refugee does to the human heart? If so, what will it do to mine?

BOOK FIVE

SEPTEMBER

35

HILMA

The Vathi courthouse reminds me of an Argentinian hacienda: tall, elegant, and painted pale yellow. It stands behind a cast-iron fence, cornices gracing its windows like arched eyebrows, marble steps mounting to its yellow front door. It even has an upper-story window and a balcony perfect for a senorita tossing a rose to a suitor.

The date of the court hearing has at long last arrived. It's been an excruciating wait—five entire weeks since I hired Despina, seven since I rescued my little fish. But I am ready.

It took me hours to find the right outfit to wear, given that I, of course, didn't pack for Samos expecting to end up in court. I wanted something that would make me look sturdy and reliable, as an adoptive mother should, but also chic in a way that would speak of financial security and status. All I could find in Vathi, though, was either nightclub sexy or linen-sack frump, local taste being execrable—unless it's the taste of the tourists who shop here. I had to drive to more sophisticated Karlovassi again, where I was at least able to find a passable dress; three, in fact, just in case. The dresses are my armor and my only support, aside from Despina, Kosmos having gone into a sulk. My note seems to have done nothing but enrage him. He's such a sore loser. No matter. After the little fish and I are settled, I shall find other, less myopic friends.

I had to go to Karlovassi for another reason, too: to sign the papers for the house, the owners having happily accepted my deposit. The place is not cheap, but it's perfect and all mine, minus an official stamp or two. A home for my little fish and me! I can't wait to settle her there, to fill it with her shells and my paintings, make her happy again. Her little almond of a face, her questioning eyes. I can't wait to dress her in joyous clothes, teach her all she needs to know, replace her tears with laughter, erase her past with a future.

Inside, the courtroom surprises me. I had expected it to be old and battered, like so much else in Samos, to wear the burden of centuries of justice and its reverse. Instead, it's modern and bright, entirely furnished in light brown wood, the floor and rows of chairs included. Even the wooden railing cordoning off the audience looks new, while the walls are a spotless white and the windows large and plentiful. Clearly the place has just been renovated, Greek austerity notwithstanding.

The judge's bench, which reaches from wall to wall at the far end of the room, is elevated so high it forces one to crane up to look at it, as if at Mount Olympus—how the Greeks do love their gods. On the right side is a smaller desk for lawyers, and in the middle a little podium—more like a pillory—for witnesses and defendants. But there's no place for a jury because, as Despina explained to me, juries aren't used in the courtrooms of Greece. "But I thought the jury system was invented here," I said. She shrugged.

I'm so early that nobody else is here yet, aside from two pudgy police officers, so I choose a chair under a window, which is open, even though the air conditioning is turned up high, and try to calm my breathing. I've never been in a courtroom with a true criminal before, having always found a way to evade jury duty, much to Theo's disgust. The last time I was sitting in on a trial like this, the criminal was me.

When I hear people start to file in a few minutes later, I refrain from turning my head, although the tension in my neck is radiating into a headache. A sweat breaks out over my lower back, trickling under my dress. I look down at my wrists and pluck at my *lulaki* bracelet, which I wore for good luck. My ribs knit together and squeeze.

"*Dear Theo,*" I wrote in an email this morning. "*I know it is unbearably painful for you to see me, but I hope you will at least approve of what I'm doing, you who care so much about trying to make the world more humane. I, also, am trying now, in my own small way. For you and Megan, for me. For Linnette.*"

36

FARAH

Allah, I beg you long and hard in my heart to show me mercy. Forgive me for my anger against you, but please don't let my daughter be taken from me again. *Please.*

I roll up my prayer mat, lie back down on my lower bunk and prepare to wait through these last hours before the hearing, trying to refrain from tearing open the scabs on my cheeks. The dim light crawls like a spider up the gray metal wall. The movement and talk of other people press in around me. Each second stretches into an hour, each hour into a hundred days.

"Farah, *omri*." Mother touches my hand after a thousand such days have dragged slowly by. "It's time to get ready."

❧

Larisa Diamandis is already sitting at the lawyer's desk when we arrive, as is another female lawyer beside her, with hair like a yellow helmet and a face like a fox. The woman who rescued Dunia and now wants to steal her is here as well, in a chair on the far side of the room—it must be her because she looks so rich and out of place. Avoiding her eyes, I glance around quickly, hoping to see Kareem or one of the other people from Turkey, even somebody from the boat. Not one of them is here.

The chairs where we are supposed to sit are divided by a middle aisle, so I take the side near the door, as far from that terrible woman as I can. Mother sits to my right, dressed in her best midnight blue galabeya and matching hijab, faded though they are. Hazem and Majid nestle beside her, both in clean T-shirts and shorts, eyes roving curiously around the room. Amina and Sadek take the chairs on my left, while on the far side of them sits the Greek, whose interest in us I still do not understand. Between us, we fill an entire row.

I only hope that you, Allah, are here with us too.

Larisa Diamandis is wearing white slacks and a sleeveless yellow shirt, which puzzles me; I had expected a more authoritative outfit and wonder now whether she's a true professional. She and the fox-faced lawyer, who is also in surprisingly casual clothes, chat and smile as if they're friends, not adversaries. At one point they show each other their cell phones, leaning over the screens with their heads touching, like teenage girls. Otherwise the room is hushed, except for the sounds of our shuffling feet and the deafening racket of my heart.

Not long after we have taken our seats, Larisa Diamandis beckons me, Amina, and Sadek over to her. The three of us stand again, which means the Greek has to stand as well so we can edge by him, the noise of our scraping chairs against the wooden floor echoing like thunder in the near-empty room. We pass through the gate in the wooden railing that separates us from the judge's bench and walk up to her, my heart louder than ever.

"Good morning, Farah, are you feeling ready?" she says to me in English, standing up to shake my hand.

I understand this enough to tell her I am.

"Good. Now, you should know that the judge will be watching you and assessing your fitness as a mother. So you must remain calm, firm, and polite, no matter what happens. If you seem at all unstable or hysterical, it will count against you."

But how is a mother whose child has been stolen supposed to stay calm? I ask her. Wouldn't a calm mother seem not to care, wouldn't she seem false?

Sadek translates again.

"The law is not a psychologist, Farah, only a set of rules."

But what are we to do without any witnesses? O Allah . . .

"Please, keep your voice down. Now, go sit. And good luck."

I turn, aware of the other lawyer examining me closely, and walk back to my seat. How do they expect me to remain quiet with that child-stealer only an arm's reach away? I fix my eyes on her, no longer wanting to avoid her but to pierce her to the soul. She pretends not to notice, but I see her skin glistening with sweat, the hair on the back of her neck growing damp. She's old—much too old to be Dunia's mother. She's also thin and stringy, if elegant. A white linen dress, as if she were an angel—a calculated effect, I'm sure. Fashionable blue sandals. A matching leather handbag. A blue and white bracelet and even blue earrings: strings of shimmering beads long enough to brush her shoulders. Her hair, tightly curled and sprinkled with gray, is cut into an expensive crop that even I know is chic. It's been many years since I have seen such glamor anywhere but on television.

I, on the other hand, am in a mix of clothes I borrowed from Mother and Amina—a dark brown skirt and matching hijab, a white blouse and sneakers. I thought I looked respectable, but now I see that I look just as poor and powerless as I am.

Allah, help me.

"Farah," Amina whispers, "I've seen that woman before. We spoke once. She seemed friendly then. She even took our friend Nafisa out for coffee."

That may be so, I reply. But now she's a thief.

We wait for half an hour. The room, full of sunlight, grows hot in spite of the air conditioning. One of the police officers guarding the door walks over and shuts a window. We watch him in silence. I pick furtively at my scabs.

We wait another fifteen minutes. I'm thirsty but have no water. The thief shifts in her seat. Her earrings flash.

We wait a further half hour. Mother leaves to use the toilet off the corridor, as does the Greek. Otherwise we all sit and study the air. We do not talk. We do not move. My cheek is bleeding.

The thief looks down at her lap and fiddles with her bracelet.

Larisa Diamandis, too, looks impatient, shuffling through her papers, squirming in her seat, drinking water, shuffling again. The other lawyer scowls down at her phone and keeps crossing and recrossing her legs, revealing a short white skirt and a shoe with a heel as sharp as a knife. Even our Greek friend seems annoyed, red and sweaty and muttering to himself. The thief keeps looking at him with a hatred even I can see. He avoids her eyes.

Mother hands me a tissue. "Fix your face," she whispers.

The door opens at that moment and we all turn. I'm hoping to see Kareem, at least. But no, the person who walks in is Haider.

I grow so dizzy I have to clutch the sides of my chair.

Without even glancing at me, he strides to the far side of the room and sits behind the thief, slouching down in his seat and stretching his legs out into the aisle. He folds his arms over his chest, his biceps as thick as my thighs, sinks his bearded chin into his neck and stares at the floor.

"What's he doing here?" Amina whispers, echoing my thoughts. "Did you know he was coming?"

I shake my head and start to pick at my face again. She pulls my trembling hand from my cheek, moves it into her lap and holds it there.

After we have withstood yet another stretch of waiting, a police officer enters the room and gestures at us to stand. A door I hadn't noticed before opens behind the judge's bench, and at long last the judges walk in, like actors making their entrance onto a stage. There are three of them but only one is draped in a black robe; a tall, white-haired gentleman who looks just as severe as I'd expect for someone about to play King Solomon. The other two are women, the first with the face of a grandmother, the second more like an executioner. All three look tired and annoyed.

When Solomon had to decide between two women claiming the same baby, he only discovered the true mother by threatening to slice the infant in half. Will these judges be so cunning? I clutch Amina's hand.

The male judge sweeps back his robe and sits in the center, the women on either side of him, nodding at the rest of us to sit as well. There follows a barrage of talk. The judge talks. Larisa Diamandis talks. The fox-faced lawyer talks. But although the Greek does his best to whisper a translation into English and then Sadek to Arabic, there is so much being said so fast that all they manage is snippets.

After each lawyer has spoken at length, waved papers about, and answered the judge's questions, I am beckoned to the stand.

Withdrawing my hand from Amina's, I walk through the gate to the front of the courtroom, feeling the eyes of Haider and the thief rake the skin on my back. Stepping onto the podium, I look up at the judges above me. Never have I felt so small, so insignificant, or so determined. I set my jaw, ready to fight, praying to you, Allah, and summoning Hassan's spirit to my side.

The judge glances about. He asks a question of Larisa Diamandis.

"*Ochi*," she says.

The judge looks over at the other lawyer and asks her a question, too. She also says, "*Ochi*."

The judge sighs. Then he waves me back to my chair without having asked me a single question or allowing me to utter a single word.

"May they all shit donkeys!" the Greek explodes.

What's happening? I ask Sadek when he relays this. Why didn't they ask me anything?

He turns back to the Greek for explanation. "They have no translator to Arabic," he tells me.

But what does this mean?

"It means they have to postpone. They can't hold the hearing until they find a translator from Greek to Arabic, or at least from Greek to English to Arabic."

But why don't they use you and Kosmos? You could both do it.

"Because the translator has to be appointed by the court."

But I can't wait anymore! I need Dunia back! She needs me!

"Shh." Mother puts her hand on my arm. "Shush, *benti*, remember the lawyer's words."

And so all of us stand to file out and wait yet again; nothing resolved, nothing achieved. I am no closer to having Dunia back than I was when the waves tore her away from me in the sea.

37

AMINA

"What news, little sister?" Nafisa asks when I toil up the scrubby mountain to visit her the morning after our debacle in court. "I'm hungry for news. The animals up here make dull company after a while."

Unsure of whether she's joking, I settle beside her bed of grass to catch my breath, wipe the sweat off my face with the hem of my T-shirt and hand her the oranges and water I brought. Each time I climb up here, I bring her what nourishment I can and try to persuade her to accompany me back down to the camp, but she always refuses. And I must admit, as much as her health worries me, she does seem happier here.

Are you all right, Auntie?

She stretches and yawns. "I'm wonderful, thank you. Now, talk."

So I tell her about the thief and the hearing, the man who is stalking Farah and the refusal of a single other survivor to testify. The thief is the same tourist who nodded at us in town, I say, the one who took you for coffee, remember?

Nafisa sits up at that, looking at me in surprise. "*She's* the one who's trying to steal Farah's child? Why?"

I've no idea, Auntie. None of us does. We only know what the Greek told us, that she's sad and a little crazy because of something bad in her life.

Nafisa shakes some ants from her skirt. "We are the ones who've earned the right to be sad and crazy. She's only sorry for herself. But why won't any of Farah's fellow survivors help her? This I can't understand."

I can't either. And every time I ask Farah, she refuses to tell me.

"Then ask her again. And come fetch me the morning of the next hearing. I'd like to go with you." Nafisa runs her eyes over my face, a smile playing across her lips. "But you haven't told me everything, have you?" Moving to a comfortable squat, she reaches out to touch my cheek, her finger as dry as a stick. "I can see in your face that all is not sorrow. I've seen it for a while. Come, child, confess."

I'm reluctant at first. I feel shy about myself and Sadek. But her expectant smile is so coaxing, I can't resist. So I tell her about Sadek and his sultan's tent, about our poetry and our plans. I even tell her that he's taught me to no longer fear love.

Is it so terrible, Auntie? I ask. Am I just being stupid? Leila would be furious if she knew.

Nafisa strokes my knee. "Take love when and where you can, my girl. You deserve it. And what else is there in a life as pillaged as ours?"

My eyes sting. I so want this not to be true.

"Come now, don't be sad." She examines me a moment. "Be careful not to fall pregnant, though, Amina, at least not yet. This is not the place or the time."

I gaze down at the earth, dry and sandy and crawling with ants. I can't get pregnant, I tell her. Because of the prison. I haven't had my menses for almost two years.

Nafisa clucks her tongue and lies down again, wriggling back into the grass the way one snuggles into a mattress of furs. "I'm sorry to hear that, little one, but don't worry, it will return when you put a bit more flesh on your bones and are able to live with less worry. Now, let me sleep."

🙐

The two weeks until the next hearing creep by as slowly as if time has turned back to eat its own tail. Again and again, I beg Farah to tell me why her companions won't help her, yet she still refuses to answer. We also keep trying to talk to Kareem, but whenever he sees us approach, he hurries away with the same terrified expression as before. And when we attempt once more to persuade *Oum* Aziz and *Oum* Mahmud to testify, they only turn their backs, while *Ammo* Salman is nowhere to be found.

Meanwhile, the man Farah tells me is called Haider will not leave her alone. Even when Sadek and I are with her, as we are most of the day now, he follows a short distance behind. Finally, I can stand it no longer.

Farah, I say to her one evening in our metal box, you have to stop being so stubborn and tell me who Haider is and why he's persecuting you like this. And you have to tell me why the other passengers refuse to help you. If you explain all this now, we might be able to do something about it. But if you insist on keeping silent like this, we won't be able to help you anymore. And then you'll never get Dunia back.

She sits without a word for a long stretch after I utter these threats, hunched on her bottom bunk, plucking at her fingers. "Please don't be angry," she mumbles eventually and covers her face with her hands. "It's just that I'm so ashamed."

I gaze down at her little body and, for the first time, my sympathy for her is stained by suspicion. Did she commit a crime while she was in Turkey, is that why the others are shunning her? Did she betray someone, cheat or steal or cause harm to one of her companions? But then I reject these uncharitable thoughts and bend to touch her shoulder. Farah, I say, sitting beside her, you can trust me. Please, unfold yourself and tell me the truth. We have no more time to waste.

It takes a further stretch of patience and talk, and yes, even more threats, to persuade her, but, at last, she relents, sits up, and gives me her story, much as I gave mine to Leila and Nafisa, although her voice is a whisper and she can't stop shuddering as she speaks. "Haider made me look so low with his lies, Amina. He made everyone despise me." She gazes at me, her eyes beseeching. "You do believe me, don't you?"

Of course I do, I assure her. I've heard about men like this who become so obsessed by a woman that they'll stop at nothing to possess her, even murder. One of the guards in my prison was like that with me. But what about Kareem? Surely he doesn't believe Haider?

"I thought he didn't, but now I don't know." Farah's voice shakes. "I'm so afraid of what will happen if Haider comes to court again. Oh, Amina, what will he do to me next?"

I can't answer this, of course, but it frightens me too.

I think we should go to Larisa, I say then. Maybe she can ask the police to make him stop threatening you.

"Please don't." Farah clutches her scarred cheeks. "Don't tell Sadek or Mother, either, or I could never look them in the face again."

I pull her hand away. You've got nothing to be ashamed of, Farah. But I have to tell them. Sadek will understand. He can help me speak to Larisa.

Farah hesitates for a long spell, biting her fingers. But in the end she agrees.

For the remaining eleven days before the hearing, Sadek and I seek out Larisa at her hidden office every morning and afternoon. Each time the door is either locked or we are told that she's off the island or in court. "The lawyers, they rent here," a woman explains in basic English when we find her mopping the hallway. "On mainland they live."

Sadek also tries numerous times to call and text the number Larisa gave us. She never answers. The Greek tells him that he can't reach her either. "These lawyers they only work for the exact hours you pay them. I am afraid I could not pay very much."

"Not all lawyers are as bad as that," Sadek says. Kosmos only shakes his head. Sadek even approaches Haider, first trying to talk some reason into him and, when that fails, threatening him with refugee justice—that is, a beating by Sadek and a group of his friends—unless he leaves Farah alone. Haider's response is to laugh in his face.

"Hedgehog, that man is seriously insane," Sadek tells me after this encounter, looking shaken. "I don't understand him at all."

ॐ

When at long last the Monday of the second hearing arrives, I climb the mountain once again to fetch Nafisa as I promised, afraid, as I always am when I visit her now, of what I might find. But no, here she is, awake, upright, and expecting me. "Ah, little Amina. Is this the day?"

It is, Auntie. We have to be in court by eleven.

"Good. Only I must change into fresh clothes; I can't go like this." I say nothing but it's hard not to agree. Her skirt and blouse are stained with soil and her hair is threaded with pine needles.

I lead her gingerly down the long slope, my arm linked into hers, my heart aching with love for this woman who has become my second mother. She's so much taller than I am that once I wouldn't have been able to keep up with her, but she is slower now, and weaker. Her hand is like a cluster of twigs.

After some thirty minutes or so, we reach her old tent, only to find that the few clothes she left there have been stolen and that somebody else has moved in.

Wear mine, Auntie, I say, bringing her inside my container. I know I'm half your height, but you're so thin now.

She shakes her head skeptically, ignoring the stares of my neighbors, but she does welcome the chance to wash the earth off her limbs and the needles from her hair in our shower, which is mercifully working today. She even consents to step inside my curtain of blankets and try on my longest skirt, ankle-length on me but shin-length on her, and a white tunic that fits her like a shirt. "I'm sure I look like a fool," she tells me, "but at least I'm a clean fool." We comb and tidy her hair and apply a light touch of the rouge a neighbor lends us, until I can see again traces of the elegant and beautiful Nafisa I saw in that photograph.

Auntie, I say, you don't look like a fool. You look like a queen.

"What nonsense you talk." She pats me on the head and pulls herself upright with a wince. "*Yalla*, I'm ready." So, with my arm linked again in hers, we make our way down to the port, where the courthouse sits opposite the Greek coast guard, the police, and Frontex, as if all the authorities of the island need to huddle together and conspire.

Once we are again inside the courtroom of wood and glass, we find Leila, her boys, Farah, and Sadek already sitting in a row by the door, along with Kosmos, every one of them looking tense and nervous. Then, just as we feared, Haider walks in again.

Farah darts him a terrified look but he ignores her and lumbers over to drop into his seat behind the thief.

Nafisa bends to kiss Leila and the boys, and we edge into the row of chairs with them, where I sit between Sadek and Nafisa. Sadek and Kosmos, who have never seen her before, stare at her sunken face in alarm. I think again of the photograph in which she looked so regal in her sky-blue toab. I wish they could have seen her as she was then.

Are you all right, Auntie? I whisper because she is breathing heavily. She squeezes my hand and nods.

Larisa arrives a few minutes later, to my relief—I was growing afraid that she had run off with Kosmos's money—and once more beckons Farah, Sadek and me over, so we stand again with a great scraping and banging of chairs and file through the little gate to her desk. There, she tells us that the court has finally found a translator from Greek to Arabic, although she's unsure how good a

20 of 302

translator he is. But this, she assures us, should at least allow the hearing to continue without further delays.

"Miss Larisa," Sadek murmurs, leaning toward her. "Do you know what that big man over there is doing here? He's been following and threatening Farah ever since she arrived on this island. He's extremely dangerous."

Larisa looks disturbed. "Why didn't you tell me this before?"

"We tried to call and tell you many times, but you didn't answer." Sadek pauses but Larisa neglects to answer this, either. "Do you know why he's here?" he persists.

"He is a witness."

Farah's face lights up at that. "Have you persuaded him to tell them that I'm Dunia's mother?" she asks eagerly, Sadek translating.

Larisa looks disturbed for the second time. "Oh, no. No. I'm sorry. He's a witness for my colleague. The other side." She takes in Farah's bewildered expression. "Don't worry. Now that I know he's threatened you, I should be able to discredit anything he says in his testimony."

Farah nods when Sadek translates this but I can see she is crushed. We return to our seats for another wait. What this Haider plans to tell the court, I don't know, but it is certain to be a lie.

When, after another long wait, the judge appears at last and settles into his seat on the bench, he's flanked by the same two women as before, all three looking every bit as weary and annoyed as they did last time. What is it about us that wearies and annoys them so? If anyone deserves justice, surely it is refugees from war and mothers who are claiming their own children. And isn't it the job of judges to deliver justice?

I glance over the aisle at the woman Farah so rightly calls a thief. She is not wearing white this time but dark blue, a tailored dress made of linen and lace.

She looks, if anything, more deadly than ever. It is hard to believe that she is the same woman who saved Dunia from the sea.

I glance at Haider, too. He is again slouched in his seat, legs splayed, huge arms folded over his chest. His face is as flat as a shovel, his narrow eyes cold, his beard full and dense. He reminds me of my brother Abdullah. If he's married, I pity his wife.

Kosmos, who is sitting beside Sadek, avoids looking at Haider, the thief, or her lawyer. Instead, he studies the string of amber beads in his hands, which he rubs one by one between his thumb and forefinger, as if counting the odds against us. Baba used to worry his beads like that; his *masbahha*. Tahar told me once that in the company of other men, Baba would sometimes dance with those beads, twirling them wildly as he jumped and kicked. "*Baba* dances?" I exclaimed. I could not imagine him as anything but bad-tempered or weary. But Tahar said that Baba often displayed a joy and liveliness with men that he never revealed to me or Mama.

Sadek reaches for my hand and squeezes it until Leila eyes him, forcing him to let go.

The judge has begun to speak. He opens the hearing and beckons the translator to step up to the bench. To my dismay, he's the very same incomprehensible Egyptian who refused to let us touch him. Is this the best they can do? I whisper to Sadek.

The judge calls Farah to the witness podium once again and I watch her step onto it to face him, trying her best to pull her tiny frame tall. Larisa walks over to stand beside her. I can't see Farah's face, only her back, but I knead my hands and, unbeliever though I might be, I pray.

The trial—if that is what this is—opens with the judge swearing Farah in, making her promise to tell the truth and nothing but. He then fires a series of questions at her, each filtered through the translator from Greek to Arabic, her answers filtered back in reverse, all of which slows the proceedings down to a pace that makes every one of us writhe in our seats.

First, the formalities:

"What is your name?"

"Farah al-Haaj, Your Honor."

"Where do you come from?"

"The city of Homs in Syria."

"When did you arrive in Samos?"

"On the twenty-first of July this year."

"What is your age?"

"Twenty-five."

"What is your marital status?"

"I am a widow, Your Honor."

"What is your asylum status?"

All this and more she answers in a voice so thin and tremulous I can barely hear her. I glance at Nafisa to see what she is thinking. Her eyes are closed, her chest heaving.

Next come the questions at the root of the matter, all delivered and answered with the same excruciating delays, the translations plodding clumsily back and forth:

"Are you the mother of the child?"

"Yes, Your Honor."

"Where is your child's birth certificate?"

"Lost at sea, Your Honor."

"Where is your marriage license?"

"Also at the bottom of the sea."

"And your identification papers?"

"Those, too, sank, Your Honor. I had them hidden in my clothes but the water took them anyway."

"Just answer the questions. What do you call this child you are claiming?"

"Her name is Dunia al-Sarrot. She is five years old. I gave birth to her in Aleppo, Syria, on the sixth of December."

My hope springs up at this. Surely the fact that Farah knows Dunia's name, age, and birthplace should be proof enough that she is the mother.

The thief's lawyer suddenly asks to speak. The judge grants her permission. Greek words rattle through the air like bullets. The judge then turns to Larisa and says something to her at an equally percussive speed. She looks humbled.

Surely Kosmos is not paying Larisa to look humble.

What are they saying? I whisper to Sadek. He confers with the Greek.

"He says the other lawyer claims that the child has never told anyone at the shelter her name or age, so there's no telling whether Farah is right. She said the girl has refused to speak since she was found."

Dunia, that little chatterbox, that lover of riddles, will not speak?

Larisa retreats to her desk.

Now it is the other lawyer's turn to stand beside Farah, and soon this lawyer has the judge smiling and nodding, conversation passing comfortably between them. Then she asks Farah a question, the translator once more filtering it into his heavily accented Arabic.

"Can you explain, Miss al-Haaj, why none of the other persons who were held with you in Turkey or who were passengers on your boat are willing to testify that you are the mother of this child?"

A long and terrible silence. I might not be able to see Farah's face but I can see her trembling.

"Miss al-Haaj, could you please favor us with an answer?" the judge intercepts.

Another long silence.

"I will give you one more chance."

Farah remains mute.

"If you have nothing to say to us," the judge pronounces, his voice wearier than ever, "you may sit."

Farah turns, her torn cheeks ashen, and stumbles back to us, unable to meet our eyes. Leila covers her face with her hands.

Why didn't Larisa step in to save her? Why didn't she say that Haider has been threatening Farah and probably the other witnesses, too? Is the woman asleep?

The thief's lawyer calls Haider to the stand next. Up he strides, jaw flexing. And when he swears in and is put through the routine questions, echoed again by the translator, we can hear his answers only too clearly because, unlike Farah's timid murmur, his voice booms across the room.

"Mr. Akil, were you on the boat with the claimant, Farah al-Haaj?" the thief's lawyer asks.

"Yes, madam."

"And were you also on the boat with the child in question?"

"Madam, I was."

"Do you know this child?"

"I do."

"What is her name?"

"Her name is Dunia al-Sarrot. But everybody knew that."

"Is the claimant here the child's mother?"

"No, madam. Her mother drowned. This woman Farah is a known liar and a fraud. A known whore . . ."

I gasp at this just as Larisa finally jumps up. "Objection!"

Farah is shrinking under her hijab, once again a snail.

The judge nods. "Sustained. Answer only the questions asked, Mr. Akil, and watch your language. We are in a court of law. Explain how you know who the real mother was."

"Your Honor, we were held captive together for five months in Turkey before we crossed the sea. We knew each other well."

"And how do you know the mother drowned?"

"I saw it happen in front of my eyes, may Allah have mercy on her soul. She was a widow, Your Honor, by the name of . . . Yasmin."

"He's lying!" Farah screams, leaping to her feet, her face no longer ashen with defeat but scarlet with fury. "I am Dunia's mother! He's making this up! Yasmin's the name of a girl he loved as a child—there was no Yasmin with us in Turkey! Ask anyone, they'll tell you!"

The judge glowers at her and barks something in Greek. The Egyptian translates: "Be quiet and sit down or we'll have you arrested!"

Farah glares at them but sit she does. The judge returns his attention to Haider.

"Mr. Akil, you are under oath. Was this woman Yasmin truly the mother of the child and did she really drown?"

"Yes, Your Honor, what I say is true."

"Very well. You may return to your seat."

How did all this come to happen? How is it that Farah, having lost her daughter at sea, is now being treated as a criminal?

I glance at Nafisa beside me. She is sitting up tall, watching all this with her eyes narrowed.

It is Larisa's turn again now and this time she calls Leila to the stand. Leila approaches the judge's bench and steps up on the podium. Again comes the swearing in and the questions regarding her identity. And then the ones for which we are here:

"Explain your relationship to the child in question."

"Explain your relationship to the claimant."

"Do you swear that this child is indeed the claimant's daughter and your granddaughter?"

"Do you swear that you took no money to make this appearance today in support of the claimant?"

Leila answers all this calmly and directly. She tells them the details of Dunia's birth, who her father was, who her mother is, how they were separated from us on the beach, and that although she has a copy of Farah's birth certificate, she does not have Dunia's. She tells the lawyers and judges all they allow her to tell. But somehow I can sense that, just like Cassandra, she is neither believed nor even truly heard.

Leila is sent back to her chair much too soon.

When will they call me? I whisper to Sadek. Larisa said I'm a key witness. He shakes his head.

But I am not called. The thief is, to present her petition to adopt, Sadek explains in a whisper. It is she who has the court's ear now.

I look at Nafisa again. She's leaning forward, staring at this woman who once bought her coffee.

When the thief rises to her feet, she turns out to be surprisingly small—no taller than I am—even if her fashionable clothes give her the illusion of height. She walks a little unsteadily toward the witness box and climbs up onto it. I glance at Kosmos's scowling face. He is the color of eggplant.

The judge nods at the thief and asks Larisa a question.

"*Ochi*," she says.

The judge asks the other lawyer a question.

She, too, answers, "*Ochi*."

The judge sends the thief back to her seat and closes his file.

"Not fucking again!" Kosmos splutters . . . or I surmise he does, because a minute later Sadek says, "Another postponement! This time because they don't have a translator from Greek to English. How can they be so incompetent? This island's full of people who speak English!"

Farah breaks into tears. The thief glances at her with a frown. Kosmos jumps to his feet and rushes out of the room.

The judge adjourns the court and gathers his papers as he and his colleagues prepare to leave, so we have no choice but to stand and file out as well. Farah and Leila are both crying now, while I'm in such a rage that I can hardly see my way through the tangle of chairs between me and the exit. "How can they torture us like this?" Farah moans through her tears. "Have their hearts dried to dust?" Haider is staring at her from across the room, his eyes alight with satisfaction.

A commotion arises outside the courtroom just then and Kosmos reappears at the door, wearing a peculiar expression. Gesturing at us to wait, he opens the door wider to usher in a woman I've never seen before: a stolid, middle-aged Greek in a baggy pink dress, with a cap of rust-colored hair plastered to her head. She stops in the doorway, looking lumpy and a little frightened, and stares at us while we gaze back at her, waiting for her to move out of our way. After a moment, she turns around and holds out a hand.

A child walks in.

For a long, still moment, the entire room goes silent and dark in my eyes, as if all the daylight has seeped out of it except for one bright spot: her little olive of a face.

And then, pandemonium.

"Mama!" Dunia cries and runs at Farah, dodging chairs and legs and grasping hands.

"Dunia!" Farah shrieks, stumbling forward, stretching out her arms.

"Dunia, *hayati*!" Leila shouts, rushing toward her, stumbling over a chair in her haste.

"Dunia!" the boys squeal, grabbing onto me in their excitement.

The woman who brought Dunia tries to catch her, the court police officer tries to catch her, the two guards in the rear try to catch her, but Dunia evades them all, reaches Farah, jumps into her arms and breaks into sobs.

The court erupts. The judges are shouting, the lawyers are shouting, the police are shouting, Kosmos is shouting, the boys are shouting, the thief is staring, Leila is crying, and I, too, have, at long last, rediscovered my tears. Even Sadek wipes his eyes. Farah hugs Dunia tight and tighter while Dunia clings to her, her arms around Farah's neck, her legs clamping her waist, crying with such passion that her tiny body shakes.

A policeman rushes at them then, seizes Dunia around the waist and, just as the smuggler did on the beach all those months ago, tries to rip her from Farah's arms.

"Mama!" Dunia screams, kicking wildly at the man.

"No!" Farah shrieks, trying to fight him off. But he only pulls the harder—so hard that I'm afraid he will tear Dunia in two.

"*Stop!*"

The voice is so loud that everybody freezes and turns.

Nafisa is standing by her chair, her skeletal figure erect, her eyes fixed on the thief. She turns to address the judge.

"I know this woman, Your Honor," she says in Arabic, pointing at her. "She killed her own granddaughter. She told me so herself. She should not be allowed to take this child from her mother. Ever."

We all turn to look at the thief. She grips the back of a chair, her cheeks draining to gray. "What's happening?" she asks in English, her voice small and shaky. "What is she saying?"

The only person willing to answer is Sadek. "Is it true about your granddaughter, madam?" he says when he finishes translating Nafisa's words.

She takes a long time to reply, the lines deepening in her thief's face. But finally, she speaks.

"It was an accident." Her words are barely audible. "A horrible car accident. I loved my granddaughter more than . . ." Her voice cracks. "The car rolled backward down the hill . . . I must have forgotten the hand brake, I . . . She was crouched on the driveway, her back to it, examining something on the ground, an insect, I don't know . . . I was standing by the house talking on my phone . . . I looked up. The car rolling and rolling toward her, faster and faster. I wanted to run, grab her, snatch her out of the way. But I froze. I couldn't move. The car rolling and rolling. I just watched, paralyzed, I don't know. I tried . . . didn't try . . . I couldn't . . . I did nothing . . . Yes, it's true."

An excruciating wait ensues while Sadek tells us what she said in Arabic and the Egyptian repeats it in Greek for the judges. We all turn our eyes to the woman again, the judges included, the only sound the sobs of Dunia in Farah's arms.

"Please," the thief says then, her voice trembling, and we need no translation now. "Can we stop this? I've made a terrible mistake. Please. Give the child back to her mother."

BOOK SIX

SEPTEMBER 2018-FEBRUARY 2019

38

HILMA

Kosmos has offered to drive me to the airport this morning. "That clown car you rented, Khilma, she is not safe," he announces as we sit on his terrace one last time, only we're drinking coffee rather than ouzo. "I will drive her back to the *malakas* at the rental office for you and say to her goodbye."

"If you insist."

"You have somewhere to live in when you return?" Kosmos has taken to treating me like an errant child since I went off the deep end.

"Yes. Maybe. My husband says I can come back. At least till I sell my house here and recoup my money."

"No divorce?"

"I don't know about that yet."

"You want to go home to him?"

"Kosmos, is this your business?"

He looks genuinely puzzled. "Of course. I want for you to be happy and stop, how you say, hitting yourself up? I want you to be wife and mama and grand-ma again. And I want you to paint. You know, my friend Khilma, we Greeks, we understand these things. To be forgiven, you must be ready to accept the forgiveness."

"And to accept forgiveness, you first have to forgive yourself?"

"Exactly!" He beams, his leathery face triumphant. "It was an accident, Khilma—you said this yourself. Even your New York court said this, even the newspapers. A horrible accident, yes, but not your fault. So yourself you must forgive."

I look down at my lap. I'm dressed for my flight in khakis and a blue shirt, having asked Kosmos to give away the fancy outfits I bought for the Hacienda courthouse. "Yes, I've heard all that before."

Standing, I walk to the edge of the terrace to gaze out at the Aegean blues for a last goodbye while Kosmos loads my suitcase, laptop and notebooks into his car. "Are you ready, my friend?" he says gently. "It is time we go."

"Yes, I'm ready."

He helps me into the passenger seat by an elbow, as if I'm suddenly an old lady, and takes off with a jerk and a squeal of tires. "You will come back to our beautiful island of Samos one day?" he asks brightly as we hurtle down his needle-thin driveway, barely missing the trunk of a pine tree. "Come back this time for real holiday and no more fishing?"

I wince. "I don't think so. No, I think I'll concentrate on fixing my life at home."

He sighs. "*Dax.* This is good. But I will miss you, even with all your trouble bringing."

"You are a kind man."

We drive in silence for a time after that, the traditional Greek music Kosmos finds on the radio belting out of the car windows. Soon we pass the back entrance to the refugee camp, more people than ever streaming up and down the road: a gray-haired man limping on crutches, children bowed under backpacks, youths hefting wood they must have scavenged from the abandoned houses around town. Grandparents clutching the hands of toddlers. As I once did.

I will never forgive myself. Never.

"Kosmos?" I say after a while, leaning forward to turn down the volume. "I do have one more favor to ask you."

He crosses himself. "God in Heaven help me." He chuckles. "Of course, *Amerikanikh*. What is it you need?"

"I want to give some money to Dunia's family. Not because of the harm I did—"

"You saved the life of a little girl, Khilma. This do not forget. True, you went, how you say, down the wrong back road after that. But this, it does not undo the good. So not all harm, no."

"Well, anyway, they can't know it came from me. That would seem . . ." I swallow. "Can you find a way to get them the money anonymously?"

Kosmos looks pained. "They are not stupid, they will know."

"Then pretend it comes from you. You've already helped them so much, maybe they wouldn't suspect. And if they won't take it, give it to Metadrasi. Your friend there was so good to bring Dunia to court—I know she must have risked her job to do that."

Kosmos gives me no answer, only pulls into the airport, screeches around a traffic circle, and jerks to a halt in front of Departures. The airport is so small that the division between Departures and Arrivals is somewhat conceptual. He jumps out of the car and trots around to the trunk, slinging my bags over his shoulder as if they weigh no more than popcorn.

"I'll carry that," I say, eyeing my laptop case in alarm.

"You carry nothing. Come, I bring you to checkout."

"In."

"Pardon?"

"Never mind." I follow him through the glass doors, his Bilbo feet padding firmly across the macadam in chic leather loafers, I clumping behind him in my dusty hiking boots, too bulky to pack. "You haven't answered my question."

He takes me inside—a garage-like room with a few plastic chairs along the walls, nearly empty but for an elderly woman and a man I guess is her son, who seem to be in the middle of a quarrel. Kosmos puts down my bags and opens his arms wide. "Hug. In Greece you must hug and kiss many times like the French, only better."

He smells terrible—no deodorant—but his arms are solid and warm. He squeezes me hard. "You are the most trouble woman I have ever met, except for maybe my Eleni, who I loved but who was big headache. Well, maybe you are bigger. But I will think about the thing you ask and I will write to you a letter with Yiannis on the computer. Not through air-bee-and-bee, though."

"Oh? Why not?"

He squints at me, his weathered face somehow more handsome than ever. "Because, my friend Khilma, air-bee-and-bee and me, we are, how you say? Finished."

39

AMINA

Now that February is here, the summer heat has long since given way to lashing winds and a rain that seeps into every window, tent, coat, and shoe. We've been on this island for an entire year as of today, Leila, her boys and I, like passengers waiting for a train that never comes. The twenty-first: our anniversary.

To mark the day, I climb all the way up the mountain to visit Nafisa. I pat down the soil around her bed, pull out the weeds, brush away leaves and ants. Lay sprigs of wild thyme on the earth where she once slept and water her memory with the tears that are mine again, for even though her sickness finally won, sending her first to the hospital and then to a cemetery below, I know her spirit lingers here. Pulling my collar tighter against the wind, I sit on the ground and tell her our news.

Farah has set up a little school for her brothers and Dunia, I say. Dunia suffers from nightmares and refuses to let Farah out of her sight, but her liveliness in the day has coaxed the boys out of their shells at last. Every morning they sit under a tree up on the mountain here while Farah teaches them their letters and numbers, tells them the stories her husband used to tell, and draws maps in the dust to show them the shape of the world. Leila and I help when we can, as does Kareem. I wish you could see Dunia now, Auntie, this child who survived so many hours alone in the sea and yet can still laugh. I think she would remind you of Amal.

Kareem says he had always intended to testify for Farah until Haider held a blade to his throat. We think Kareem is in love with her, although she finds him too young. As for Haider, he's been put into prison. For a fight, for theft, for possessing weapons, we don't know. Nor do we know how long his sentence will be. But while he is gone, Farah can at least breathe.

Majid has finally seen the doctor for his hearing—a wait of nine hours—but alas, there's nothing the doctor can do. Majid needs a specialist, and for that, Leila must go to Athens. But she lacks permission to go to Athens, so for now, he reads our lips and pulls his ears.

The thief went back to America. She tried to give us five hundred euros through the Greek. We refused to take it.

The wind picks up, rustling the trees around me and raining pine needles over Nafisa's bed. I move over to the boulder she always said guarded her like a faithful dog and lean my back against it.

We have at last been given the dates for our asylum interviews, I tell her then. Leila's is in six months, Farah's in two years. Mine, Auntie, is in three.

I pause and shift on the wet ground, listening in spite of myself for her reply. Plucking out a few blades of grass, which the winter rains have dyed from yellow to green, I braid them the way she used to until I've made a tiny rope. A drop falls on my cheek. I must hurry.

Sadek won his open card at last, Auntie. He left for Thessaloniki. He gave me his quilt, his lamps and books, and his old phone so we can keep in touch. But he took with him his circus tent and my heart. When we stood on the dock to say goodbye—my own farewell at last—he promised to write to me and save the money to bring me to him, once he has a job and I have permission to leave Samos. He did indeed know the language of escape.

That was four weeks ago. He has not yet found a job, or even a home.

I fall silent, pull my knees to my chest, and gaze out to the horizon, that door to the rest of the world I so long to reach. The sea glistens in its myriad blues below, free as we humans will never be.

That is all the news I have, Auntie, I say then. There is nothing more to tell you. Our stories are over for now, dried up and gone.

All we have left is the wait.

Author's Note

For readers who wish to know more about refugees in Greece and elsewhere and would like to help, here are some suggestions.

Donate or volunteer to work with refugees:
Doctors Without Borders/MSF (https://www.doctorswithoutborders.org)
Florence Immigrant and Refugee Rights Project (https://firrp.org)
HIAS (https://www.hias.org/where/greece)
Indigo Volunteers (https://www.indigovolunteers.org)
International Refugee Assistance Project (https://refugeerights.org)
International Rescue Committee (https://www.rescue.org)
MADRE: Global Women's Rights (https://www.madre.org)
Ruth's Refuge (provides furniture and basic home supplies for asylum seekers in the New York area) (https://ruthsrefuge.org)
Samos Volunteers (https://www.samosvolunteers.org)
Still I Rise (education for refugee children) (https://www.stillirisengo.org/en/)

Help refugees find a home, or invite them to dinner:
In the United States:
Welcoming America (www.welcomingamerica.org)
The Borgen Project (https://borgenproject.org/3-ways-to-host-refugees-in-your-own-home/)
The Welcome Corps (https://welcome.us)
In Europe or the UK:
Refugees at Home (https://www.refugeesathome.org)
www.unitedinvitations.org
Refugee Action (www.refugee-action.org.uk/heres-can-help-refugees)

Keep up with what is happening to refugees:
Aegean Boat Report (https://aegeanboatreport.com)
Amnesty International (https://www.amnesty.org/en/)
AYS (Are You Serious) Newsletter (https://medium.com/are-you-syrious/ays-newsletter-ays-special-from-bosnia-the-game-bdcadd6b9c3)
Doctors Without Borders/MSF (https://www.doctorswithoutborders.org)
Human Rights Watch (https://www.hrw.org)
International Rescue Committee (https://www.rescue.org)
Reliefweb (https://reliefweb.int)

Further Reading

Liberty Walks Naked by Maram al-Masri

The Boy on the Beach by Tima Kurdi

The Crossing: My Journey to the Shattered Heart of Syria and *A Woman in the Crossfire: Diaries of the Syrian Revolution* by Samar Yaztek

No Turning Back: Life, Loss, and Hope in Wartime Syria by Rania Abouzeid

The Home That Was Our Country, A Memoir of Syria by Alia Malek

Asylum by Edafe Okporo

Somewhere in the Unknown World by Kao Kahlia Yang

The Ungrateful Refugee, and *Refuge* by Dina Nayeri

After the Last Border: Two Families and the Story of Refuge in America by Jessica Goudeau

The Beekeeper of Aleppo by Christy Leferti

HB 2024

Acknowledgments

Eyad Awwadawnan, Ayad to me, you were my inspiration, my first reader, and my companion in Samos and beyond. Thank you, my friend. This book is for you.

Hasan Majnan, thank you for your trust, your friendship, and all your tales of Manbij, your native city.

Ali Jallow, Evans Atagana, Guilia Cicoli, Nick Vander Steenhoven, York Kamara, Dan Chapman, and many of the other wondrous souls I met on Samos, without your friendship, knowledge, and generosity, these pages would have been blank and my heart would have been poorer.

Stephen O'Connor, Eyad Awwadawnan, Matilde My, Zainab Sultan, Becky Stowe, Charlotte Innes, Sarah Van Arsdale, Ru Marshall, Barbara Friedman, what would I have done without you to read this and help me get through the stubborn thickets of my mistakes?

Tommy Olsen, who founded and runs the Aegean Boat Report all on his own, you are a hero.

Mazin Sidahmed and your Sudanese family: Nafisa and I thank you.

Yaddo, Blue Mountain Center, VCCA, I-Park, La Joya, Blue Cactus all gave me residencies of beauty and peace in which to write.

I am grateful also to the War & Peace Initiative at Columbia University and the PEN Jean Stein Grant in Literary Oral History of 2021 for funds to take me back to Greece. Also for permission to quote from: "15th March 2013: 5,000 Women in Syrian Prisons" by Maram al-Masri, published in *Liberty Walks Naked*, trans. Theo Dugan. Southword Editions, 2018; and from "The Heart of a Woman" by Lateef Helmet, published in *Flowers of Flame: Unheard Voices of Iraq*, trans. Soheil Najm. Michigan State University Press, 2008.

And of course to Steve, Emma, Simon, Iggy, the family and loves that hold me up.

Samos, island of beauty, island of sorrow.

Biographical Note

Helen Benedict, a novelist and journalist, has been writing about refugees and war for many years, most recently in her nonfiction book, *Map of Hope & Sorrow: Stories of Refugees Trapped in Greece*, published in 2022, and in her critically acclaimed novels, *Wolf Season* and *Sand Queen*. A recipient of the 2021 PEN Jean Stein Grant for Literary Oral History, the Ida B. Wells Award for Bravery in Journalism, and the James Aronson Award for Social Justice Journalism, Benedict is a professor at Columbia University and lives in New York. For more information, visit www.helenbenedict.com.